Power Play

A Novel

Nikki Vilendrer

Copyright © 2015 Nikki Vilendrer

All rights reserved. No part of this book may be reproduced by any mechanical, photographic, or electronic process, or in the form of a phonographic recording, nor may it be stored in a retrieval system, transmitted, or otherwise be copied for public or private use, other than for "fair use" as brief quotations embodied in articles and reviews without prior written permission of the publisher.

This book is a work of fiction. Names, characters, places, and incidents either are products of the author's imagination or are used fictitiously. Any resemblance to actual events or locales or persons, living or dead, is entirely coincidental.

ISBN 13: 978-1-59298-890-7

Library of Congress Catalog Number: 2015900937

Printed in the United States of America

First Printing: 2015

19 18 17 16 15   5 4 3 2 1

Cover and interior design by Laura Drew.

Beaver's Pond Press
7108 Ohms Lane
Edina, MN 55439–2129
952-829-8818
www.beaverspondpress.com

*To my parents.
Thank you—for everything
and for all the wonderful family trips.*

Chapter 1

She saw the mob and groaned, "I don't need this right now!"

Dani O'Brien was running on caffeine fumes and in no mood to face the press corps blocking the way to her office. She'd already survived a horrible morning commute thanks to an overnight snowfall. And now she was contorting her legs to hide a run in her pantyhose and trying to ignore the audible protests her stomach was making after skipping breakfast and lunch because of meetings. All she wanted was to grab a sandwich and get to her desk to tackle the mounds of paper that awaited her. It looked like that was going to be a challenge.

Taking a deep breath, Dani started charging the horde to create a path.

Despite her irritation and low blood sugar, her curiosity was piqued when she realized that reporters from every major Twin Cities and national news agency were part of the blockade. It took a good amount of people to fill the wide, Italianesque marble-lined corridor of the Capitol, and there were enough members of the media present outside the pressroom to do just that. It wasn't clear if they were waiting to enter the pressroom or watching for someone else to enter it. She couldn't remember reading any media advisories in her recent emails, but judging from the assembled swarm something big was happening.

She came to a stop mid-stride when with a flash, literally, the group turned her way. Cameras whirred and people started rushing toward her, but she soon gathered she wasn't their target. Following the direction of the dodging traffic, she turned around and immediately understood the reason for the mayhem.

"Oh my," she whispered.

Growing up in a sports family and working in the legislature meant she'd frequently been in the presence of well-known athletes and public officials. Though Dani wasn't often starstruck, the sight before her was impressive: two of the biggest names in hockey and a political legend of a mayor were standing ten yards in front of her.

Having a mayor in the Capitol wasn't unusual, but witnessing the hockey stars inside its walls was a shock to her system.

The press were going crazy at seeing Bill Wallace, the longtime mayor of St. Paul, standing next to Lars

Nelson, the state's professional hockey team's coach and a retired, two-time Stanley Cup champion. But Dani's eyes were immediately drawn to the figure on the right: Luke Coffey, all-star center of the Minnesota Blizzards. Here he was in the Capitol, looking downright sexy in his fitted navy suit and wearing a guarded expression.

She just stood there, wedged next to one of the Capitol's famous marble pillars, trying to make sense of the scene.

Luke was scanning the fast-approaching newshounds when he caught her eye. To her surprise, his gaze stopped when he saw her and his guarded expression turned into surprise. At least she interpreted it as surprise, given his sudden wide-eyed stare. Even more surprising, she thought, was that she couldn't look away.

There wasn't much time to process that realization before a reporter nudged Dani in his zealous efforts to get to the stars. Unfortunately for her, the unintentional push sent her straight into the immovable marble pillar. As she worked to regain her balance, she looked up to see Luke moving to approach her as he scowled at the aggressive reporter. Their heights allowed them to maintain eye contact above the crowd of newsies, but it was clear that the mob wasn't going to allow him anywhere near her. Luke apparently realized the same thing and gave her a tentative smile.

She hesitantly responded in kind. It wasn't like her to be so timid. Usually she'd waste no time before flashing a megawatt grin, but she had good reason to be wary—a few good reasons, actually.

Her dating history was proof that history repeats itself. The pain had diminished over the years and eventually ceased, but the memories of her past relationships with athlete ex-boyfriends had left scars. She reminded herself not to forget what she'd learned the hard way: athletes do not the best boyfriends make.

Her objective side, the part she relied on for her job, argued that she shouldn't judge a book by its cover; but the unpleasant memories made her lose the tentative smile she had going. Without sparing her favorite Blizzard another glance, she pushed herself away from the marble column and headed toward her office, which was, conveniently, in the opposite direction of the hockey legends.

"Get it together, Dani." She couldn't stop the muttered reprimand as she approached the elevator bank. "He's just like every other athlete." She stepped into the elevator and pushed the button for her floor. "You've been down that road before—numerous times. Stay focused!"

She certainly was focused ten minutes later as she perched cross-legged on her office floor with piles of legal-sized manila folders surrounding her. She looked up when she heard a knock at her door. Tyler, her fellow committee colleague, had a bemused expression on his face as he looked at her sorry state and nodded toward her antique of a television.

"Dani, your TV isn't on?" Tyler asked with laughter in his voice.

Dani turned back to her files as she mumbled, "No, I didn't want any distractions while sorting these legislative requests. The Revisor's Office just delivered another huge stack of bills and amendments."

"Trust me, Dani, you should turn on the TV." Tyler was already reaching for the old boxed TV sitting on one of her file cabinets when he made his statement. "Because this directly impacts your life for the next couple of months."

Dani sat up straight to try to relieve the knot of dread that had settled in her stomach at Tyler's words. The dread was quickly replaced by aesthetic appreciation as she saw Luke Coffey's face displayed on the TV. She may not be keen on getting chummy with him in person, but that didn't mean she couldn't appreciate him from afar. Tyler turned up the volume just in time for them to hear the mayor of St. Paul respond to a question.

She almost missed what the mayor was saying while she grudgingly observed that the old adage of the camera adding ten pounds obviously didn't apply to this group. But as she scanned the three healthy-looking men on the screen, she thought ten pounds could do the mayor some good. He was practically dwarfed by the hockey stars. And to her, Luke Coffey, with his broad shoulders and proud stance was by far the most commanding of the group. Then the mayor's next comment penetrated her distraction and snapped her back to reality.

"Our proposal includes a significant commitment from both the City of St. Paul and the Blizzards. Since the whole state will benefit from this arena expansion, we believe we're justified in submitting this request for funding."

Tyler fought back a laugh as Dani sprang up from her sitting position.

"You're kidding me!" she screeched, her voice jumping up an octave in her panic. "The Blizzards are proposing an arena expansion?" She walked to her office window to look out at the building in question. "I heard rumors, but nothing came through—"

"They must have been waiting for the right time to drop the puck, if you will."

Dani heard the laughter in Tyler's voice, but she couldn't find the humor in his lame joke.

"Well, how nice of them," she said snidely. "They wait all session to throw this bombshell into the mix." Dani raised her hands to her head and ran her fingers through her hair—a nervous habit from childhood.

"You, Kim, and I need to sit down to develop a game plan." Cringing as she realized that Tyler wasn't the only one who could throw out lame puns, Dani pulled her left hand down from her head to look at her watch. "You grab Kim, I'll secure the provisions, and we'll meet in the boss's office."

Turning around, Dani stalked over to her goody drawer. This news definitely called for chocolate—lots and lots of chocolate. When she was satisfied she had enough goodies for the three of them, Dani grabbed her ever-present notepad and cell phone and headed into their representative's office. She sidestepped the more formal meeting table and headed right for her favorite leather wingback chair.

Dani and her two coworkers made up the committee staff for the Minnesota House of Representatives' Bonding Committee. Along with their counterpart in the Senate, their committee was responsible for requesting state funding in the form of bonds for local projects that would then need to be approved by the legislature and signed by the governor. The arena expansion proposal would need to be reviewed and evaluated by their committee, which meant her job had just gotten a lot crazier.

Dani was just settling into the comfy leather chair when Tyler and Kim walked in. She was sure her expression matched the serious one Tyler was sporting—she figured the gravity of the situation had finally hit him—but the same couldn't be said about Kim, their committee page.

"Dani, do you know who's in the building?" Kim asked almost breathlessly. "Luke Coffey!"

No need to ask Kim how she felt about that bit of news. Her enthusiasm was palpable. Dani couldn't even respond to Kim's question before she excitedly continued.

"I snuck into the packed press-conference room to see him. He is so hot!" Kim practically leaped onto the couch in excitement. "Sorry, Ty. I'm sure you don't want to hear this stuff."

Ty, a salt-and-pepper-haired father of three girls, just waved off Kim's comment.

"I know." Dani replied as she tried to redirect the conversation, and then paused as she mentally replayed Kim's comment. "I mean, I know that he's here, not that he's hot." She paused. "He's just a guy." She sounded a little surly, but she couldn't help it.

Kim was aghast. "Just a guy? You're crazy!"

Dani knew her experience with athletes backed up her statement, but she wasn't about to share her reasoning. "Did you hear why he's here?"

"I couldn't." Dani thought that Kim sounded way too disappointed. "The room was so packed I had to sneak out before my claustrophobia kicked in."

Out of the three staffers, Kim was the newest to the legislative realm. She was a college senior who was helping them during the current session by serving as a page. Dani thought Kim was a great asset to the team, and she appreciated Kim's strong will to learn. Apparently, though, she was also prone to being starstruck.

Dani reached forward to grab a handful of the chocolate caramels she'd brought to the meeting. "Had you stayed in that press conference a little bit longer, you'd have heard that the City of St. Paul and the Blizzards are submitting a bonding request for the Rink."

Kim sat up a bit taller in her seat. "Really? To our committee?"

"Yes, so that means that we're adding a little more to our workload."

"How many bills do we have to hear before the deadline, Dani?" Tyler asked.

Even though she held the senior staff position of the trio, Tyler was a legislative veteran and Dani would be relying on him heavily these next few weeks to make sure everything went smoothly.

Setting down her pen, Dani eased back in her chair and looked at the two people she'd be spending almost every waking minute with in the upcoming weeks.

"Members have another three weeks to introduce a bill if they want it to be heard in committee and moved to the floor." Tyler knew this information, but Kim needed a refresher, so she started with the basics. She appreciated Tyler's efforts to listen carefully.

"We've received about two hundred bills from representatives requesting money for projects in their districts. Most requests we received early on, but we may get a few more small proposals for trails and such. My guess is we'll end up with about two hundred and twenty bills. Right now I'm getting a lot of revisions of and amendments to the bills we already have on file. I assume the Rink will be a large ask from the state, but most of the other bills won't be."

No one in the room needed to be told that the Minnesota State Sports Center, known among locals simply as the Rink, was the home of the Minnesota Blizzards Hockey Club and a year-round entertainment venue. Situated in the heart of St. Paul, the Rink was a major attraction. Ice hockey was the official state sport, and Minnesotans traveled from far and wide to get a glimpse of their beloved home team.

Kim sank down into her chair. There was no sign of her earlier enthusiasm.

"Seriously? Two hundred bills?"

Dani sent a reassuring smile her way. She understood the tinge of panic in Kim's voice all too well after being a legislative virgin herself last year. The legislative process was definitely not as easy as the civics books led students to believe.

"Don't worry, I promise we'll survive." More than anything, Dani wanted that to be true. As a new committee administrator in the House, she was out to prove that she could not just do the job, but that she could do it well.

"Even though this proposal is coming later than we'd like, we'll treat it like every other bonding request. No special treatment just because they're the Blizzards."

Dani's college acting classes must have been paying off. She saw some of the panic fade from Kim's face, which suggested her own terror wasn't on display. She was relieved to calm Kim's worries, but her heart sped as she looked down at her own notepad and saw "200 bills" underlined four times. She tried to push any worry from her voice.

"The last couple months of this session are going to be grueling. We have to be on our A games. Never be afraid to ask questions. It's a learning process, but hopefully not a public one. Thanks in advance for being such good sports. We're all going to be pulling long hours from here on out, and we shouldn't hesitate to ask for help. And if you ever need a little sugar rush, you both know where my candy drawer is. Deal?" Despite their less than enthusiastic responses, Dani really hoped Ty and Kim registered her sincerity.

As Tyler and Kim stood up, Dani remembered one last crucial issue she needed to discuss with them. This was directed more at Kim than Tyler, but Dani didn't want to single her out. "Oh, one last thing. Well, two things actually."

She stood so she could look her fellow staffers in the eyes to telegraph her seriousness. "Once we schedule the Rink bill for a committee hearing, the media will go crazy. I peeked at my email before coming in and I already had messages from three reporters looking for a scoop. I can only guess that this will be the bill of choice for the media."

Some of Kim's excitement reemerged at the mention of the media.

"Do you think we'll get to be on the news?" Kim asked eagerly.

Dani shook her head. "Being highlighted on the ten o'clock news really isn't in our job description, even during this whole crazy process. If the media approach us, we can take messages for the boss or we can refer them to our communications department.

"Second, when speaking to the public we need to remain professional at all times. Even if people get emotional or agitated, just reassure them that we'll take a message and pass it along to the boss. Given Luke Coffey's presence today, I think it's safe to expect that we'll see a player or two around promoting the proposal, but we'll remain professional. We can't favor one group over another."

Dani saw Kim's animated face dim a little upon hearing the instruction.

"Are we all on the same page?"

Tyler and Kim both nodded and left the office, looking as overwhelmed as she felt.

Dani mentally prepared a list of tasks as she checked her phone for missed messages. Sadly, relying on her memory to store her to-do list just wasn't cutting it anymore. That's why her notepad was always within arm's reach.

After jotting down her must-dos and collecting the few remaining chocolate caramels, Dani headed back to her own office. It wasn't as swank as the boss's, but it was a private office and she was thankful for that. And she was even more grateful for the porthole of a window that overlooked Minnesota's capital city. A number of great landmarks—the Minnesota History Center, the Cathedral of St. Paul, and the Rink, ironically—were visible from her office window.

Dani sat down in her desk chair and dropped her head into her hands. "It's okay, Dani, you'll get through this. You're a professional. Just push through it!"

Talking to herself was another habit that stemmed from childhood. Just as she started scanning the plethora of emails that had come in, an IM box appeared on her screen: *"Oh dear. I think we may need to start stocking your chocolate drawer with wine. I assume the Blizzards bill will be coming your way?"*

Despite the gravity of the situation, Dani smiled at the notion of wine in her goody drawer. She only wished. Piper, her colleague and friend, always had a way of lightening her mood just when it was needed.

Dani started typing her response: *"You bet it is. First I've heard anything about their proposal. How considerate of them, right?"*

"Totally!!!" read Piper's quick reply. *"I must say, it was pretty strange watching Luke Coffey giving a TV press conference from the Capitol pressroom instead of from the rink or a locker room."*

Dani would have preferred to speak to her friend in person, but since their offices were on opposite sides of the Capitol and she had a stack of papers calling her name, IM would have to suffice.

"Agreed. And you know what's even more strange? I saw Luke Coffey when I was downstairs. And he saw me. And for whatever reason, I couldn't look away. I mean, I couldn't. That sounds clichéd, I know. And this is me—we both know how I feel about athletes. But our

eyes connected and I was caught. But then some photog pushed me into a marble pillar and I was able to get my senses back. Weird, right?"

Piper's response was instantaneous: *"Really? Did anything else happen?"*

"What do you mean, did anything else happen?"

"You know…. Did your heart race? Did your breath catch? Palms sweat?"

Maybe it was a good thing she hadn't gone to see Piper in person. In person, she probably wouldn't be able to sell the lie she was about to tell her best friend. *"Don't be silly."* Because Dani knew her breath had caught, and she was sure she'd sported a full-body blush. She couldn't explain it, and she didn't care to further examine the situation.

"You know I love ya, Pipes, but I need to start going through a barrage of emails. It's going to take hours. Talk soon!"

"Think about that wine idea!"

Closing the instant chat, Dani chuckled until she saw just how many emails had come in. Her email count had more than quadrupled since her arrival this morning. No time like the present, she thought as she opened the oldest email. And just then, as she was reassuring herself the day couldn't get any worse, she heard an achingly familiar voice from her doorway.

"Well, aren't you a sight for sore eyes."

She was wrong—the day had just gotten worse. Much worse.

Chapter 2

She may not have heard that distinctive deep voice for years, but Dani knew immediately who was waiting for her attention. Slowly and reluctantly, she turned toward the man who had broken her heart years ago. He was leaning against her doorframe and looking at her as if nothing had changed.

But things had changed. For one, she was smarter now.

He gave her the smile that used to make her melt. "It's been too long, Dani."

His comment almost made her smile. Almost. She'd argue it hadn't been long enough.

"Why are you here, Sean?"

Her terse reply didn't seem to faze him. He removed himself from the doorway and approached her with a swagger that used to make all the girls, including her, swoon. "Well, Dani dear—"

She used to love it when he called her that; now it made her jaw clench and her teeth grind.

"It looks like we'll be seeing more of each other in the near future."

Dani tried not to blanch at his statement, but she wasn't sure if she succeeded.

He held out a large folder emblazoned with a Blizzards logo that was shining proudly in the fluorescent lights. Her stomach dropped painfully.

"As a member of the Blizzards organization, I am officially delivering our proposal."

Obviously, Dani thought. This was a familiar scene, except most other groups had dropped their proposals off many weeks or months ago. They also hadn't accompanied their delivery with a massive press conference. The only thing that annoyed her more than the proposal's eleventh-hour arrival was that it was being delivered by Sean Williams, her high-school sweetheart, or so she'd thought at the time.

"I saw the press conference earlier," she said nonchalantly, masking her true feelings. "But I didn't see you down there." Dani saw Sean's smug grin fade a little as she reached forward to grab the folder. She'd hit a nerve. He'd always been a proud one. "I take it that all the information is in here?"

Sean nodded. "Yes, it is!" he exclaimed excitedly. "And it's a great proposal. If I do say so myself."

Of course you do, she thought.

"I'm sure everyone says that, but this is legit."

Sean's smug tone didn't escape her. He'd always been too cocky for his own good. Once she'd found it enthralling, but now it was just obnoxious.

"And as you can see," he started, reaching over to open the folder and point to the cover sheet, "this is a joint effort with the City of St. Paul. We have some great people working on this project—analysts, consultants, and Blizzards players, including our star center, Luke Coffey, who"—Sean's voice dropped a little in what sounded like annoyance—"is downstairs enjoying some attention from the fans."

Of course he is, she thought. He's an athlete. He thrives on the glory.

"It's fiscally sound for all partners. This," Sean continued to boast, "is a great project for the state. Not only will it benefit the city and the team, but also many local communities and families. Maybe even yours."

For the second time that day, Dani congratulated herself on the foresight she'd shown by enrolling in an acting class back in college. At the time it had seemed a pleasant way to satisfy an arts requirement, but today it was paying off in unexpected ways. It took everything she had to ignore Sean's fishing attempt. At least she thought he was fishing, until he just came right out with it.

"Granted, it's been a while since I've played with any of you O'Brien's, but we've had our eyes on one or two of your brothers. Sam has done a scrimmage or two—he's got potential. I'm sure you know that a number of teams, including the Blizzards, have been tracking his college career." He leaned forward to place his elbows on her desk and his smug smile widened as he continued, "Wouldn't it be great to see him play in front of a hometown crowd in a newly expanded arena? An expansion you helped make happen. You and your parents could catch all his home games."

Dani tensed as she processed exactly what he was saying. He thought he could use her to help move the project forward. She was offended by his audacity—pissed off by it, if she ignored her inner censor—but she would never give him the satisfaction of knowing that. If Sean, Luke Coffey, or the Blizzards thought that she could be manipulated or bought, they had another thing coming.

She couldn't quite hide the anger from her voice as she responded. "What my brothers do with their careers is none of my business. Just like my job is none of theirs." She put the documents on her desk, stood up from her chair, and motioned toward the office door. "Thank you for dropping these off, Sean. I'll be sure to share them with the representative when he's available."

Sean looked startled by her abrupt dismissal. He seemed a little wary when he responded. "Could we set up a time to bring some of the Blizzards back to meet with the representative? And you, of course."

She wanted more than anything to say no, but she had a job to do. "Sure." Dani stepped out from behind her desk to lead Sean to Ty's desk. "Tyler here can help you with the scheduling. Nothing gets on the representative's calendar unless he puts it there." She looked at her colleague, who was honing his own acting skills by not letting on to her lie. "Ty, this is Sean Williams from the Blizzards. He'd like to set up some time soon to meet with the boss." She tapped the desk and was turning away when Sean stepped in front of her.

"It was great seeing you, Dani," Sean added emphatically.

She couldn't make herself say the same, so she nodded instead. "We'll see you soon," Dani replied. It was a heroic moment since, truth be told, what she really wanted to do was ask Capitol Security to escort him from the building. It probably wouldn't have worked anyway. Even though she was on good terms with the security guards, they needed due cause to go to such an extreme and she figured Sean's arrogance wouldn't technically qualify. A girl could dream, though, and the thought of him being tossed out of the building made her smile.

Holding on to that image and without looking back, she headed to her office and closed the door. She needed a little time to cool down.

A few ideas came to mind of how she could deliberately delay the Blizzards' efforts by keeping the proposal away from the boss and committee—a misplaced hearing request perhaps, or an incorrect hearing notice—but the ideas didn't sit well with her. Sean

Williams may stoop to that level, but she was better than that. She'd do her job, and she'd do it well, because that's the only way she knew how to do anything. Dani wouldn't sabotage the project, but the Blizzards wouldn't get any special treatment. Which is why she pushed their proposal to the side and returned to the queue of emails that she'd been answering before Sean Williams slithered back into her life.

Her breathing had evened out and she'd finally pushed the conversation from her mind when Dani felt her cell phone vibrating. She quickly answered it when she saw who was calling.

"Hi, Mom."

As soon as she put her phone to her ear, Dani could hear a swooshing in the background that sounded suspiciously like the exhaust fan from her parents' stove.

"Hi, sweetie, I know you're busy, but your dad and I are wondering if you're still going to be able to make it home for dinner tonight?"

Dani glanced down to check her watch and felt a stab of guilt when she saw the hour. "Sorry, I lost track of time. I'll close down and will be there in thirty minutes. Is that too late?"

She could hear her mom's excitement. "That's just perfect. And don't stop to pick anything up, we already have everything cooking and I baked a dessert earlier."

Dani couldn't help but smile. Her mom was always cooking—usually way too much. She forgot that not all seven kids lived at home anymore. Dani routinely left her parents' home with enough leftovers to cover her lunches for a week. They weren't low-fat meals either. It didn't do much for Dani's diet, but she didn't mind. Running around the Capitol to and from meetings kept her in decent shape. She welcomed her mom's leftovers with open arms.

During their conversation, she'd walked over to check the traffic on the interstate, which was visible from her office porthole. She was just about to hang up when she saw a massive light show begin on the roof of the Rink just beyond the interstate.

"Oh, awesome!"

The background swooshing continued as her mom stayed on the phone. "What's awesome? My cooking?"

Dani couldn't help but laugh as she responded. "Your cooking is awesome, Mom, and you know it. But, I mean that the Blizzards must have just scored. The strobes and spotlights are going off on top of the Rink."

"Ahhh. That must be why the boys are cheering in the next room. All right, sweetie. I'll hang up so you can leave work. See you soon."

"Yep, love ya. See you soon."

Dani sent off a couple of quick emails, turned off her computer, and started locking her file cabinets. Once all of her end-of-day tasks were complete, she grabbed her jacket and prepared herself to face the Minnesota winter. She was praying the evening commute would be much quicker than this morning's version.

Glancing out the porthole again, Dani smiled when the light show erupted, again, across town. She may be annoyed by their grandstanding, last-minute submission to the bonding committee, but that didn't stop her from cheering for her hometown team. She was a Blizzards fan at heart, and they'd just scored two goals in less than five minutes. She couldn't resist a cheery "Go, Blizzards!" as she closed her office door.

Chapter 3

Scoring a goal in any arena, or on any hockey rink, was a great feeling, but scoring one at the Rink was especially thrilling. And scoring two goals in the first period sent the fans into a frenzy.

Sports columnists claimed that the Rink's great atmosphere was a combination of the fans' energy and the design of the arena. Whatever it was, Luke Coffey knew that scoring a goal in front of the Minnesota home crowd was unlike scoring one in any other arena.

Skating toward the Blizzards' bench, Luke lifted his fist to receive the glove bumps of his teammates, who were waiting at the wall with their gloves raised.

"Yeah, man!"

"Sick shot."

"Way to earn that 'C'!"

Grinning as well as any guy could around a mouth

guard, Luke responded to his teammates' accolades with their usual game patter.

"Someone has to carry your sorry butts," he managed to garble out. Luke knew his teammates would take the statement for the jest it was. They were a competitive bunch and used good-natured razzing as encouragement.

After finishing the last glove pound, Luke entered the bench enclosure and took a seat. The crowd was still going wild, but they momentarily hushed to hear Luke's play finalized over the PA system.

"Scoring his second goal tonight for Minnesota, with twenty seconds left in the power play, Luke Coffey!" The crowd's excited eruption was so loud it was hard to hear the announcer finish. "And the score is now two to zero."

Guessing that the cameras were on him, Luke lifted his head slightly and gave a nod to the fans. He tried to appear completely in the zone, concentrated on staying mentally in the game, but he was rejoicing. His two quick goals went a long way in reassuring him that today's foray into politics hadn't thrown off his game. While his teammates were arriving at the Rink to prepare for the night's game, he'd been dragged to the Capitol for a publicity stunt. Luke's ritual of arriving to the Rink early and leaving late was well established, but management didn't seem to think that disrupting his game-day pattern was a big deal.

A couple of periods later, Luke and his first-string line were back out on the ice for the remaining minutes of the game. Their opponents from Indianapolis had scored a goal in the second period, so all they had to do was hold them off to avoid overtime play.

Indy pulled their goalie in the final minute. Luke had trained himself over the years to block out noise, so when the crowd's roar crescendoed enough to breach his mental sound wall, he knew the game clock had almost run out.

An Indy player took an unsuccessful slap shot on the Blizzards' goal that ricocheted off the side post. Luke was perfectly placed to accept the short pass from his defender. With the puck cradled by the blade of his hockey stick, Luke skated a couple of strides knowing the clock was running down and his opponents were flanking him on the sides. Briefly seeing the red center line slide by under his skates, Luke wound up and brought his stick down perfectly to connect with the puck. It got air heading toward the goal. Next thing Luke saw was the red light on the glass going off at the same time he heard the buzzer. Lifting his stick in the air, Luke celebrated his empty-net hat-trick goal, and was quickly surrounded by his teammates.

Minutes later, the crowd was still on their feet as the team headed to the locker room. Luke came back out for an encore skate around the ice to acknowledge the fans who were waiting and then headed down the tunnel that connected the locker rooms to the ice.

Soon the press would be trying to catch players between showers and other interviews. He'd seen enough of the press earlier; he'd let the other guys handle them tonight.

Luke was removing his gear at his locker when he felt someone come up behind him.

"Pretty good night, kid!"

Turning around, Luke saw Coach Nelson. He generally hated being called "kid," but when it came from his ornery coach, Luke viewed it as more of a term of endearment.

"Thanks, Coach."

"It wasn't enough that you're already going to be in the papers tomorrow for our Capitol stop. You just had to get in there a second time with the hat trick," he goaded with a gleam in his eye.

Luke laughed at the ribbing from his longtime coach. "Well, you know, your contract is up soon; management needs to know you're doing something right. I mean besides lobbying."

In response, Coach grunted and walked away. He was a man of few words, but when he spoke, he commanded respect and his players took notice. Those who didn't soon learned their lesson after being subjected to torturous skating drills.

Coach was the only reason he'd agreed to appear at the Capitol that afternoon. Luke wasn't exactly patient when it came to politics and politicians, but when Coach had approached him after his initial refusal of management's request to be part of the Capitol circus, he couldn't turn his back on his mentor and friend.

He sat down at his locker bench to remove his skates and remembered the day's earlier events. Even knowing that he was doing it as a favor to his coach, Luke still resented having to make an appearance at the Capitol when he'd wanted to focus on tonight's game. Thankfully, there had been an upside—the blonde woman in the hallway. She'd looked familiar, but he didn't know why. He was sure he wouldn't have forgotten someone like her.

He'd been surprised when he couldn't break eye contact with her. That is until she'd turned her back on him. He wasn't a cocky guy—well, maybe a little—but her rejection stung. It wasn't his habit to chase after women; they chased after him. Maybe her indifference was what had him thinking about her now. He couldn't stop. She certainly was beautiful, but he knew this wasn't just lust.

He had looked for her again during the press conference, but he hadn't seen her. So she wasn't a reporter, which was good for him. Reporters weren't his favorite people. He'd been burned by one too many in the past.

So why was she there? She could be a politician, albeit a young one. But given his disdain for politics, he hoped that wasn't the case. Even if she wasn't a politician herself, if she subjected herself to that world, she probably loved the partisan, political atmosphere that he found frustrating.

He thought she could have been there as a member of the public, like the kids he'd chatted with after the press conference. The media tried to corner him as he left the pressroom, but he saw the school kids across the rotunda and made his way over to them. But unlike the kids who looked around the Capitol in awe, the mystery blonde had seemed undaunted by a manic scene in the landmark building.

Visions of her as she was forced into the pillar once again floated across his mind. As he sat on the bench facing his locker, he had to shake his head in frustration. "Get it together, man. It's not like you'll be seeing her again," he whispered in a low voice.

He figured that was a good thing. He had the playoffs to prepare for, but right now the steamers called his name.

After a long, hot shower and a few sly moves to bypass the few remaining reporters who were trying to flag him down, Luke was again at his locker, having just slipped on his pants when he felt someone come up behind him. Expecting it to be a particularly persistent reporter, Luke turned around and was surprised to see Jim Keller from their executive offices. Suits didn't typically hang around the locker room, which made Luke assume the visit was about his pending contract renewal.

"Luke, great game tonight."

"Thanks, Jim." Not knowing what else to say, Luke remained quiet.

Jim didn't keep him waiting long. He cut right to the chase in a solemn voice, "Luke, you are well aware that you are one of, if not *the*, most popular players this franchise has ever seen. With that status comes a certain amount of responsibility."

Jim grabbed a seat on the bench in front of the neighboring locker. "You did a great job today, despite your reservations about politics. You're a great spokesperson for the team." Jim didn't seem uneasy at all about the situation. His voice was calm and direct. "In your position as captain, leading point scorer, and face of the team, it would seem odd if you weren't involved with this project going forward. That's why we in the front office think it would be appropriate for you to be at the meetings to promote the arena bill. The first will be with the chair of the House committee, Representative Johnson, on Thursday."

Luke had been in the process of sitting down when Jim presented the request—or *demanded* might be the better term. He stopped midway between standing and sitting as he mentally replayed the last statement, then dropped down to the bench with a thud. When Coach had asked him to join the group today, he'd expected that a repeat performance was a possibility but, given their imminent playoff run, Luke didn't think the suits would expect routine appearances.

"Jim, I'm a hockey player," Luke announced tersely. He hoped his tone would leave no room for doubt. "I let you parade me around the Capitol once, but that was it. I need to be focusing on the game. In case you forgot, the playoffs are just around the corner."

Luke ran a hand through his hair, trying to come up with other reasons to avoid the Capitol. "Not sure if you've looked at a calendar recently, but we play Chicago on Thursday night. That's gonna be rough. I need to focus on my job—which is leading this team, not playing lobbyist. Plus, I don't know much about politics or care for politicians."

Luke told the lie without flinching. Although politics gave him a headache, he followed the news closely and kept on top of what his own legislators were doing.

Despite Luke's best efforts, Jim seemed unaffected.

"I figured you'd say that, but we need you to be there, Luke. We're expecting it. The team has a much greater chance of getting this bill passed successfully with you involved. The media and public love you—and frankly, we can use the positive spin. I'll make you a deal: you only have to meet with House members. We won't make you handle the Senate committee too. Our political consultants tell us the House will be the tougher ask, so we only ask that you be there for that."

Jim must have been able to sense his continued opposition because he played his trump card. "Rest assured that management will keep your efforts in mind as we work with you and your agent on your contract negotiations."

Snapping his head to the left, Luke stared at the unflinching Jim. He wanted to believe he'd misunderstood. "Are you holding my contract hostage?" Luke asked.

Jim shrugged and continued in his deadpan voice. "Be here at noon on Thursday and we'll take a car up to the Capitol. This will be good for you, Luke." With that, Jim turned to leave the locker room.

Unwilling to give in without a fight, Luke tried one more time. "Jim, I don't think—"

The suit didn't even glance back when he cut him off. "Noon on Thursday, Luke. See you then."

Luke was left standing in front of his locker, shaking his head in dismay.

"Great game, LaFrey," Jim said as he passed their goalie, Marc, who was returning from the showers.

Marc and Luke had been teammates and friends for years. He wasn't surprised to see his friend still here. As goalie, Marc often took a bit longer thawing out after games. Looking at his friend, Luke didn't even try to hide his displeasure at his recent assignment.

"You won't believe…" Luke trailed off as he heard his friend chuckling.

"I overheard as I was walking back. Sucks to be the team's golden boy, don't it?" Marc teased—not feeling the least bit guilty. "I told you that your good-boy image was going to come back to haunt you someday." Marc sat on the seat that Jim had just occupied and faced his locker to begin dressing.

Luke knew he was joking, but it still stung. "Screw you. This is the last thing I need right now, not to mention the team."

Marc's nod signaled his agreement. Both men were very serious when it came to the playing level of the team. The playoffs were coming up soon and although they looked like strong contenders to move into the post-season, if the guys started getting distracted there wouldn't be a post-season.

"Tell the suits to forget it." Marc advised.

"I tried. Jim claims it falls under my responsibilities as captain. And get this: it could play into my contract."

Marc raised his eyebrows. "Haven't heard that one before." He paused for a moment while he processed the unusual stipulation. "Run it past your agent."

Luke started emphatically shaking his head. "No way. I can just see him agreeing with this. He'll say it's a great PR opportunity." He was starting to feel resigned. "No good can come from this."

In a flash the pretty blonde popped into his mind. He wasn't sure he liked it, but he'd felt something in his gut when their eyes met. And he was feeling it again just thinking about her. His chances of running into her at the Capitol again were slim, and if she were a politician, their chances of getting along we're almost nonexistent.

Marc nudged him to get his attention. "Come on, I'm done with this sweathouse."

Chapter 4

The Minnesota State Capitol was an impressive sight from the outside and even more so from the inside. Luke would say that much for the stately house. He still thought he worked in the state's coolest building, but the Capitol ran a close second for the title. After registering his surroundings, Luke's mind quickly returned to his most pressing concern: tonight's game.

As the Blizzards delegation made their way to the Capitol's third floor, Jim directed the group around various sculptures and busts. While passing through an archway into another hallway, Luke saw a sign on the marble wall announcing that the offices of Representative Johnson were located at the end. Seconds later, they entered the offices and a middle-aged man greeted the group as he rose from his desk.

"You must be from the Blizzards. My name is Tyler," he began eagerly as he circled the group and shook hands. "The representative was held up in committee. If you'd like to grab a seat in his office, he'll be right with you." Tyler motioned the group to the office just left of his desk.

Pausing in the doorway, Luke felt himself smile as he caught his first glimpse of the politician's office. It was easy to deduce that the man was a big outdoorsman. Given the stuffed wildlife on the walls, Luke would wager heavily that the representative was a good friend of his taxidermist. The office wasn't what Luke was expecting.

The team didn't even have time to sit before they heard a booming baritone. "Welcome, everyone."

The group turned to see a man with broad shoulders, a friendly smile, and silver hair enter the office and set some papers on a side table. "Sorry I'm late. Committee ran over."

"Thank you for meeting with us today, Representative," Jim said.

"Please call me Scott, and the pleasure is all mine. I enjoy meeting with folks who have proposals coming before our committee." Johnson shook Jim's hand and began to move around his office to acquaint himself with everyone else in the group.

Jim seamlessly began the introduction process. "Let me introduce you to everyone. I believe you've worked with Meg Dwight in the past; we've recruited her to help us with the project given her extensive history here at the Capitol, and with sports and economic development issues. Next to her is our public affairs director, Sean Williams, who along with me will be our team's main contact on this proposal. Next to Sean is Sara Smuth from Mayor Wallace's office. And last but not least, Luke Coffey, our team captain."

After handshakes were shared with all, Johnson turned to Luke.

"I'm sorry to say that I don't get much time to watch hockey during the session months, but I hear you're doing good things for the Blizzards this year, Luke. My wife and I have season tickets to the U's hockey games. We've had them for years. I remember watching you play back in your college days."

Even though he still wasn't happy about being part of the arena pitch, Luke smiled sincerely at the mention of his glory days. "Thank you, sir. Those were some fun years. They prepared me well for the Blizzards."

Johnson shook his head in the affirmative. "Your stats sheets would agree."

Turning back to the whole group, he motioned toward the chairs, "We'll get started soon; we're just waiting for my committee administrator. Dani ran over to Senator Gilbert's office to discuss some things with our counterparts, but will be back any second. Please feel free to grab a seat or look around the office. I'll be back in a minute."

Trying to keep his mind off the fact that he could be preparing for that night's game instead of wasting his time there, Luke took a closer look around the office.

He headed toward the back of the room, which was lined with pictures and certificates. They were mostly community awards and local-event recognitions. The representative's election certificate hung in the center of the back wall. Out of the corner of his eye, Luke saw Sean approaching. He'd never gotten along with this particular suit.

Feeling a bit annoyed, Luke didn't look up. "So much for this meeting going quickly," he muttered. "This Danny guy better get here soon."

"Oh, I don't think you'll mind the wait," Sean said smugly.

Luke did turn to Sean then, not knowing how to interpret that comment. It looked like Sean was fighting back a grin. Not that interested in knowing why and not wanting any reason to extend their conversation, Luke turned back to the representative's plaques and certificates while Sean approached the representative, who'd just come back in.

On days like today, as the precipitation alternated between snow and sleet, Dani nurtured a love-hate relationship with the tunnel. It kept her dry and warm as she raced back and forth between the Capitol and the State Office Building, or SOB, as the insiders affectionately called it. But she wasn't keen on having to wade through the musty, damp passageway—especially when it was crowded with other staffers also trying to avoid the unpleasant weather.

It didn't help that some Senate committees had just adjourned and members were heading back to their offices in the SOB. Human roadblocks kept popping up in the tunnel as lobbyists jockeyed to catch a word with senators while they walked.

Dani rose up on her tiptoes to see how the tunnel traffic was flowing. Personally, she figured that if the Blizzards waited this long to bring their proposal forward, a few more minutes weren't going to make a difference. But as happy as she was to make Sean wait a little bit, she didn't want her tardiness reflecting poorly on the boss, so she started to hustle.

"Excuse me, I just need to sneak past you quickly. Oops, sorry, Senator, didn't mean to bump you! Excuse me—thank you so much!"

Having taken this trip many times as a page the year before, Dani's weaving skills were well polished.

"Finally!" she muttered after encountering a break in the traffic. Darting as fast as her three-inch heels would allow, Dani booked it to the next elevator bank. She hoped her mental note to buy some flats would soon stick. She was already a little wary about meeting with the Blizzards given her last meeting with Sean, and feeling rushed and unsteady on her feet wasn't helping. Dani lunged to stop the elevator door that was closing a few feet in front of her.

She received a few annoyed glances from the people occupying the elevator. And the woman she plastered herself against so the doors would close offered a very clear "Humph!" Dani pretended not to notice any of them.

Exiting the elevator on the third floor, Dani booked it to their offices. Glancing at her watch, she saw that she was seven minutes late.

"Oh well, better late than never," she mumbled to herself.

No time to stop for a sip of water or to make sure that she looked presentable—Dani headed straight toward the boss's door. Giving a quick smile to Ty, who was on the phone and unsuccessfully trying to motion to her, Dani grabbed the door handle and put her weight into it.

After swinging open two feet, the door shuddered to a stop as it connected with a solid mass. A mass that let out a not-so-eloquent "What the—?" at the exact moment Dani managed a very Minnesotan "Uff da" as she ricocheted off the vibrating door. She couldn't help but groan. It felt like her brothers had just caught her in a game of red rover.

Still recovering from the shock, Dani rounded the door to apologize and came face to face, or rather face to neck—a strong neck at that—with Luke Coffey. Her shock doubled upon seeing the face of the immovable mass she'd plowed into, but she was coherent enough to know that she should be contrite. Blizzard or not, she felt awful about the collision. "I am so sorry!"

Quickly processing what Luke was looking at, Dani understood why he'd been behind the door. "I was expecting you to be meeting already." And even if she'd anticipated their late start, never in a million years would she have guessed that Luke Coffey would be standing behind the office door, admiring her boss's mounted ten-point buck.

In the silence, Dani looked from the deer head back to Luke Coffey and found him staring at her with a bemused expression and rubbing his shoulder, which made her feel even worse.

"Can I get you anything? I have some aspirin in my office. Tylenol maybe? Chocolate?"

The last offering caught his attention. Before Luke could reply, the boss decided to step in. "Dani, I'm sure that Mr. Coffey is just fine. He took harder hits in his peewee games." Waving the two of them over, Johnson motioned to the table. "Why don't we all grab a seat so we can get started."

Looking back to Luke, Dani stuck out her hand and tried to save face. "I'm Dani, the committee administrator. Again, so sorry."

Luke stopped rubbing his shoulder long enough to shake her extended hand. "Luke Coffey." After dropping her hand, he motioned toward the table and answered the previous question. "And I'm fine, you just caught me by surprise. I wasn't expecting someone to whip open the door with quite that much force." She could hear the laughter in his voice as he continued. "Or offer me chocolate to ease my pain!"

Had she been alone, Dani would have hung her head in mortification. But, chocolate always made her feel better, so she could only imagine it would have the same analgesic effect on others.

Luke pulled her back to the moment. "The more important question is, are you okay?"

She could only nod her head. Amazed that the hockey star was being so understanding about her clumsiness, Dani was touched that he was concerned about her. Looking back at Luke, Dani mouthed "Sorry" again and turned before he could notice the inevitable blush. Her fair skin never missed an opportunity for a good blush. Turning to face the other meeting participants, Dani began introducing herself like the professional she was trying to be.

"Dani, very nice to meet you. I'm Jim Keller from the Blizzards. This is Sean Williams, our public affairs director. I believe you met last week."

They'd actually met more than a decade ago, but no one needed to know that, no one but the boss. She'd explained the situation to him, though she'd intentionally left out Sean's attempt to persuade her to support the proposal. She could handle Sean on her own. The boss, as always, was understanding and said the old connection with Sean or her family's hockey presence wouldn't cause problems. The disdain in her voice as she spoke of Sean no doubt further comforted the boss about her impartiality.

Dani looked over the visitors and assessed the others during introductions. Jim struck Dani as a true businessman: impeccable grooming, a nice pinstripe suit that was perfectly tailored, and an overall confident presence. He had an aura of experience. From his build, she assumed he'd been an athlete himself back in the day.

Dani turned to greet Sean. She drew on her acting skills again and delivered a performance that had no one suspecting he was currently on her do-not-like list.

He moved closer to her as he shook her hand and flashed his cocky grin. "Nice seeing you again, Dani." He tilted his head as he asked her a question that was clearly audible to everyone in the office. "You still go by Dani, don't you?"

Since he had called her by that name last week, she was confused by the question—until she saw the gleam in his eye. If Sean was trying to make known their prior connection for whatever nefarious reason he had in mind, she was having none of it. "That is my name," she replied tersely.

Dani extracted her hand from Sean's grip and moved to meet Meg, who had heard their exchange. "Is Dani short for something?" Dani had met Meg a couple of times before at the Capitol, but they had yet to work on a project together.

"Danielle. I'm the fourth of seven kids and the only girl." Feeling like people were waiting for more, she felt the need to explain her name further. "I think my parents thought I was going to be another boy and had their hearts set on Daniel. Once they saw that I was in fact a girl, they added a couple of letters but kept the nickname the same. I only go by Danielle when I'm in trouble."

Like everyone in the room, Meg chuckled at the quip. Just as she was about to move on to Sara, Dani caught Sean giving her body an once-over. Growing up with brothers, she knew the way guys acted, but to check her out in the middle of a professional meeting was too crass for Dani's liking. Her blush was returning, but this time it was anger, not annoyance, bringing the heat to her face.

She heard Luke clear his throat. Maybe he'd noticed Sean's rude survey as well.

Before letting her go, Meg said, "Wow, seven kids, and you're the only girl. Must have been interesting growing up in your house."

"It had its moments!" Dani responded with laughter in her voice. In truth there were more outrageous moments than she could ever recall.

Dani moved to greet Sara so the meeting could get underway. Time at the Capitol during session was precious. Dropping Sara's hand, Dani circled the table to grab her seat, which she made sure was not next to Sean.

"Was that often?" asked Luke.

Hoping that either her blush had faded or the lighting in the office was dim enough that he wouldn't notice it, Dani turned to the hockey star who she would admit was way too good-looking to put any woman at ease.

She was confused by his question. "Excuse me?"

"Were you in trouble and called Danielle often?" Luke clarified.

Looking up at Luke, Dani would have bet her favorite pair of shoes that Luke was trying to hold back a smile. "Only when I ran into people with doors!"

Luke let out a bark of laughter. It was a genuine, booming laugh and not one of those fake sounds people made to stay in character. His reaction made her smile, but she wasn't letting her guard down for one second around this group. She picked up her pen and put on her game face.

Chapter 5

"I'm sorry, Jim. Would you repeat those last figures?"

Dani liked to think of herself as someone who kept her cool no matter what was going on around her. Growing up in family of nine had made her immune to distractions, or so she'd thought. But with an ex-boyfriend a few seats away, an all-star hockey hunk across the table, and a massive bonding proposal on the table before her, she was definitely fazed.

The situation was only made worse when she glanced up from her notes and made eye contact with Luke. She had a sixth-sense feeling that the gorgeous center was looking at her. He hadn't spoken since their exchange about her name, but he seemed to be making an earnest effort to follow the discussion. If his vaguely irritated expression and rigid posture were any indication, though, Luke was not all that eager to be at the meeting. Unlike Sean, who was inserting himself into the conversation at every opportunity, even when his perspective wasn't needed. Luke, she realized, didn't need to be the center of attention.

A few minutes later, the sixth-sense feeling was back. Glancing around the table, Dani saw that Sean was also looking at her. He always had a lot going for him in the looks department, and if Dani were honest with herself, she'd have to admit that he was more classically beautiful than Luke, but he also had an extremely unattractive amount of cockiness. Something that Luke was missing. Surprisingly. Sean had given her the impression that Luke was an active member of the project, but all indications today suggested the opposite.

Quickly glancing back at Luke, Dani recognized that she was on the receiving end of two very different looks. Like his once-over of her body before the meeting, Sean's gaze was definitely a leer. Luke's gaze was more difficult to define. Although not unfriendly, his look was somewhat reserved. Or maybe confused, she thought. It was as if he was trying to process something. Just like she should be processing what Jim was saying, but was instead fancying herself a mind reader.

"So, in a nutshell," she started, hoping she had caught enough of the conversation to summarize correctly and not sound like a buffoon, "there isn't anything structurally wrong with the Rink. This proposal is to enlarge the facility. Correct?"

"Correct," Jim elaborated. "Right now our arena holds about sixteen thousand people. As you probably know, we've sold out every home game for the last seven years—a major feat for any sports team. Knowing a significant number of fans are being turned away every game, we decided to do an impact analysis to determine how many fans were unable to attend games due to capacity restrictions. Then we calculated the coinciding revenue losses."

Sean enthusiastically jumped in, again. "Not only are we losing ticket sales, but the city and state are missing out on the extra revenue that would come from the taxes on ticket sales, parking, hospitality taxes, and so on. Additionally, many entertainment acts don't even consider doing a show at the Rink because it's too small. If they know they can sell out a twenty-thousand-seat arena, they aren't going to look at venues that max out on capacity so far under their average."

"Do you have data to back that up?" Dani hated to be a stickler for detail, but this was a pretty big selling point of their pitch and she didn't want it to be false—like some of Sean's other statements.

If Sean was surprised by her request for proof, he didn't show it. "We do. We have communications from at least five acts who visited Minnesota last year." Sean then proceeded to list the acts, which Dani took down in her notes. He handed out a financial breakdown before he continued. "The Rink is a great venue, but the Center across the river in Minneapolis holds about six thousand more. We'd like to help the state and city capitalize on the potential of bringing more marquee acts to the capital. And keep the success of the Blizzards going, of course."

Dani peered up at Sean from her notes. "I see."

He'd always been a smooth talker. Sean still had the ability to frame any situation to benefit him. It was a highly valued and exploited skill in politics.

"So how many extra fans are you hoping to pack in the house with this expansion?" the boss asked. Though he never took notes, the representative had a canny knack for remembering figures and anecdotes, a trait Dani envied.

It was Meg's turn to discuss the infrastructure. "The Blizzards and the city recognize that one of the reasons fans and performing acts are drawn to the Rink is its size and ambiance. We certainly don't want to change that too much. These drafts," Meg continued as she passed out some small-scale blueprints, "show a seating increase of slightly over thirty-five hundred seats. That would make the Rink's capacity just under twenty thousand. We believe an expansion of this size would substantively enlarge the facility while maintaining its famous atmosphere."

Jim took over. "According to the analysis and surveys we contracted, the team is well positioned to fill the additional thirty-five hundred seats every game. And this number brings us more in line with the Center in Minneapolis, making the Rink more marketable for big traveling acts."

"Your proposal seems to be contingent on the Blizzards continuing to sell out every game." She directed her question to Jim, Sean, and Luke. "How can you be sure that the team will continue to accomplish that feat?"

She wasn't surprised when Sean was the first to speak up. "Of course, there's no way to know for sure. The economy has a hand in things like this, but we have a ten-year waiting list for season tickets and a rush line that's out the door and around the block for every game. And as you know"—he nodded at Dani—"we have a great team with a number of great new player prospects on our radar."

Dani's expression remained unchanged, but she didn't miss that Sean had addressed that last comment to her.

Sean's gaze didn't move from hers as he continued, "Minnesotans love hockey, and we have players, like Luke, who really appeal to the fans."

Everyone turned toward Luke who, to his credit, Dani thought, looked slightly embarrassed. Dani didn't doubt for one minute that Luke appealed to thousands of fans—especially the female kind.

"Why are you looking to the state to help you bond for this project?" Dani inquired. Usually the boss asked the questions, but she just couldn't stop herself with this group. She wasn't trying to imply anything improper was going on, but the Blizzards were obviously a successful organization and she wanted to know their motives. "The state gets numerous proposals every year for capital funding. Is this something just the city could take on since they're your local partner?"

In a voice slightly scratchy from being quiet for so long, it was Sara's turn to join the conversation. "The city is very supportive of the proposal. However, due to the current economic situation of our state and city, it would be difficult for St. Paul to cover the entire project. We are willing to help with a significant portion, though."

"As are we," added Jim. "We know this expansion could lead to a great deal of new revenue for our team, but we also believe it will be a great benefit for the public agencies. We're committed to maintaining our positive relationships with our host city and the state."

"Well, everything has been presented here very well," chimed the boss. "Luke, you're the only one who hasn't spoken up. Is there anything you'd like to add?"

Dani thought Luke seemed a little taken aback by the question. But if he was nervous or unsure of himself, it wasn't apparent in his voice when he spoke. "Nothing that you haven't already heard at this meeting. I'm not familiar with the studies that have been done, but I can speak from personal experience about the lack of seating from chatting with the fans."

"Captain Luke here saves the day and gives away tickets for almost every game," chided Sean. "Always a do-gooder."

Not sure if that was supposed to be a jab or an accolade, Dani remained quiet but looked back to the man who was making her second-guess her preconceived notions about pro athletes. She thought she caught a flash of annoyance in his eyes, but Luke just shrugged and looked around the table. She wasn't sure what to make of him yet.

Dani broke the awkward silence and changed the topic. "Typically we create tours for members to visit the bonding proposal sites around the state. Most proposal sites were visited late last year since it's so hard for members to get away from the Capitol during the session months. And," she could resist adding, "most proposals were submitted with plenty of time for review." She turned to look at the boss, who understood her silent question.

"But a proposal this big warrants a tour," Representative Johnson offered. "Dani, if you could set something up, that would be great. Some members might not be able to make it, given our sometimes inflexible schedules."

Before she could respond, Sean spoke up.

"That's great. Dani, I can work with you—"

The rest of his offer was lost as Tyler knocked and poked his head in the office. "Sorry to interrupt, but your constituents are here, boss. They have to catch their bus to head back in twenty minutes. I put them in the conference room down the hall."

"Thank you, Tyler. I'll be right there."

Standing up to close the meeting, Johnson turned to Jim, "Well, thank you, everyone. I look forward to working with you in the upcoming weeks. Dani can set up a tour."

After a quick round of handshakes and thank-yous, the group left the office. Before they moved very far, the main door to the office swung open. Shirley, the tenacious reporter from Channel 3, practically skipped into the office as she realized she'd hit the jackpot.

"Oh, isn't it my lucky day!" She clapped her hands in excitement. "Did you just meet with Representative Johnson? About the Rink? Do you mind if I ask you a few questions on camera about how it went?"

Shirley asked her questions so quickly no one could respond, but once there was a break in her barrage, Sean took charge of the situation. "Sure, if you wouldn't mind giving us just a couple of minutes. We'll meet you out in the hall."

Shirley's smile stretched from ear to ear. "Sure," she said, heading toward the door. "We'll get everything set up out here."

Once she'd exited, Jim turned to Dani. "I would really like to set up that tour."

"Of course! If you'll just come into my office, we can discuss details."

Following Dani the few yards to her office, she swung open the door and felt the overwhelming need to apologize.

"I'm sorry about the stacks of files," she said, motioning to her office floor. "I'm organizing bills for upcoming hearings. I swear there's a method to my madness!"

Making her way to her desk, she saw that the others were taking the liberty of looking around her office. Although the space was small, it was professional with a scattering of some personal touches—like a picture of her and her six brothers decked out in their hockey gear. That was currently being analyzed by Luke. Their mom had taken the picture after a particularly satisfying three-on-three match-up with her as goalie. It was hard to make out all the details, but you could definitely tell she was in the middle, flanked by three guys on each side.

She thought it was far too convenient that Luke went right to that picture. Especially since it was on her bookshelf, which meant it wasn't so visible to guests but she could see it from her desk. She wondered if Sean saw the picture when he dropped off the proposal and mentioned something to his Blizzards colleague. Was Luke also going to try to exploit her hockey connection? Dani didn't know what to make of the wave of disappointment that washed over her at the thought.

"Is that you?" asked a quizzical Luke.

Dani wasn't offended by the surprise in his voice. She also wasn't convinced of its sincerity. She sometimes worried that her more famous brothers would be recognized, but so far that hadn't been an issue among the few people who'd noticed it, and the photo was her absolute favorite. Given her state of dress at the time—sweat-matted hair, wind-chapped cheeks, and no makeup—she was surprised her pride let her keep the photo displayed.

She nodded, "With my brothers." She didn't say who they were, since she was fairly confident Sean had already shared their history and his connection to her family. "We had just finished one of our three-on-three matches with me between the posts."

"Pretty and a hockey lover. That's a rare combination. Just my type." Sean's inappropriate comment had everyone turning his direction. He just smiled and she had to fight back a gag. He really was a piece of work. History had proven that she wasn't his type. They had fundamentally different views on fidelity, but he must have forgotten about that. She could feel her face reddening.

Thankfully, Meg spoke up. "Not so rare in Minnesota. Many girls play hockey," she scolded. "Both of my daughters are on their school team."

Dani was so thankful that the mom in the group had spoken up. Trying to backtrack, it was Sean's turn in the hot seat.

"Of course. I meant it as a compliment. It's nice to know that we'll be working with someone who appreciates and understands the game of hockey. From the picture, I'd say that Dani and her family appreciate the sport."

The jerk had real boundary issues, Dani thought. Before she had the chance to respond, Jim steered them back to the business at hand.

"As you know, Dani, the team is almost at the end of the regular season. We're a contender to make the playoffs, which would mean the Rink would be off limits." He pulled out his smartphone and started hitting some buttons. "I know this is late notice, but how about a tour early next week? The team will have a couple of days off, and we can get the legislators in."

Dani cringed at the mention of next week. They were nearing bill deadlines and schedules were packed.

"Next week really is short notice," Dani said with no sympathy in her voice. "Maybe next Friday? Or early the week after?"

Jim shook his head. "Friday won't work. We have a home game, and then the team has an away series. I worry if we push it back more, we'll have conflicts with committee deadlines."

He didn't need to tell her that. She was well aware of the tight time frame their late submission was forcing.

"We usually have committee on Monday afternoon, but we haven't sent the agenda to members. I'll send out a notice today that we'll be heading down to the Rink and see who's able to make it."

That seemed to appease the team. Dani could see Jim and Sean both nodding their heads. It was a good thing that Dani was already planning to come in this weekend to get some work done. Otherwise preparing for this new committee tour would have ruined any plans she'd made.

"Do you need anything from us?" asked Jim. "We'll have parking all set for you. Sean or I will follow up with you Monday morning." Upon seeing her shake her head in the negative, Jim extended his hand, which Dani took after rising from her chair. "Thank you for your help, Dani. I look forward to seeing you on Monday."

"We'll see you Monday, Dani, won't we?"

Turning from Jim to Sean, Dani answered the latter's question. "Yes, I'll be there. It's my job." She didn't mean to sound so harsh but she'd had enough of Sean for today. Trying to be a bit more amiable, Dani added a personal insight. "It's a great perk. I get to travel around the state to visit all the proposal sites."

The group headed for the main office door, where Shirley was undoubtedly waiting. Following Jim and Sean as they exited the office, Meg and Sara shook Dani's hand as they moved out of the small room. That left just Luke and Dani.

Lifting her head to look up at Luke, Dani thought she'd apologize one last time before politely ending their conversation. "Again, so sorry about running into you with the door. I hope it doesn't affect your game."

Dani was surprised to realize that Luke Coffey had a breathtaking smile with perfect, white teeth — not such a common thing among hockey players.

"I wouldn't expect anything less from a woman who can hold her own on a rink with six guys. Especially since they all look like gladiators."

His comment was so unexpected it almost caused Dani to laugh out loud. She was a woman with curves and muscle. Her brothers all outweighed her by quite a bit, but she could hold her own.

He motioned back to the picture. "That's a really great picture of you and your brothers."

She interpreted his repeat mention of the photo to mean he was fishing for more details. She wasn't going to give him any more than she needed to be polite. "Thanks. They're a great group of guys. The best, actually." The pride she had for her brothers was hard to mask even though she was wary.

"You're lucky."

As easy as it was to hear the love and pride in Dani's voice, it was just as easy to hear the melancholy in Luke's. If Dani remembered correctly from his player profile, Luke was an only child. After growing up with six siblings, Dani couldn't begin to imagine what her childhood would have been like as an only child. All of her favorite childhood memories included at least one of her brothers.

"Luke, we really need you out here." Sean's sharp voice came from Tyler's desk.

Extending his hand, Luke grasped Dani's hand with a firm handshake. "It was very nice meeting you, even if I will have a bruise." Luke smiled as Dani winced, and he gestured to the piles of paper on her floor. "Good luck with all of these bills."

Her smile returned. "Thanks, I'll need it!"

And with that, Luke Coffey walked out of Dani's office.

Dani watched as the group made their way out of the main office. She saw that a few other reporters now joined Shirley. Word of the Rink delegation's meeting had spread among the Capitol press corps as quickly as usual.

Closing her door, Dani grabbed a seat at her desk, logged on to her computer, and tried to push aside the riot of thoughts and emotions running through her. She especially tried not to think about Luke Coffey, even though she could still feel his hand holding hers. She told herself years ago that she was done with athletes. Sean's recent actions were reaffirming that plan. So her mixed feelings about Luke really made no sense. Especially since she didn't know him. And then the hypocrisy hit her like a brick: she didn't know him and yet she was judging him. She should feel bad about that, but her past wasn't letting that happen.

Twenty new emails were vying for her attention, but five minutes later she was still staring blankly at computer monitor picturing Luke Coffey and his gorgeous smile.

"Nice meeting, everyone." Jim folded his tall frame behind the wheel of the black SUV. Everyone else climbed into the remaining seats to head back to the Rink.

Sean was peeling off his jacket in the front passenger seat when he turned around to look at Luke, who'd taken one for the team and was sitting in the middle, allowing the ladies to take the window seats. "Maybe after your playing days, Coffey," Sean said mockingly, "you should transition over into the lobbying world. You seemed pretty comfy today."

Leaning forward to allow his elbows to rest comfortably on his thighs, Luke grunted noncommittally. He'd admit that today wasn't as bad as he thought it was going to be. Representative Johnson seemed genuinely nice, but the real surprise had been Dani. When she'd shyly poked her head around the door after whaling him with it, he'd been dumbfounded. Now he knew why he'd seen her at the Capitol before the press conference. And having seen how she'd handled the meeting, and how she didn't seem taken in by Sean's smarmy suaveness, Luke was impressed with her professionalism and intelligence.

Sean cleared his throat and Luke realized he was still waiting for a response to his last statement. "The political world may be for some people," he said, motioning to the ladies sitting next to him, "but I'll stick to the sporting world."

"Don't be naïve," Sean mocked, "you can be connected to hockey and work in politics. Just look at Dani."

Luke had never liked Sean. They'd first met when Luke was drafted and Sean was interning with the team out of college. Being almost the same age, Luke always got the impression that Sean was engaged in some kind of competition with him. They were in very different positions, but both were successful at what they did. Luke knew he shouldn't let the jerk rile him but Sean knew just how to push him. His current condescending tone was a good example. And how he'd targeted Dani with insinuations and leers during the meeting.

His irritation with Sean made him a little slow to process his latest jibe. "You're saying Dani's connected to both because she plays hockey with her brothers?"

Sean snickered. "You really didn't do your research before this meeting, did you? I saw you looking at that photo, but you must not have looked close enough."

The cocky smugness permeating from Sean was almost too much for Luke to handle. He didn't know what the jerk was getting at. He'd looked at that photo closely, but his attention had been focused on the blonde in the middle of the group. Any woman who could hold her own with six guys on the rink certainly had his respect and admiration — even if she worked in politics.

"Dani is from a very well-known Minnesota sports family." Jim decided to step in to defuse the tension that was no longer under the surface. Luke caught his glance in the rearview mirror. "You may have noticed that she didn't say her last name when she introduced herself. It's O'Brien. One of her older brothers is a professional baseball player, Jake O'Brien. Her younger brother, Sam, is currently at your alma mater and one of the Blizzards' top prospects. Her parents own Bats and Blades, the sporting-goods store, and are former sports standouts themselves. You could say she comes from something of a sports dynasty."

Sean turned around and smirked at the shocked expression on Luke's face.

Luke had no idea. He'd barely glanced at the faces of her brothers in the photo. He'd only wanted to look at her. The revelation hit Luke hard. That's why she looked familiar, he thought. He'd played a scrimmage with her brother Sam last year. The family resemblance was definitely there. His feeling of ignorance quickly transformed into additional annoyance toward Sean.

"Why didn't you mention something before the meeting? Isn't it your role in public affairs to prep us on these things? I've even played with her brother." He leveled a sharp stare at Sean. "Your mistake," Luke challenged.

The man in question just shrugged his shoulders innocently. "Everyone is swamped right now with extra work. I wasn't able to get out briefing books. Like I said, you should have done your research, captain."

Luke wondered what the punishment would be for decking the jerk. Thankfully there were ladies present and he wasn't in the most advantageous physical position.

"Don't feel bad." Meg patted Luke's arm like the concerned mom that she was. "I never would have known if it wasn't for the Capitol rumor mill."

Luke turned to Meg as she continued. "I've only spoken with her a few times since she hasn't been around the Capitol long, but she never brings up her family. She seems very private, very reserved about sharing any personal information."

Luke understood that sentiment completely. He'd experienced exploitation firsthand more than once. Thinking about it, he appreciated that she was so reserved about her family. It would undoubtedly be easier to network and move up the political chain if she were willing to name-drop, but it sounded like Dani was trying to do it on her own. He admired her for that.

Traffic was moving smoothly, so Luke let himself relax as best he could in the uncomfortable middle seat and think about the meeting. As soon as she'd rounded the door and started apologizing, he'd been stunned into silence. He'd recognized on first glance that she was physically his type. A little shorter than him, a healthy physique—not too skinny, athletic—

and the most gorgeous amber eyes he'd ever seen. He kept looking at her during the meeting just to catch a flash of their color, and her smile was just as impressive.

Luke heard someone clearing his throat. Snapping out of his daydream, he realized they'd reached the Blizzards ramp and parked. Everyone had exited the vehicle while he stupidly remained inside daydreaming. Sliding across the seat with as much grace as he could muster, Luke extracted himself from the vehicle and tried to save face.

"Sorry… I was thinking about some player reports for tonight." And wasn't that the real kicker. He hadn't once thought about tonight's game since being attacked by the door-wielding Dani.

Everyone was already heading toward the elevator. None of them seemed all that interested in his excuse. Except Sean, who was smirking—again! Sean said just loud enough for Luke to hear, "Player reports, my ass!"

Realizing that it wasn't worth the effort to argue with Sean, physically or verbally, Luke kept walking toward the elevators. It occurred to him that his annoyance wasn't just a result of Sean being his normal arrogant self. It also stemmed from the fact that Sean's assumption was right. When he should be focusing on tonight's game, he was picturing Dani apologizing to him for the third time while trying to hide her blush. He needed to get on the ice, and fast.

Chapter 6

Dani learned early in her legislative career that long hours and session went hand in hand. What she was begrudgingly learning in her new role was that those long hours extended through the weekend and into Monday. With no weekend to speak of, and a morning that flew so swiftly Dani almost forgot to eat lunch, Monday afternoon was upon her.

She looked at her clock and willed it to turn back ten minutes. She'd give anything for a catnap, but the clock wasn't yielding. Almost robotically, she started packing up her things for the rink tour when a telling question came to mind: what were the odds of her seeing Luke today? It wasn't so much the question that caught her off guard, as it was the excited feeling that she got about the prospect.

"Oh, Dani. What are you doing?" she muttered. Much to her chagrin, she couldn't answer her own question.

After posting an away message on her instant messenger, Dani was set to head to the Rink. She had emailed the committee members with instructions to meet in front of the Capitol where a couple of vans would take them downtown.

She walked out the main doors of the Capitol and saw Shirley speaking with one of her committee members on the marble steps. Not wanting to appear in any footage or be interviewed, Dani intentionally went wide of the cameras and hurried down the steps to the driver's door of her family's van, which her parents had graciously lent to her to serve as a car pool for today.

Opening the door to put her folder on her seat, she grabbed her list and pen and started checking that everyone was present and accounted for. Her boss came to stand next to her and glanced down at her checklist. To be safe, Dani double-checked her list before confirming with her boss. "We're all here, Representative." She saw him nod while he turned to bellow at the members.

"Times a wastin', everyone. Let's get this show on the road. Some of us need to be back in time for evening committees."

Although his personality reminded Dani of a teddy bear, her boss had a deep voice that reeked of authority. Everyone hurried into a van.

A couple of minutes later, the two vans—one driven by Dani and the other by a representative—pulled away from the Capitol and headed downtown. In no time, they entered a parking ramp located under the Rink. Spilling out of the vehicles, everyone moved toward the elevator bank. Waiting for them as they stepped out of the elevator cars were Jim, Sean, and Sara.

To Dani's unwelcome disappointment, Luke was nowhere to be seen. She decided she should be grateful for the improved peace of mind. But disappointment dominated again when she spotted Sean.

Jim held out his arms in an inviting motion to formally welcome the group. "Welcome to the Rink, everyone. Thank you for taking the time to come down and tour our facilities. My name is Jim Keller. I'm the vice president of public affairs and government relations with the Blizzards. The gentleman next to me is my associate Sean Williams, and next to him is Sara Smuth, representing the City of St. Paul."

Smiles and waves of greetings were shared before everyone returned their attention to Jim.

"I know we're on a tight schedule today, so we're going to head to the seats by the glass so we can describe the proposed expansion, and you can get a feel for the magic that happens on game nights."

His comments brought smiles from the members. Glass seats were a dream for hockey fans.

Jim began walking backward, leading the group as he continued, "After we've discussed the proposal from the rink level, we'll walk around the basement level to show you the upgrades that would be needed down there. Then we'll come back out here to one of the meeting rooms right behind us and get you on your way back to the Capitol."

Dani tuned out their hosts as she looked around the Rink. She enjoyed all the times she'd come here for games with family and friends, but was amazed at how different it looked when the concourses weren't packed with fans. She focused her attention back to the group as she saw Jim disappear down some aisle stairs.

She hung back while the representatives headed toward the prime glass seats. Her smile couldn't be contained as she heard an elderly representative swear under his breath at the intimidating sight of all the stairs. Dani was the last of the Capitol group to begin down the steps. She felt her smile fade as Sean fell into step beside her.

"I've seen you more these past two weeks than in the past two years, Dani," he said as if they were long-lost friends. "We appreciate you putting this together on such short notice."

Sean may have appreciated her organization skills, but she most definitely did not appreciate him putting his hand on her back while she was walking.

"Just doing my job."

For someone who considered herself an amiable person, she hated how annoyed she sounded. But between the leers and the unwelcome touch, he was getting way too personal. She was determined to be professional and not let Sean Williams get under her skin. She forced herself to keep her voice upbeat. "I'm happy that we got such a good turnout. I thought more members were going to have conflicts, but people seemed excited about coming."

His cockiness was evident as Sean responded, "I'm not surprised. You and I know how people love their hockey."

She rolled her eyes without worry, knowing that Sean was oblivious. He was in his own ego-driven world.

As he stepped down another riser, he reached into his pocket. "Before I forget, I wanted to give you my card. Feel free to email or call me anytime if you have any questions or need my help. I also put my personal cell on the back—it's changed over the years. Maybe we could meet up for a drink or dinner."

Her job required her to maintain an extensive business card collection, but this wasn't the usual kind of networking. She'd never had to field an offer for a date along with a business card before, so she treaded lightly. Her shock caused her to slow her descent. She reached for his card but couldn't make herself grab it. Instead she just stared at it until she could formulate a response that would put Sean in his place.

"I'm sure I won't have too many questions, but I can contact Jim or one of the ladies as well."

Looking a little put off, Sean held the card out a little further and tried again. "Really, call me anytime day or night."

Dani was absolutely certain that she wouldn't be doing that. She made herself grab the card as she forced out a laugh that hopefully didn't sound too fake. "I don't believe that's appropriate, and I don't foresee that happening—but thank you for the offer." She hoped it didn't escape his notice that she'd emphasized the impropriety of the moment.

Sean hesitated just enough on a stair that Dani thought, or rather hoped, that he'd gotten her meaning. Thankfully she didn't have to stay around to find out because they'd arrived at the glass. Members were taking seats to hear the next part of the presentation and Dani literally threw herself into an empty seat next to one of the members. It was on the aisle so Sean couldn't sit next to her.

For the next twenty minutes, Jim, Sean, and Sara talked the members through the expansion proposal as they motioned around the arena.

A rink filled with ice was fifteen feet away, but sitting in a seat with a thick peacoat wrapped around her, Dani was getting uncomfortably warm. Privately berating herself for not leaving her coat in the van, she shimmied out of the wool and threw it across the seat behind her.

After a few more minutes of Jim speaking, the group was invited to walk along the glass and enter the lower-level Zamboni entrance to check out some infrastructure changes that would be required. Dani stood up and would have normally let the members walk in front of her, but not wanting to get stuck with Sean, she made a quick move to be in the middle of the group.

She started chatting up one of the rural members who was new to the committee and one of the younger members in the House.

"What do you think of the tour so far, Representative Burns?"

"Very interesting! My boys—they're nine and seven—are really jealous that I'm here without them."

Dani smiled as she pictured two pouty boys. "Do they play?"

"Of course, and they're shamelessly lobbying me for a yes vote. But I'm not sure yet," the representative replied cautiously. "I need to see a bit more of the finances, but it sounds like that's the final pitch while we're here."

Dani nodded. The representative was known for being methodical, and she appreciated that. "I'll ask Jim to call your legislative assistant to set up a time so he can follow up with you."

The representative smiled in response. "Thanks, Dani. You're the best."

After touring the unglamorous parts of the Rink, which included the utilitarian hallways and HVAC areas of the lowest level of the arena, the group was ready to hear the final pitches. Sean was holding the door open to an inside staircase that would lead everyone back up to the main concourse. Just as she was approaching the stairwell Dani realized that in her hurry to avoid Sean, she had left her coat by the ice.

"Oh shoot," she muttered, causing Sean to stop in his tracks. "I forgot my coat on my seat. I'll grab it and meet you upstairs."

Dani saw his eyes light up in anticipation.

"Why don't I come with you?" he offered.

No, her mind screamed. She didn't want to be alone with Sean—at all—so she waved him back. "Oh no, you go with the members. Someone may have a question that you can help answer. Actually, you may want to chat with Representative Burns." Dani would say an extra rosary at church on Sunday for throwing the kind representative under the bus, but she was desperate. "She has some questions about the finances."

Sean looked like he was still going to object so she cut him off. "I remember my way back to our section; it'll just take me a second to find my coat." Already heading away from the group, Dani looked over her shoulder and waved at Sean. "See you in a few."

In no time she was back at the ice and making her way along the boards. From her vantage point she saw that a player had taken the liberty of using some ice time since their departure minutes ago. While she walked toward her previous seat, she kept her eye on the shooter. He was extremely accurate with his shots, until he got to the lower right corner. With the handful of shots she saw him take to that side, she noticed he wasn't quite as accurate.

He was wearing an unnumbered practice jersey that left her wondering who he was. But then he turned around and started skating her way. In an instant, even without the number or captain's C to identify him, Dani knew with absolute certainty that Luke Coffey was the skater in question. And he was heading toward her.

Without thinking, she ducked. She stayed crouched as she debated her options. Knowing that her coat was just a section away, she took what she thought was the best course of action. She started duck-waddling along the boards to stay hidden. She knew she was being ridiculous, but she didn't want Luke to think that she was spying. She valued her privacy and assumed that he did the same. In that moment it made complete sense to waddle to her coat and then run up the stairs when he started shooting again.

Taking a peek over the boards, Dani saw that Luke was still skating laps around the rink, which prompted her to keep waddling up the steps. She was almost to her jacket when she heard the unmistakable sound of blades scraping along the ice as someone came to a stop. She cursed under her breath.

Dani knew she was caught. Instinctively, she turned while crouched in anticipation of sprinting up the stairs. Realizing at some point she'd have to face the music, she straightened to her full height and faced the man who had her rethinking her self-imposed boycott on athletes.

Well, she thought as she stared into the light-brown eyes of the man on the ice in front of her, at least he didn't look upset to see her.

Most players took advantage of non-game days by spending time with their families or girlfriends. Since Luke's parents lived out of state and he was currently single, he decided to head to the Rink to catch a bit of alone time on the ice.

The team had taken a beating on the road yesterday. It had been an old-fashioned mauling in Toronto, and Luke needed to vent some frustration. Heading into the final weeks of the regular season, the team needed every win they could get to keep their playoff momentum going.

Scoring the lone goal for the Blizzards didn't make the loss any less painful for him. He was obsessing about a couple of shots that just missed the mark.

As Luke was walking to the ice after putting on his gear, he stopped at an equipment locker and pulled out a net. Other than his gear, the net was all he needed to play some "around the world." With his stick in one hand and the net in the other, Luke headed out onto the glassy surface that was like home to him.

Thinking that he saw some people in the mechanical area on the home side of the rink, he skated toward the Blizzards' side, not wanting to disturb the engineers he figured were working. Setting the net on its pegs, he began to warm up by skating around. When his limbs had been sufficiently loosened, Luke went to the team bench to grab a bag of pucks and dumped them in strategic locations around the ice. Once everything was in place, he started his practice set.

After shooting nonstop slap shots for a few minutes, Luke took a break from shooting and skated around, rolling his shoulders to stay loose. Mentally replaying the missed shots from last night, Luke restaged his puck drops to be similar to those plays. He was missing the two-hundred-pound goalie whose sole goal—his lame attempts at hockey humor always astounded him—in life was to stop his shots, but re-creating the mechanics of the shots was important.

Sixty or so shots later, Luke took another breather. Needing to shake out his limbs, Luke skated some laps around the rink. He thought he saw a flash of yellow on the other side of the glass, but then it disappeared. Making another swing around he saw the yellow again. It kept appearing and disappearing along the boards.

As he skated toward that side of the rink, he realized it was a blonde head. His gaze focused as he moved closer and saw that the blonde hair was attached to a body fitted with a white sweater and moving up the stairs while staying crouched. Letting his gaze dip lower, he noticed that the sweater led to black pants that were hugging a very nice figure. Thinking it was a reporter hoping to catch some personal ice time with Luke, or a fan trying to sneak some photos, Luke skated up to the boards with every intention of instructing the intruding blonde to leave.

The figure grabbed for something on the seat just as he skated to a stop. He patiently waited for the blonde to turn around. Her reluctance signified to him that she knew she was caught. Fully intending to demand the unwanted guest leave immediately, he couldn't hide his surprise when she finally turned around. For the third time in two weeks, he was looking into the beautiful eyes of Dani O'Brien. They were the same apologetic eyes that had looked into his after she'd blasted him with the door last week. He was surprised, but in a good way. And he definitely didn't want her to leave.

It took everything she possessed to not run up the stairs as fast as she could. She probably could have made it—she'd had the foresight to wear flats today—but she couldn't make herself flee the scene. Besides, she grew up with six brothers. Dani knew she could hold her own, so she straightened and squared her shoulders.

"Umm. Hi, Luke." Really, Dani, she thought, if that's the best opening you can come up with, you deserve any ridicule he sends your way.

It looked like Luke was getting ready to respond, but she plowed ahead, hoping to keep his ridicule at bay. "I wasn't spying on you," she blurted. "In case you were wondering. The committee's touring the Rink and I forgot my jacket on the seats where we started and had to run back."

While she was finishing her explanation, Luke started moving slightly to his right, leading him to one of the team benches. He stepped into the bench area and moved toward the door that would lead him out into the stands and right in front of her.

She was preparing herself to be reprimanded for interrupting his practice, so she was completely surprised upon hearing Luke's warm welcome and seeing his genuine smile. That smile, she was quickly realizing, made her feel slightly light-headed.

"Dani, it's nice to see you." Her blushing presence was the last thing he was expecting during his private practice, but he was genuinely happy to see her again. "And I didn't think you were spying," he lied. "I forgot about the tour. Usually I check the ice schedule, but today I didn't. I just had to skate."

Glad to hear he wasn't upset about her interruption, Dani was playing mental chess, trying to determine the best move. She knew she should be reserved and somewhat annoyed since he'd conspired with Sean, but he was making it difficult with his candid reactions.

"The tour went really well. Or is going well… At least I think it is still going." Great, she thought. First she was mumbling and now she was rambling. Where was her confidence when she needed it? "It was going, anyway, before I came back for my jacket." She picked up said article of clothing. "I had to run back for it." And now she was repeating herself.

Dani knew she should say good-bye and head back up the stairs, but she was reluctant to cut off the conversation with Luke so quickly.

"Do you come in often on your off days?"

She realized that the question was kind of personal. She hoped her attempt to prolong their conversation didn't offend him.

Leaning back against the glass, Luke didn't seem annoyed by the question. In fact, Dani thought that he looked as reluctant to leave her company as she was to leave his.

"It depends how I played the previous game. Yesterday wasn't my best showing, so I wanted to come in to practice and blow off some steam. It's hard to get much useful ice time when I have to share it with the rest of the guys."

"I used to have to fight my brothers for every inch of the ice growing up," Dani emphasized. "As for yesterday, congrats on the goal!"

"Thank you. The goal was nice, but I missed some shots." Feeling completely at ease around Dani, Luke shared one of his biggest personal critiques without even thinking about it. "I tend to go wide when I'm shooting for the lower right corner."

He tensed immediately after sharing his insecurity when he saw Dani start to smile, afraid that he'd inadvertently given her some fodder for exploitation, but his concern faded when he saw the sparkle in her gorgeous eyes.

"Me too! That's my worst area of the net. My brothers have used it against me since they realized that years ago. It is frustrating as all get-out."

"Your brother, Sam, doesn't seem to have a problem with it," he stated simply.

It was her turn to tense. "That's right, you know all about my family."

Luke heard the animosity in her voice and saw it in her eyes. He didn't like whatever caused the change.

"No, I don't." When he saw the animosity change to speculative disbelief, Luke knew he had to do something to change her misconception. "Don't believe me? Then how's this for knowing your family: I thought you were a guy!"

He was so emphatic about that statement, Dani had to smile. Then she mentally replayed the beginning of her conversation with Sean in the representative's office as a confused Luke looked on.

"I don't know, Luke. Sean implied that you both thought passing the arena bill would be a great way to entice Sam to play for the team."

"What?" Luke had the good grace to look genuinely outraged. "That pompous—" He stopped himself before really speaking his mind. "I never would have known who you were had Sean not told me in the car *after* we left the Capitol."

Dani hadn't taken her eyes off of Luke. "Was that after the press conference?"

"No, after you whacked me with the door," Luke

teased. "But it could have been after the press conference. I was going to go with Sean when he was meeting with 'Danny,' *the guy*, to drop off the expansion proposal, but I ran into some school kids at the Capitol for a visit. So I hung around to chat with them."

Flashing back to her first conversation with Sean, she remembered him mentioning that Luke was hamming it up with some fans. He failed to mention that those fans were idolizing kids. Luke's story was making a lot of sense, except one last part.

"Why did you go to the photo in my office? Did Sean tell you about it?"

Luke leveled Dani a gaze that was direct but soft. "I'm a hockey player, Dani. I saw something that was hockey related." He took a couple steps, which landed him on the stair below Dani, making them stand eye to eye. "But believe me, I didn't notice anyone in that photo except the beautiful woman in the middle decked out in goalie gear, with a smile so warm it could melt ice."

Dani's breath caught. She opened her mouth to say something but nothing came out.

While he watched her process his telling compliment, Luke remembered something about his playing time with Sam. "Have you ever noticed that he leaves himself open on the right side while skating?"

Dani heard her voice catch as she responded. "Wh-who?

"Your brother Sam. I was able to steal a couple of pucks from him in an exhibition game at the U. He didn't see me coming up behind him. It just took a little nudge. You should try it sometime."

Dani was touched. He wasn't leveraging her for something that would benefit him or the Blizzards; he was offering information that might help her best her brother in a family skirmish. He was so unlike Sean and so different from the type of guy she'd thought he'd be. "I'll remember that." She was going to thank him for his honesty when she heard an unwelcome voice from above.

"Dani, are you ever coming back?" Sean yelled from the top of the stairs loud enough for anyone in the arena to hear. "The representatives are waiting for you."

Feeling slightly guilty, Dani glanced at her watch; it had only been five minutes but she could have stayed there for another hour talking to Luke. It felt so natural.

"I'm being summoned," she announced begrudgingly as they shared a smile. "I should get back; I've been neglecting my duties for too long." She motioned to head up the stairs. "I'm sorry that I kept you from your practice." She paused for a moment that she knew was telling. Turning around, she started ascending the stairs. A few steps up, she whipped around. Luke was watching her. "Luke?"

"Yes."

Her voice was soft but firm when she said, "I believe you." And with that, she started running up the stairs, leaving Luke with an excellent view of her backside in motion. He took some time to admire the sight before glaring at Sean. He saw the suit place his hand at the small of Dani's back as she approached and his hands reflexively clenched into fists in his gloves.

"Damn," he muttered. He skated back onto the ice, charged a puck, and sent it sailing—all the while imagining Sean's face on the flying puck.

Chapter 7

"Kim," Dani said, shuffling through papers on her desk without looking up, "did we get the new version of the amendment for the trail bill?"

Out of the corner of her eye, Dani could see Kim flying around the office.

"Yep, I have fifty copies down at the printers. Running to grab them."

"Fabulous!" She heard the office door close, finished sorting a pile of papers, sat back in her chair, and leaned back to take a few deep breaths and rest her eyes.

The week after the Rink visit was a crazy time at the Capitol. The day that every Capitol reporter was waiting for and the day that had caused Dani to miss many hours of sleep had finally arrived—the Rink bill was being heard in her committee.

Dani had been glued to her phone all day. And

when she wasn't on the phone or talking to people in her office, she was tracking down Ty and Kim to make sure everything was set for committee.

She'd hardly set foot in her apartment that week. Committee had been meeting all day, every day, to begin hearing all two hundred and some odd bills. It had been a marathon of a week and Dani knew that this was only the beginning.

Today's committee would hear the four largest bonding requests, which included the Rink expansion. Each group was limited to fifteen-minute presentations but the question-and-answer session with the members was a bit more difficult to restrict. Often, there was no stopping the members when they were on a roll.

While downing a meal shake she'd stocked in her food drawer for moments like these, Dani checked, again, to make sure she had the proper documents for each proposal, including the summaries she'd created of every tour.

It had taken her hours to write all the summaries, but Dani was thankful she had. There had been so many visits and most had happened months ago, so it helped to have a detailed record for reference.

The tour of the Rink had taken place last week and would be fresh in everyone's mind, but she included her notes on that too, just to be safe. She had certainly been thinking a lot about that last tour in the past week. Even though it made her feel like a bad administrator (but a perfectly healthy, single, twentysomething female), she wasn't remembering the parts of the tour that related to the bonding request. She was replaying her conversation with Luke. More times than she cared to admit.

Mentally revisiting the conversation one last time before committee, Dani couldn't believe just how easy it had been to talk to him. He seemed so easygoing and genuinely interested in talking with her. His amiability was making it really hard for her to remember her self-enforced rule. And there was her dilemma: last week's conversation with Luke, and her discovery of Sean's most recent lies, proved to her that Luke wasn't like Sean or many of the other athletes she knew. But she wasn't sure it was enough to rethink her universal sanction against dating athletes.

Her head was hurting and she groaned audibly. "Keep it together, Dani. You're in the middle of session, he's in the middle of the season, and you don't have time for distractions right now."

Her lecture was obviously not successful because she was still excited about the prospect of seeing Luke later. She shook her head at her lack of self-control, but she didn't have any more time at the moment to continue berating herself.

Looking at her watch, Dani saw that committee was set to begin in two hours and the House was just starting session. She knew two controversial bills were set to come up on the floor, so committee might be delayed or postponed if the debate went long.

Much to her chagrin, ninety minutes later, session was still going strong.

"Ty, I'm going to head over to the floor and talk to the boss." She approached Ty's desk, sat down a chair in front of it, and rested her forearms on its smooth surface as she watched the live stream on his modern flat screen. "I'm thinking we'll have to push back committee a bit, but I want to get his approval before sending out the notice."

Ty nodded his head while still watching his TV screen. "It's looking like they could go for a while. Smythe is on a soapbox again, and I just heard them say they have twenty amendments at the desk."

"Well, that probably confirms it, but I'll run it past the boss anyway. Be right back!"

Dani headed the short distance over to the chambers—conveniently located just a floor down. Entering the House floor from the side hallway, Dani went to the boss's desk and knelt by his side. Leaning in slightly to chat with him, it took Dani less than a minute to get his approval and discuss session drama.

The boss nodded toward the back of the chambers. "Have you seen the crowd in the rotunda?"

"No," Dani answered as she looked toward the gated entrance, "I came down the back way. Crazy out there?"

"Pandemonium. The Blizzards are here."

Minnesotans loved their hockey. "Crazy indeed!"

Sneaking out the side door, Dani was able to avoid

the crowd and make it back to her office in one piece. Once there, she sent out a notice that committee would begin after session adjourned. Unfortunately, people wouldn't have much forewarning about the change of plan.

Her insight was validated as Jim Keller led the group who would be representing the Blizzards proposal into their offices. She was neutral about seeing Jim and most of the others, instantly annoyed by Sean, and slightly giddy at seeing Luke in the middle of the group. She really had to work on controlling this ridiculous crush.

It was never fun to tell people they were going to have to wait for committee; she hoped they'd understand. Letting out a sigh, Dani stood up from her desk and headed toward the group.

"Hi, everyone. Nice to see you again. I'm not sure if you know, but session is running late. It's looking like we're going to be postponed for a bit." With a slightly awkward wave, Dani motioned toward the chairs. "Feel free to grab a chair or mosey around the Capitol. We'll start about fifteen minutes after the House adjourns so the members can grab something to eat."

If Jim was annoyed by the delay, he didn't show it. Sean, on the other hand, was an open book. Jim obviously knew how the place operated and spoke up before his colleague could share his obvious frustration. "Thanks for the update, Dani. We could hear the House as soon as we walked into the Capitol. They're a lively bunch!"

"That's definitely true! Much more so than the boring Senate." That statement got a few smiles from the group. "By those last nights of session, everyone is so tired that any remaining decorum goes out the window. One member even brought a Segway at the end of last session for us staffers to try out. It was awesome, but probably entirely inappropriate."

"That's a nice story," Sean replied with no feeling. "Since committee is delayed, why don't we head downstairs and chat with the media?" Dani could practically see the opportunities flashing in his eyes. "That way we can hit the media before and after."

While the group seemed receptive to the idea, Luke hung back and surprised many when he spoke. "I'm going to wait around here until committee. I'll meet you down there."

Dani was already walking back to her office when she heard the announcement and whirled around. Her gaze flew to Sean. She could tell he was not happy. Having seen that same look so many times as a teenager, when he tried to convince her to do whatever was on his agenda, Dani knew Sean was trying to glare Luke into submission.

"We could really use you for all the interviews, Luke. It would be great for the team."

Luke shook his head in the negative. "I'm sure you can handle it. If this was going to be an interview about the team or our playing mentality, I'd be more than happy to help. But I think you guys are the better spokesmen on the expansion proposal. Anything I have to say would be exactly the same as what I said a week and a half ago at the press conference."

Sean started to respond, but Jim cut him off—he obviously knew when he could and when he couldn't push their star player. "That's fine, Luke. Just take a breather up here and we'll see you downstairs for committee."

Obviously not happy with the decision, Sean reluctantly followed his boss outside. Dani was standing in the doorway of her office when Luke turned around to ask if she needed help with anything. Surprised by the unexpected question, it took Dani a few seconds to respond. She assumed he'd just relax in one of their comfy office chairs and kill time on his smartphone, but he proved her wrong again.

"Thanks for offering, but I think we're all set. Ty and Kim will be heading down soon to get everything set up and I'm just going to keep watching session to see how it goes. Feel free to grab a seat anywhere."

Luke scanned his options before turning back to her. "Could I grab the one in your office?"

Was the Pope Catholic? Dani had to bite back the gasp that threatened to erupt. She silently wondered what woman would ever turn him away. Then she remembered that she should be that woman, but she wasn't going to do it.

"Sure, come on in. As long as you don't mind having session on in the background." Dani saw Luke shake his head. "Hopefully this won't go too much longer. Grab a seat!"

She closed the door as Luke got comfortable. Dani didn't even give herself a moment to relax before she started stressing about what to say. She usually was naturally at ease when talking to guys, but this was different—especially after his compliment last week. She could have fallen back on hockey talk, but she guessed that he got that all the time. She could do better.

"Chocolate?" Dani offered her guest as she reached into her drawer for a few pieces.

Luke's eyes flared with amusement as he reached forward to grab one of her favorite candies.

"Thanks, these are my favorite," Luke responded as he tossed the chocolate caramel into his mouth. "How was your weekend?"

Considering it was midweek, Dani was a little surprised by the question. Maybe he was a little nervous as well.

While she contemplated that reassuring thought, she considered her weekend. It had consisted of coming into work both days and then having a marathon of *The Golden Girls* each night while she stayed home and heated up leftovers she'd received courtesy of her parents. There was no way she was going to own up to those unglamorous details.

"Oh, you know, probably the same as you."

As soon as she spoke she remembered the team

had been away in New York over the weekend. Between the sites, the game, and the hotel swarmed with fans—especially the female kind—she was absolutely certain their weekends were far from the same.

She looked to Luke from the TV and saw a wicked grin forming. She probably couldn't even begin to fathom what he did when on the road. Well, she had brothers; she could guess. And she didn't like it. She could feel the heat start to deepen on her Irish skin. She dropped her gaze from his and mumbled, "Or not."

Dani could hear the laughter in Luke's voice when he spoke. "Well, after the game at the Garden, which we won, I headed back to the hotel and watched a *Star Trek* marathon." He was grinning while he spoke. "Were you watching the same thing?"

Her head snapped back up. What an enigma. Shrugging her shoulders, she tried to look bashful.

"Actually, it was *The Golden Girls* for me."

Luke threw back his head and laughed, causing Dani to smile.

"Great game, by the way. You guys played well. How's that right corner treating you?"

He shrugged his broad shoulders. "It's an ongoing project. I have years to perfect it."

She thought that was a telling statement. "Does that mean you see your whole life in hockey?"

For the first time in the conversation, Luke looked a little hesitant. "I love the game." He paused and held her gaze before continuing. Cautiously.

"You've probably read that I'm in a contract negotiation right now. Once my playing days are over, I'd like to stay close to the game—and the Blizzards. Whether that means coaching or managing or recruiting, or pulling a Brett Favre and coming out of retirement to play, I guess time will tell."

Dani could sympathize. "My brothers have similar sentiments."

Luke glanced at her hockey photo. "Are you close with all your brothers?"

Dani's grin was instantaneous. "We're one of those weird, ridiculously close families. The seven of us are only separated by about ten years, so we grew up doing just about everything together."

"I've played with Sam, and I know about Jake. Obviously sports run in your family. What about your other brothers?"

Fair question, Dani thought. "We grew up in a very sports-driven home. But even with that commonality, we're all pretty diverse. Chris is the oldest. Although he had a lot of interest from colleges for football and hockey, he had a higher calling."

Luke raised his eyebrows in a questioning gesture. "Did the league try to draft him right out of high school? What's his name? I don't think I know of him. Is he over in Europe?"

Dani smiled at Luke's assumption that the pros were the higher calling.

"No, actually his higher calling was from God.

He's a Catholic priest."

Dani felt her smile grow as she saw the surprise flash across Luke's well-structured face. Chris's choice of profession had surprised a lot of people, especially the scouts who'd tried to recruit him. Many thought he was crazy to give up a life in professional sports, but she knew he didn't regret his decision. And lucky for her, he'd attended an in-state seminary and was currently working for the local archdiocese so she got to see him often.

"Next to Chris is Andy. He played hockey and football in college, but followed a different family tradition of entering the military. He's an Army Ranger now. Jake is currently wreaking havoc on the baseball diamonds. Sam, who you know, is next youngest after me. And then the babies—Nate and Patrick. They're twins. They're in college now and athletic standouts. Who knows what they'll do. I just hope the world is ready for them."

Luke looked impressed. "That's quite the lineup. Your parents must be proud."

Dani glanced at another picture, one she kept on her desk and had taken of her parents on the lake years ago. She was pretty confident her parents were proud, but she gave a slight nod and muttered, "Hopefully."

Checking the TV to make sure session was still going, Luke switched the topic to her specifically. "So you took a little different path. Were you always interested in politics?"

She smiled as she thought about the past few years. "Honestly, no. I entered college planning to go into sports management and business. I thought I'd help run the stores one day, but I became really interested in the policy aspect of things—how laws are made to serve communities, all that stuff. So when I finished undergrad, I came home and started taking some public-policy classes. I took a shot and applied for a page position here last year as I was finishing my last year of grad school. It was only for the session, but at the end of session the CA—committee administrator—for this committee was retiring, so I applied with the representative and he took me on. A big leap of faith on his part!"

Luke didn't let her take a shot at herself. "Don't sell yourself short, Dani. He knew what he was doing when he hired you."

"Thanks, that's nice of you to say, but I'm sure it has been a little rough for him with a new administrator this year. I'm grateful that I've had this opportunity. And to think—"

She trailed off as she heard the Speaker of the House ask if there were any other announcements. "Oh, they're about to adjourn. That's our cue. We can take the back way to avoid the public traffic."

Luke's thanks came in the form of a sincere smile that had Dani practically melting. "That would be great. I try to avoid the cameras any chance I get."

Humility was a quality Dani admired in anyone. He was becoming more appealing to her at every moment, which meant she was in trouble. "I imagine in your line of work that's easier said than done."

Grabbing her folder and locking the office, Dani led Luke to the wood-paneled committee room. No surprise, it was a packed house. She came up with a bogus excuse to talk with another staffer so Luke could walk in before her. She didn't want people to see them together.

After she put her materials down on the committee table, Dani checked in with Ty. Everything was set to go; all they needed to do was have a majority of the members present and they could begin. A few minutes later, they had a quorum and the boss was rapping the gavel to begin.

On a normal legislative day, a committee-room audience mostly consisted of smartly dressed lobbyists tapping away at their tablets or smartphones along with a handful of citizens who were there for an issue on the agenda. Dani looked around the room and saw that today's audience was very different. Every age group, from elementary-school kids to senior citizens, was represented. Most were dressed formally, but a number were wearing Blizzards jerseys. Dani thought the room looked great. This is why she loved her job. She loved seeing people witness and participate in their government's process.

Although all four proposals were requesting funds for large projects, the first three proposals were completed in less than forty-five minutes. The last item on the agenda was the Rink proposal. People instantly became more alert.

Dani began typing the minutes for the proposal as Jim took the lead for the Blizzards and explained the bonding request. Sean sat at the table with him, as did Sara Smuth. Joining them was Representative Rice, whose district included downtown St. Paul and who was the chief author of the bill. The Blizzards were the face of the proposal, but the representative had the legislative responsibility for the bill. He'd been doing a lot of the behind-the-scenes work with other legislators. The last person at the table was Luke. Dani couldn't help it; her eyes kept going to him. She thought he looked like a seasoned pro, very composed and absolutely stunning in a dark gray suit that offset his gorgeous brown eyes.

Like every other project, the Blizzards had ten minutes to present their proposal and then it was a free-for-all for questions from members. Jim and Sara fielded questions on the logistics of the proposal and Sean interjected whenever he could. One of the northern Minnesota representatives asked Luke why he thought the project needed to happen.

The room got noticeably quiet. Everyone wanted to hear what Luke had to say.

Taking a second to clear his throat, Luke's smooth voice took over. "Mr. Chair, members, I've been to a few arenas in my life in hockey." People chuckled quietly at Luke's understatement. "Some professional venues, some amateur venues, but nothing compares to the Rink. To be honest, I don't know if I can put into words what makes our home so unique. But I can tell you a lot of it has to do with the fans. Minnesota's hockey fans are the best in the league."

An overzealous hockey fan sitting in the audience shouted, "Damn straight!" Representative Johnson rapped the gavel and explained that there was to be no commentary unless it came from the testifier's table, but not before everyone in the committee room had a good laugh. "You were saying, Mr. Coffey?"

Luke continued, "Fans are the reason we show up to the Rink every day. Without the fans, we wouldn't have a team. In the Rink's current configuration, we have to turn fans away at the door because we reach at capacity every single game. It's been that way since I started with the Blizzards. It's terrible to see a young fan come to the Rink hoping to see his first Blizzards game, only to be turned away at the door.

"The proposal before you wouldn't alter the Rink enough to change its ambiance, but it would provide extra seats per game to ensure our fans have a greater chance to experience the atmosphere. This bill would allow that." Luke looked at all the members before turning to Dani. "Thank you."

Dani was caught off guard by the sense of pride that overcame her. The papers had always been favorable to him, and Dani used to think it was because he was the Blizzards' poster boy. She was forced to emend her initial opinion of him and admit that he was just a good guy. She was learning that he just didn't like being in the spotlight, which was impossible to avoid with this project. But he was also smart—something the papers rarely highlighted. He spoke eloquently and had no problem with the formality of committee. As much as her sense of self-preservation didn't want it to be true, Luke Coffey was turning out to be the antithesis of everything she thought he'd be—arrogant, rude, and obnoxious. All the traits Sean had been showcasing during the process.

Since no other members had further questions after Luke's off-the-cuff speech, the boss thanked the Blizzards and the other groups for coming and adjourned the meeting. Everyone made a beeline for the testifier's table. Dani was going to say "nice job" to Luke, but people flanked him on all sides. She knew he'd have to do interviews since he'd bypassed them before. Thinking that there was no way to extend her congratulations, she headed back up to the office, fighting her disappointment at the realization that she wouldn't see Luke again for some time.

Once upstairs and unpacked from committee, Ty and Kim headed home. The boss had an off-site dinner that he had to head to, so Dani quickly ran a few things past him for the next committee meeting. Then she returned to her own office.

Dani unlocked her door, set down her notes and other paper, and began going through emails. A few minutes later, she ran down the hallway to make copies of a document and when she returned, Luke was in her office. Stumbling as she entered, Dani tried to hide her surprise.

"Luke," she finally managed to say, "I wasn't expecting to see you back up here. It looked like you had enough media down there to keep you busy for hours."

"I snuck away first chance I could. Sean had the press under control. He loves that." He bent to grab something on the chair. When he stood up, Dani saw that he was sporting a devious smile. "I left my jacket, so I took the back way up here."

The smile told her the jacket excuse was a ruse, but she played along with the meaningful fib. "It's a lifesaver!"

Their gazes locked in the same way they had in the packed Capitol lobby just a couple of weeks ago. Dani could have stayed that way indefinitely had Luke not broken the moment by dropping his gaze as he shifted his weight from one foot to the other.

"So... how did I sound?"

Dani was shocked to hear the nervousness in Luke's voice. He hadn't sounded at all nervous forty minutes ago in front of a whole committee that she knew for certain was being broadcast by at least a dozen news stations. She felt humbled that he sought her opinion.

"Honestly?"

Luke nodded.

"You did great!" she said with sincere enthusiasm. "Your group presented a concise proposal, and your speech at the end added a great personal touch to it. I was watching the audience while you spoke. You really resonate with people. That's a gift!"

Luke tried to wave off her compliment.

Again, his humility was endearing. "Do you know the next steps from here?"

"The boss puts together a bonding bill from all the proposals he's heard this session and then brings it before the committee to be voted upon. The Rink may or may not make the cut."

He nodded. "Well, it is what it is. No use losing any sleep over it. Jim mentioned something about coming back to meet with your boss and the other members of the committee again. I'm not sure if I'll be at those."

"You don't sound too happy about that prospect."

Luke couldn't hide his frustration. "Right now with everything so close, I wish I could just focus on my team and our playing. But these schedules coincide and nothing can be done about that."

"If the legislature has taught me anything, it's that you can't stress over things you can't change. And your playing has been great lately. You don't want to second-guess yourself there. You're a solid player."

Luke looked at Dani and knew that there was no false facade with the woman in front of him. Everything she'd achieved, she'd earned on her own. She could have fallen back on her family name, but she hadn't. That impressed the hell out of him. He met so many women who saw him as just a hockey player, or a checkbook, but Dani had sincerity written all over her. And he liked it—and her—a lot. He decided to take a gamble. They didn't have a game tonight and he wanted to spend some more time getting to know this sincere, amazing woman who chose to work in the frustrating, backstabbing world of politics because she loved the policy side and thought she could make a difference.

"Thankfully, there has been one positive thing about this whole experience."

Luke was looking at Dani so intently, she had no doubt he was talking about her. Damn her fair skin. She could feel her face growing warm.

He must have taken pity on her because he continued without waiting for her to reply. "I hope that this isn't too forward, Dani, but would you like to meet later for dinner?"

Even though it went against her grain, she'd been secretly hoping he'd ask. And now that it was out there, she had no idea what to do. Could she risk dating an athlete? Had she learned nothing? Would it be unprofessional? Thankfully, she had an excuse that would buy her a bit more time to decide.

"I can't. I already have plans for tonight." The regret she heard in her voice was genuine.

Luke's face fell as he assumed the worst. "Oh. I'm sorry, of course you're seeing someone. I'm an ass for thinking otherwise—"

Wanting to stop his misinterpretation, Dani cut him off by waving her hands in front of her. "No, no, no. That's not it at all. I'm very single." She cringed at how desperate that made her sound. "This is going to sound weird, but I'm in a dodgeball league with some work friends and we play tonight."

Dani saw Luke's eyes go from dim to lit. "Dodgeball? Really? I didn't even know they had leagues for that."

"City champs!" she stated proudly.

"You did it again," he laughed.

"Did what?" Dani asked as she tilted her head to the side.

"Impressed me!" He'd been holding his coat, but now he started to put it on. "We're heading out for a road series so I won't be around for a few days. Maybe we can connect when I get back?"

Heaving a sigh of relief, Dani knew she had a few more days to decide the victor of her internal debate and get her emotions in check. "Sure!"

And with that, Luke said good-bye to Dani and left the office.

As soon as she heard the door at the end of the hallway close, Dani snatched up her desk phone and called Piper. It took less than a ring for her friend to answer.

"You looked great on TV. How'd it go?"

"In a word, crazy! But what happened before and after took the cake. I know we have our game soon, but can we do a tunnel walk now? Please? This is major."

"Sure. Meet you by the stairs in five?"

Dani glanced at her watch. "See you in five!" She hung up her phone, reached under her desk and pulled out the pair of sneakers she kept around for situations just like this. She laced up and headed out. The bills could wait until tomorrow.

Chapter 8

"You will not believe what just happened!" she told Piper. Frankly, Dani couldn't believe it had and she'd been a witness. She had met Piper by the stairs and they were making their way down the marble spiral staircase to the basement of the Capitol.

Regulars around the Capitol knew the two women were close friends and often took walks, so any staffers passing them in their tennis shoes wouldn't think anything unusual was going on.

Paying close attention to the steps, Dani couldn't hold back the news until they made it down the four flights of stairs, even though the staircase had a terrible echo. Not taking any chance of the gossip hounds overhearing, Dani dropped her voice to a whisper. "I know this is cutting it close, but I can't wait to tell you. Luke asked me out!"

Piper slipped down a step and gasped. Dani wasn't sure if it was from the near fall or her announcement. In an attempt to catch her friend, Dani grabbed Piper's arm. In this position, if one went down the other would as well, but she wasn't letting go of her friend. "Careful, Pipes. Are you okay?"

Waving off Dani's arm, Piper regained her balance and her voice. "Forget me. Luke Coffey asked you out?"

Making sure they both had a solid footing again, Dani continued downward while maintaining a death grip on the banister. "I know. I can't believe it. He took me completely by surprise. He came back to my office after committee."

"Wait, back up? Was he there before committee?"

She nodded. "I'll come back to that later. Anyhow, he came up and we kept talking and then he said he hoped he wasn't being too forward, but he asked me if I'd like to meet him later." Dani broke off her explanation as her friend started clapping. Piper was a clapper. "I froze for a second, not knowing what to say. Then I remembered that we play tonight and I used that as an excuse."

Piper stopped on her stair and threw her arm out, effectively blocking Dani. "Do not tell me that you turned down a date with Luke Coffey to play dodgeball!"

Piper practically shouted the statement, which was then amplified by the enclosed spiral staircase. Dani cringed, hoping none of the Capitol gossips had heard.

With a shushing noise, Dani tried to rein her friend in. "Keep it down, will you! The gossip hounds can't know. I'm already treading on thin ice." Playfully pushing aside the arm that was blocking her, Dani continued down the last flight of stairs as she let out a frustrated groan. "I'm such a hypocrite, Piper. I practically vomited when Sean invited me to meet up for drinks to discuss the proposal. I told him that I didn't think it would be appropriate. And now I'm totally willing to throw 'appropriate' out the window because this time it's Luke asking. He's the athlete, Sean isn't. At least not anymore."

Piper snorted, which made Dani smile. "Slight difference though, Dani. Sean put your heart through a blender years ago. He doesn't deserve a second chance—you gave him plenty. And those other athletes you dated in college, you saw them for what they were early on. They were trying to use you to get close to your family's connections. Luke, at least from the stories you've told me, doesn't seem to be anything like Sean or those other guys. If it makes you feel any better, I'd be doing the same thing. Choosing Luke over Sean I mean, or I like to think I would."

Dani smiled at Piper. They'd become fast and firm friends over the past year and had shared so much. For Dani, it meant telling Piper about her family and old boyfriends, including Sean. For Piper, it meant telling Dani about her lack of opportunities with guys. Dani had learned over the course of their friendship that

Piper was painfully shy around guys, but she was trying to overcome it. If that meant talking big to try to convince herself, Dani was all for it.

They reached the basement level of the Capitol and set off toward the SOB. Dani knew they had about fifteen minutes of tunnel to talk. In addition to connecting the two buildings, the tunnel continued past each to connect a total of five government buildings accessible by key cards, which they had.

The tunnel made a circle that was just shy of a mile. People used it in the winter to avoid the weather, others used it year-round as a way to get in a bit of exercise on their breaks. Dani and Piper often walked the route as an excuse to catch each other up on the day's events and just get away from their desks. Sometimes, like now, girl talk was on the docket.

Speeding up to pass a slow walker, Piper looked at Dani. "Okay, maybe you should start from the beginning and tell me what led up to this. Don't leave out even the most minute detail."

Having already told Piper about the first meeting at the Capitol as well as the Rink tour, Dani filled her friend in on the day's events. She told Piper about the small interaction with Sean, about Luke's desire to wait out the delay in the offices, even about his offering to help—and, of course, she shared her biased opinion of Luke's great appearance in committee. Piper, being the friend that she was, assured Dani that she wasn't being biased. Piper, as well as everyone else in the Capitol, had tuned in to watch the committee and agreed that his speech was the standout.

"I can't believe that you told him no. And to say it was because of dodgeball? Come on, Dani. That's an excuse I would have used, not you."

Swiping her key card at an access point, Dani laughed. "Actually, he seemed really impressed by that. He had no idea that dodgeball leagues exist. He gave us kudos on being city champs!"

Piper groaned as she answered. "You told him that?"

"Well, it's true," Dani replied defensively.

"Compared to the Stanley Cup, it seems pretty lame."

"Well, I think it's pretty great."

Dani heard her friend's audible smirk. "Okay, so what happens next? Will you see him soon? What's the deal?"

"They have a long away-game stretch, and he mentioned something about the Blizzards meeting with the boss and other members of the committee in the upcoming weeks, but he wasn't sure if those were set or if he'd be a part of them."

Piper hadn't ceased shaking her head. "I still can't believe you turned him down. You may not want to hear it, but he seems like a good guy. I haven't read anything about him causing drama. He seems to be a perfect citizen." Piper peered over at her friend. "You aren't going to let your no-athlete ban stop you from seeing him. Are you, Dani?"

Dani swiped her card again at the next security point. "It's not completely unjustified. For the past few years, that policy has served me well."

Piper snorted before she responded, "No, it hasn't."

Her friend's honesty was something Dani admired dearly. Piper didn't sugarcoat anything for her; she told it like it was.

"And you know it, Dani. Those boring academics and politicos you dated the past couple years had something missing. Personally, I think it's the sports connection. It's a part of you, sweetie." Dani felt her friend put her arm around her shoulder as they kept walking. "Not all guys are users, Dani." The empathy in Piper's voice was impossible to miss. "And I know I'm not the best person to be giving advice, since I have such little experience, but I don't think it's fair or right to judge all guys, athletes included, as an indistinguishable group. Look at your brothers!"

Piper's words hit home. Dani knew that her no-athletes argument held little weight with them in the equation. Her brothers were the six greatest guys she knew, and they were all athletes — great athletes — every single one of them.

Dani voiced the other worry that had been forming in her head. "But what if he can't live up to the standard?" She practically whispered her statement, but her friend still heard.

Piper dropped her arm and looked at her friend. "What standard?"

Dani voiced something she'd never admitted to anyone before. Her voice shook. "The standard my father and brothers have unintentionally set."

Dani looked at Piper and saw the confusion in her eyes.

"With the academics and politicos, I could convince myself that their shortcomings were okay. I couldn't compare them to my brothers, because they were so different. I don't want it to sound like I'm judging these guys, so maybe compare isn't the right word. But my father and brothers have proven to me that good, faithful, smart, funny guys exist, and I shouldn't settle for anything else. When I start seeing a guy I always ask myself, 'What would my brothers think about him? Would he get my dad's seal of approval?' Because if my guy doesn't earn my brothers' respect and my dad's blessing, he's not a guy I should be dating." To her surprise, Dani felt her eyes getting a little moist. "Given recent events, I have to ask myself what happens if Luke doesn't live up?"

Piper could hear her friend getting emotional and her heart went out to her. "Oh, Dani. I get that you want your brothers' approval. Heck, I want your brothers' approval for my future guy. But how will you ever know how they mesh and feel about Luke until you try? I'm not saying you have to introduce him to the clan right away. Keep getting to know him and see how you feel. I don't want you to miss an amazing opportunity. Give the man a chance!"

"But that is just it, Pipes. The more I get to know him, the more I'm taken with him. In no time at all, he could have my heart."

"Would that be so bad?"

Dani felt a tear running down her cheek. "Maybe."

The two were quiet as they approached the end of their trek until Piper broke the silence. "Answer this, Dani: since Sean made his pitiful attempt to reconnect with you, have you once wondered, 'Did I make the wrong decision?'"

Dani's reply was instantaneous. "Not once."

"Good, then I think that means you made the right choice years ago. Next question. If you decided not to see Luke, would you ever wonder 'What if?'"

Dani knew her silence was telling.

"It would break my heart, Dani, if you compared every future guy to Luke and constantly asked yourself what could have been if you'd just taken a leap of faith."

They were silent as they climbed the four flights of stairs back to their floor and were both trying to catch their breaths when they'd finished.

"I know you're right, Piper," Dani spoke quietly. "But it's still scary."

Piper's smile was reassuring. "Trust your heart, Dani. The risk is great, but so is the potential reward."

Dani knew that statement to be true. Unfortunately, she'd discovered firsthand the risk side of the equation in her younger years. But she'd matured since then and had more on the line now. The risk was even greater, but when it came to Luke she knew the reward could be amazing. Piper might not be worldly when it came to guys, but she had a great perspective on things.

"Okay, before people start thinking all we do is walk, we should get going to dodgeball before we're late. Want to carpool there?"

"Sure. Meet you back here in five?"

"Done."

Chapter 9

Luke absentmindedly shoved his bag into an overheard compartment as he replayed his last conversation with Dani. Again. The team was headed to Vancouver for the first game of their away series. Once he was sure his bag wouldn't fall on his head, and he'd also stored the conversation away into a corner of his mind, Luke got comfy in a seat and took out his assignment for the day's flight.

He usually tried to catch up on some pleasure reading during team flights, but today's reading consisted of his most recent contract draft. For the most part, Luke liked what he was reading. More than anything, he wanted to stay with the Blizzards, but his agent didn't want him to settle for too little. He loved the game so much he'd play for free, but as the team's top scorer, his agent believed he was worthy of a primo contract deal.

His agent was demanding a larger salary and long-standing benefits, but Luke really wanted a no-trade clause to ensure that he'd stay with the Blizzards his entire career. Playing for the Blizzards meant something to him, and their future looked good. The team had their work cut out for them to win the Stanley Cup this year, but it was possible. And they had some real soon-to-be all-stars coming up through their development league and college prospects in the system.

They were probably somewhere over Montana when Marc grabbed the seat opposite him. Facing seats was one of the things Luke enjoyed the most about their team's chartered flights. It made it easier to talk, play cards, and eat around a table.

Luke looked up to see a sour expression on his friend's face. "Did Matty take all your spending money again?" he teased.

Matt Robinson was one of the youngest guys on the team and a shark when it came to cards. As a walk-on, or skate-on, player in college, Matty didn't start out as a scholarship player, so he played in a lot of poker tournaments to help with expenses. Luke knew enough about the young gun's reputation and record to know never to play with him. He made seven figures a year, but that didn't mean he had to throw away his money.

Marc hadn't learned his lesson.

"Don't play with him, man. He takes you to the cleaners every time."

Marc's groan was one of frustration. "I thought I

had him this time. We had two kings showing in the flop and I had one more in the hole, and then *boom*. He lays down two aces to match the one showing in the river." Luke's friend leaned back, crossed his arm, and starting pouting like a schoolboy. "There goes my spending money!"

The pout was short-lived as Mark leaned over to grab a deck of cards that were lying on the table and dealt out a round of solitaire. "How was your first committee hearing as a lobbyist?"

Luke flipped another page of his contract. "It was fine. Turns out it was more informational than political. Not something I'll be looking to do after my playing days, but if it can help improve the chance of the Rink getting an update, I can stomach it."

Fanning through his contract he absentmindedly kept speaking, "Plus, I met—" Luke caught himself as he realized his mistake. He knew he had messed up; his friend had noticed the slip and wasn't going to drop it. Quickly extending the columns of his solitaire rows on the table, Marc egged his friend on.

"You met who? Don't leave me hanging like that, man!"

Cautiously, Luke proceeded to tell him about the woman who had him looking at politics in a totally different light. "I met someone. She seems—" He hesitated, not knowing quite how to define Dani. "Great." He paused and then smiled. "And funny."

"You met a girl who's great and funny. Is that it?" Marc gave him a look that seemed to question Luke's mental capacity. "Are you back in high school? Is she a *swell gal* too?"

Looking around to make sure no one was within earshot, Luke leaned across the table toward Marc. He knew that, as usual, Sean was traveling with the team and was sitting in the seat behind him. Last Luke saw Sean had his earbuds in and looked to be napping. To be safe, Luke risked a bruise along the midsection and leaned further across the table.

"Remember that night in the locker room when I mentioned that woman who caught my eye at the Capitol that first day? Thought I'd never see her again?"

Marc flipped his next trip of cards and nodded to indicate that he was listening.

"Well, I did see her again. She runs the committee the bill will be heard in. I've been getting to see her because of that." His friend looked up from his cards at that statement. "She's the reason I had that sore arm the other day."

"She's the one who barreled into you with the door?" Marc let out a bark of a laugh. "I like this girl already!"

Luke felt his irritation toward his friend lessening as he remembered the apologetic look on Dani's face. He told his friend the subsequent stories of their encounters. "Her name is Dani. Short for Danielle."

"You planning to ask her out?" Marc inquired, clearly reading his friend's interest.

Luke was embarrassed to admit that a woman had

rejected him. It wasn't because he didn't understand Dani's reasoning, it's just that it wasn't something that happened to him or his teammates and he was unfamiliar with the situation. "She shot me down, but she had a legit reason."

Luke saw his loyal friend tense up. "Another guy?"

"No, thankfully. She told me she's single." Luke was going to leave it at that, but apparently his friend wanted a specific answer.

"So what gives?" Marc continued as he surveyed his pitiful, and probably losing, solitaire rows.

Luke shrugged before responding. "She's on a dodgeball team and they had a game."

His friend took a break from his game. "Dodgeball? I haven't played that in years." Then he started laughing. "Do you realize that a girl passed up a date with you to play dodgeball?" The statement caused the laughing to deepen. "That may be the lamest and greatest excuse I have ever heard."

Frowning at his friend's poke at him, Luke wasn't deterred. "Shut it! In my defense, it was a last-minute request. I admit it was a blow to my ego, but it's decent that she didn't blow off her commitments. Level with me, Marc. Most girls we meet would blow off their dying grandmothers if given the same chance." Luke waited for his friend's hysterics to pass before he voiced another thought. "She did seem a little apprehensive about a future offer, but she has some legit reasons to be. Conflict of interest maybe?"

"Your statement was plural. Plural reasons. What's another?"

Luke's neck and back were getting sore from leaning over the table. Motioning for his friend to move over a seat, Luke stood up and scooted around the table to sit where his friend had been. Trying to get as comfortable as the seats would allow, Luke continued.

"I haven't been too discreet about my aversion to politics and politicians, but she doesn't seem to be one of those far-winged partisan junkies. Thankfully! And my apprehension to her profession doesn't seem to bother her. But that's not the big concern. You know that prospect at the U—the left winger—that the front office has been eyeing?"

Luke could see that the question caught his friend off guard, but it didn't take him long to answer. "Sam O'Brien? Kid has some skills. We'd be lucky to have him in a year or two. Why do you ask?"

"I agree that he'd be great to have, but this connection to him could hurt me now. He's one of Dani's younger brothers. She's an O'Brien."

Marc threw down his cards. "Get out!"

Luke saw some of his teammates turn to see the reason for Marc's outburst. Luke tried to stare his friend into silence, but the pointed look didn't seem to deter his energetic French-Canadian teammate.

"That means her family owns Bats and Blades right?"

Luke nodded.

"Well, you sure do know how to pick them."

Wasn't that the truth, thought Luke. "I wasn't expecting to meet anyone I'd be interested in. Especially not with the playoffs around the corner. But I'm definitely interested in this girl."

Marc wanted to pry a bit more. "So, you're physically attracted to her?"

Luke let out a slow and meaningful, "Oh yeah!"

Being the guy that he was, Luke wanted to highlight Dani's assets to his buddy. "She's a knockout, but she's doesn't flaunt it. She's tall, great legs, and a world-class ass. Her face is unforgettable. She has the most amazing eyes I've ever seen. And, she can hold her own on the rink with her brothers."

His friend looked impressed. "It helps that she understands the lifestyle."

Luke agreed. "You know hockey is our life. How could I be with someone who didn't understand my love of the game?" Although he hadn't thought about her for a long time, Luke recalled his last girlfriend. "Rose definitely didn't understand our drive. All that she cared about was the money, parties, and traveling. I just wish I'd realized it sooner."

Mark tossed a card at Luke. "We've both been there, my friend. You kicked that selfish gold digger to the curb when you realized what she was. Don't keep kicking yourself, man. It is what it is. Some people are great actors." Marc continued prodding Luke about Dani. "Do you think Dani is like Rose?"

Luke's reaction was fierce and instantaneous. Eyes blazing, Luke stared down his friend. "No!"

Marc may think that was a naïve conclusion, since he barely knew Dani. But Luke knew she wouldn't be like Rose or the countless other women who threw themselves at him and his teammates, hoping to reap some benefits of the sports world. He couldn't have said why he was so sure, but he did know he was right about Dani. And if he was wrong… Well, he didn't want to think about what he'd do if he was wrong.

Chapter 10

Having just heard the final bonding request, Dani started a trance-like walk from the committee room to her office. Once safe and sound in the comfort of her office, she plopped down on her chair in a way that would have her mom scolding her for her "unladylike" ways. But thankfully her mom wasn't around, so she kicked off her heels, stretched out her legs and lounged back as much as she could in the tight space.

Hearing hundreds of bonding requests in the last two weeks had sucked the life out of everyone in the office.

"Dani—"

Dani was too tired to even sit upright in her chair, so she swiveled to get a better view of Ty and Kim. She almost smiled when she saw that Ty was propped against the right side of the doorframe and Kim against the other. Exhaustion was clearly visible on their faces.

"We survived round one!" she exclaimed with as much energy as she could muster. Which wasn't much.

"Everything is up from the committee and put away." Ty took the lead in giving the update. Even his voice sounded tired. "Mind if we leave a little early? We're just so dead from this week."

"Absolutely. I was going to tell you guys to get going. Take off as soon as you can. I'll be right behind you."

Just as her coworkers were about to leave, Dani stopped them. "Thank you for all your help. I'm sure we made the boss proud!"

Ty and Kim mustered up halfhearted smiles before they grabbed their coats to enjoy an almost spring-like Friday afternoon. The idea of leaving early sounded amazing to Dani, but she remembered that it didn't make much sense for tonight. She wanted to whimper at the prospect of not going home, but then she reminded herself about her evening plans—going to the Blizzards game with Piper. By the time she got home, came back, and then fought traffic around the Rink, it would have been a waste of time. Instead, she thought she'd rest her eyes a bit, finish up on some work, and then head to the Rink with Piper. She was tempted to pass the tickets off to someone else and just go home to sleep, but exhausted or not, she really wanted to watch the Blizzards play—especially Luke.

Dani groaned audibly when she heard her desk phone ringing. She seriously considered not picking it up, but her long-established work ethic got the best of her.

Still unwilling to make the effort to sit up, Dani reached over to grab the phone without maneuvering to see the caller ID.

"Good afternoon, Representative Johnson's office, Dani speaking."

"Dani?" Unlike her, the voice on the line was very upbeat. "It's Luke. How are you?"

Expecting the call to be from a lobbyist or constituent group, the surprise of hearing Luke's voice sent Dani shooting up to a sitting position.

"Luke... Hi!" she managed to force out.

Dani smacked her forehead with the palm of her hand. She had a master's degree and the only thing she could think to say was "hi" while her voice jumped an octave—she sounded like she was twelve! Being frazzled wasn't a common occurrence for her. She didn't like that it only seemed to happen around Luke.

Hearing Luke chuckle on the other end of the line, Dani waited for him to say something since she didn't trust herself to speak at the moment.

"How have you been? Good week?"

Taking a deep breath, Dani willed herself to speak intelligently and calmly. "It's been insane. Lots of bills and long workdays, but that's part of the game. Oh, speaking of games, nice work up in Canada." If she could bring the conversation around to sports, Dani knew that she could hold her own.

"Hey, thanks." Dani could hear the warmth in Luke's voice over the phone. "Did you even have time to watch the games this week?"

"I won't lie," she laughed, "I didn't get a chance to watch them fully, but I caught some bits and the highlight reels on the late news. You had quite a few appearances—nice work!"

"Just doing my job! Which I'm heading to right now to get ready for tonight's game. It's actually the reason for this call. I was wondering if you would like to come to tonight's game as my guest? They're great seats! Maybe help make amends for the crappy way Sean's behaved."

"Oh…" For the second time in just as many minutes Dani found herself at a loss for words.

Hearing her hesitation, Luke tried to save face. "I'm sorry for the late notice. I didn't mean to just spring this on you."

Knowing that she had to say something, Dani tried to placate the worry she heard in Luke's voice. "I'd love to take you up on that offer, but I can't."

Now it was Luke's turn to be temporarily speechless. He could either play it cool or go for the knife to the heart. He figured he might as well know, even if it wasn't what he wanted to hear.

"Is it because you can't or because you don't want to?" Luke was happy that this conversation was happening over the phone so Dani couldn't see the look of worry that had come over his face. He hoped it was the former and not the latter option.

Luke didn't know just how much Dani wanted to see him, but she couldn't take him up on his offer for two reasons. "As luck would have it, I'm already going to tonight's game."

"Really?" Luke probably would have been annoyed with himself at how eager he sounded but he was too relieved to care. That is, until another thought came to mind. "Are you going by yourself?"

Luke was happy to know that Dani wasn't blowing him off, but he also wasn't sure if he wanted to hear she was going to the game if she was going with another guy.

"I'm heading over there with my best girlfriend from work, Piper. We're planning to work for a bit, grab a bite to eat downtown, and then head up to the Rink to cheer you guys on."

Smiling into the phone, Luke offered Dani the seats again. He wasn't lying when he said they were great seats.

"They're right where I caught you spying on me the other day!"

He had to pull some strings, but he managed to get them at the last minute. Normally he didn't like to be distracted during a game, but he wouldn't mind it at all if he looked over to see Dani behind the Plexiglas, cheering the team on—especially him.

Dani practically melted in her seat at the sentimental gesture.

"Thanks so much. I wish I could take you up on those, but I can't." Dani thought that she sounded like a broken record. But she had a legitimate reason for turning away the tickets, even if she didn't like it. "It's the law, as lame as that sounds. I can't accept gifts from lobbyists and interest groups. And because you are part of a group that's lobbying, I can't accept the seats since they could be considered a bribe."

Although she understood the reasoning behind the gift ban, this was one of those times when Dani really wished that it didn't exist, especially given the thought Luke had put into the offer. "But, I'll still be there cheering you and your boys on. We have good seats — my family has had them for years. We rotate who gets to go. We'll be nearby."

Luke liked hearing that, a lot, and immediately felt his body loosen up as he responded. "Great. Hopefully you'll be seeing a good game tonight. With those wins last week we secured our place in the playoffs, but that doesn't mean we can slack off."

With the phone to her ear, Dani saw something moving around in the office. Turning her head to look out her door, she saw Piper heading in from the hallway. Dani started frantically motioning to the phone and mouthed, "Luke!"

Piper ran the rest of the way to her office and started hopping around and quietly clapping at the same time.

Making herself focus on what Luke was saying rather than watch her friend celebrate like a schoolgirl, Dani heard his wonderful baritone voice ask the question that most women would die to hear: "Do you want to meet up for a drink after the game? It might be a little late, but it's not a school night!"

Dani froze and it didn't go unnoticed by her friend. Piper mouthed, "What?" Trying to buy time, Dani decided to tell a small fib: "Luke, can I put you on hold? The boss just walked in and I need to tell him something before someone grabs him."

Luke responded in the affirmative so quickly that Dani felt a little bad about lying. Pushing the hold button on her phone, Dani made sure that the line had clicked over. Once it had she still placed a hand over the ear receiver just to be sure. She was taking no chances.

Dani started waving her hands around, phone still attached, as her friend looked on. "Piper, he asked me to have a drink with him after the game. What do I—"

"Danielle O'Brien," Piper cut her off, "if you say no to him, I swear on my favorite pair of shoes that I will never speak to you again." She stalked toward Dani's desk and put her hands on her hips. She looked fierce and deadly serious.

"But weren't we going to go out after? I don't want to blow you off!"

Piper stared her down. "Forget about me. Plus, we'll have dinner and the game to catch up." The stare intensified. "Dani, ask yourself if you'd regret it if you said no."

Dani wanted to know when her friend started moonlighting as a relationship counselor. Giving her friend a serene smile, Dani put the receiver back up to her ear, took a deep breath, and hit the hold button again.

"Luke? Sorry. I'm back. I'd love to meet you after the game. Where's a good place?"

It was a good thing that Dani couldn't see him right now, Luke thought. He was literally grinning from ear to ear. "Do you mind if we don't go somewhere right by the Rink? They tend to be swamped and it's impossible to go unnoticed." Trying to think of a lesser-known place, he mentioned a great Mexican bar on the west side.

"Sure, I love that place!"

Luke could hear her excitement. And he had yet another thing to add to his growing list of things to like about Dani.

"Great. I probably won't get there until about an hour after the game ends. And hey, if you want, ask Piper to come along." Dani was surprised Luke made note of her friend's name. He'd obviously been paying attention. "I can grab my buddy from the team. I'm sure Marc would be game."

Dani only knew of one person named Marc on the team and that was their all-star goalie, Marc LaFrey. He was also notorious for patronizing a number of nightspots in the Twin Cities. He had a partier's reputation, the complete opposite of Piper. Maybe he was just what the doctor ordered for her shy friend.

"I'm sure Piper will enjoy that," she told Luke.

Dani looked up at her friend who mouthed, "Enjoy what?" Dani just smiled in response as Luke repeated the plans.

"We'll see you there."

Dani agreed. "Good luck!" Before he hung up, Luke gave Dani his cell number in case anything changed. She plugged it into her phone and said goodbye one more time.

Making sure the phone was securely on its holder, Dani spun around to face her friend.

"Well, Pippi, if I'm going down, I'm taking you with me." She didn't feel the least bit guilty about dragging her friend into this ordeal. "Luke and I will be having drinks at Tango Rio later and you'll be joining us."

"Dani," Piper said, looking exasperated. "I'm not going to be a third wheel at your date with Luke. You can just tell him I ate a bad hot dog at the Rink and it wouldn't have been a pretty sight had I come out."

"Oh no, Ms. Piper. You will be a third wheel—but a fourth wheel will be there too. Let's call that wheel Marc LaFrey."

Dani wasn't ashamed to feel some smugness as she saw her friend's jaw drop.

Just as quickly as her mandible dropped, Piper came back to reality and the panic set in. "Absolutely not possible! Call Luke back and tell him I won't be joining you." Panic and all, her friend's prim and proper attitude remained. "But please thank him for the invitation."

It may have made her a terrible friend, but Dani was trying her hardest not to laugh and she wasn't sure if she was succeeding. "What are you talking about? You were the one who was encouraging me to see him, and that means I'm taking you to meet his friend and be my wing-woman."

"I'm the worst wing-woman of all time and you know it!" Piper frantically announced while her gaze scanned the room. "Dani, I don't have time to run home before the game and all I brought was my throwback jersey." Piper reached into the bag that was hanging over her arm and pulled out the black jersey she had packed that morning, turning it around so that Dani could see the name and number. "Which incidentally is LaFrey's. I'm going to look like a crazed fan. This is too much. I'm not ready for the big leagues." Piper let loose a pitiful laugh. "Literally."

Dani wanted to give her friend a big hug. Though they both came from big families, Piper's had been mostly girls and she hadn't had a whole lot of interaction with guys growing up. Dani knew the jersey excuse was a cover for some deep insecurity.

"Piper, I'll be right there with you tonight. If growing up with six brothers taught me anything, it's how to get out of awkward situations. If at any time it becomes awkward or unsettling for you, I'll be right there to jump in and ease the situation. And feel free to do the same for me. And hey," she added, "my jersey is Luke's. We can both be crazed fans. And"—Dani's voice took on a conspiratorial tone—"my brother Jake did tell me once that there wasn't anything more attractive to him than seeing his girl in his jersey."

Her friend threw her hands up in defeat.

Dani just shook her head and refused to let Piper retreat. "Piper, look at me." She waited until her friend did just that. Her friend's pleading eyes almost broke her heart. "Everything will be fine. We'll have a good time. If nothing else, we know the food and beverages will be good since we're meeting them at Tango Rio."

Dani and Piper often went to the Tango after long session days. The place was something of an upscale dive bar, but they had a great kitchen and even better live music. Since it was Friday, there'd be a live band. It was also the type of place that had really dim lighting so it would be easy for Luke and Marc to go unrecognized.

Realizing that there was no out, Piper conceded. She hadn't been on a date in ages—she actually couldn't remember her last one. As scared as she was, she knew she had to start somewhere. She wanted to marry someday and have kids. And no matter how hard she wished it, the last few years had proven to her that Prince Charming wasn't going to show up at her door randomly out of thin air. As much as the prospect of that night frightened her, she had to do this for herself.

"Fine," she proclaimed. "Let's grab some food before the game. I'm starving and I'm sure I'll be too nervous to eat after the game!"

Grabbing her purse and change of clothes, Dani started packing up. Leaning over to change her shoes to something more practical for the game, Dani wondered how in the world a girl who'd sworn off athletes was suddenly meeting up with two of the best players in the NHL in a few hours. Thankfully, no one, including Piper, could hear her muttered, "Oh boy!"

Chapter 11

Much to Dani and Piper's dismay, which they shared with every other Blizzards fan, the team didn't leave the ice as victors that night.

"It's so painful watching a shoot-out loss," Piper lamented. "All that built-up anticipation, watching player after player show off their skills, and then the letdown. You know what it's like? It's like Molly Ringwald in *Sixteen Candles* waking up on her birthday expecting her family to be waiting to celebrate the milestone, only to realize that they forgot. Major letdown."

Dani agreed with her friend's analogy wholeheartedly, but also had to admit that Chicago had played a good game. She knew good hockey when she saw it. It was easy to understand why they were the Blizzards' biggest competition in the conference.

Dani and Piper walked into Tango Rio and thought it would be best to use the restroom before taking their seats. Neither would call herself vain, but they were sure they looked a little disheveled given their physical enthusiasm during the game.

They set their purses on the sink countertop and assessed the damage. Pulling her hair back into a high ponytail, Dani figured that there wasn't much more she could do. So far Luke had only seen her in business attire and now he'd be seeing her in his jersey looking like a hot mess. She didn't think that she could hold a candle next to the girls who hung around hotel lobbies and nightclubs to catch an available player. Jake had told her about those women.

"This is as good as it's going to get!" Dani muttered as she tried to apply lip gloss. The only other item available to improve her appearance was some mascara, so she threw that on as well.

Piper scoffed at her friend. "Dani, you're gorgeous," she said pointedly. "You could walk around in a potato sack and guys would be drooling at your feet."

She caught Dani's eye in the mirror and tried to stare her down. Piper knew about her friend's insecurities and how unwarranted they were. And just as Dani had challenged her to confront her own insecurities earlier, Piper was now determined to help Dani overcome hers.

"And that's because your beauty isn't just your looks, it's everything about you, Dani. You're an amazing person inside and out. You don't see that, or more accurately, you're too humble to see that, but everyone who knows you realizes it immediately."

Piper may have thought Dani was gorgeous, but growing up in house full of boys had taken its toll on her friend. Dani often questioned her "girliness," though at the same time, she was confident being who she was, even if she didn't fully understand her effect.

Dani's confidence was one of the things Piper admired most about her friend. She was never too proud or arrogant, but she had a faith in herself that was firmly rooted. If someone was wrong, Dani called him or her out on it—like she often did with her brothers—but she'd be polite while doing so. Piper had heard numerous lobbyists and staffers comment on her beauty, but Dani just didn't see it. Her humility only added to her appeal.

Dani smiled in the mirror at her friend. She appreciated that Piper was trying her best to assuage some of her fears.

Dani wasn't the type of girl to walk around in short dresses shellacked to her body or spend any more time than necessary getting ready to leave the apartment. She liked getting dressed up, but didn't overdo it for work. Dressing up was something of a novelty. Any guy she ended up with would have to realize that she was most comfortable in leggings and a tunic.

When she thought of the girls who threw themselves at her brothers over the years, just because they were athletes, she didn't even know why she was here.

The assumed dismissal shouldn't bother her, considering she wanted nothing to do with athletes, but the sense of impending doom caused a pain to start in her chest. But she didn't have time to think about it now.

Tonight, she was going to have a nice get-together with her friend and two guys. That was it. Except she could feel how nervous she was and she didn't usually get nervous for dinners. But she needed to keep it together because her friend was nervous enough for the both of them. She could practically feel the worry radiating from Piper, who was applying her third layer of lip gloss.

And with that realization, Dani knew they had to get out of the bathroom. Pulling once more at her ponytail to tighten, she rinsed her hands and caught her friend's eye in the mirror.

"All right, Pipes. You ready?" she asked.

Dani heard her friend's nervous laugh as she turned to dry her hands. "Never," Piper muttered.

Exiting the bathroom, the girls saw the sign instructing them to seat themselves, so they selected a corner table in a dim area of the restaurant. Dani and Piper sat facing the lobby so they could see the guys when they arrived.

To squelch her nerves, Dani pulled out her phone and texted Luke where they were. She added a comment at the end that she hadn't bailed. Glass to her lips, she was just taking a sip of water when she heard a familiar laughing voice reach her over the house band.

"That's good! I don't know if I could have handled losing a game *and* being stood up on the same night."

Startled, Dani's sip turned into an unexpected gulp and she tried to tame the coughing fit that erupted. Never knowing if she should remain seated or stand up for a greeting, her decision was made for her since she still was coughing as Luke approached. Piper started pounding her back. This, Dani thought painfully, had to be the least attractive greeting imaginable.

The guys had the grace to look worried until Dani was able to catch a few breaths. They removed their coats and pulled out their seats. Through her tear-filled eyes, Dani saw that they both looked ridiculously handsome in their similar outfits of gray-toned sweaters and trousers.

After being reassured by Dani that she was going to survive her coughing attack, Luke started the introductions. "Dani, this is my good friend and teammate, Marc LaFrey. Marc, this is Dani, the woman from the Capitol I've been telling you about."

Reaching across the table to shake his hand, Dani was happy to see a genuine smile on Marc's face and knew that hers was equally genuine. She had an unexpected rush of pride as Luke announced that he had spoken about her to Marc. Pride was quickly replaced by worry as she wondered just what he'd shared.

"Nice to meet you, Dani! Luke told me about your mutual encounter with the door. I can tell you that many other players in the league would have loved to be in your place. Too bad you didn't succeed at causing any permanent damage."

Dani chuckled at the quip, but she was slightly horrified that Luke had told that story. "I'm never going to live that one down, am I?"

Marc leaned back in his chair and laughed. "I hope not!"

The ladies laughed while Luke elbowed Marc in the arm.

Remembering her duties as cohost, Dani motioned to her friend. "This is *my* good friend and teammate, or rather House-mate, Piper. Piper, meet Luke Coffey and Marc LaFrey."

Piper reached across the table to shake the guys' hands as Dani shared a bit more information. "Piper is a fellow committee administrator in the House. She administers the health committee and is one of our star dodgeballers!"

"Ah, so you're also one of the champion dodgeballers," Marc stated in his ridiculously cute French-Canadian accent.

Dani thought Luke would most likely win any cuteness contest between the two hockey players, but Marc's accent certainly gave Luke's baritone a run for his money. That was saying a lot, considering that she was admittedly biased toward Luke.

Dani looked to Piper and was surprised, and relieved, to see that Piper seemed more relaxed than she was. Piper waved a hand in front of her face as if to lessen the significance of Marc's accolades as she responded, "Really not a big deal!"

Dani was incredulous at her friend's casual statement. "Hey, it is a big deal! Do you know how many balls to the face I took in that championship game alone?"

She realized her error as soon as the word *balls* left her mouth. Luke and Marc's eyes opened up like saucers and all three of her tablemates were trying to hold in their laughs.

"Oh, shut up!" she tried to save face as the group erupted. "Get your minds out of the gutter. I meant *dodgeballs* to the face!"

Although she was trying to be indignant, Dani joined in the infectious laughter.

The waiter came by for their drink order and everyone was forced to pull it together or remain parched for the remainder of the night. The group decided to start off with a round of margaritas and placed an order for some appetizers. Dani and Piper had eaten before the game, but they hadn't overindulged, knowing that they'd be going out after. It was possible that nerves played into their light supper too. She assumed the guys were starving.

While they waited for their food, the group made small talk. They chatted about current events, recent movies, and books before someone brought up the topic of vacations.

"Vacations are frowned upon during session months," explained Dani. "I'm assuming it's the same for you during hockey season?"

Both guys nodded. "Correct," Luke confirmed. "It's not acceptable to take time away unless it's an emergency. Families plan everything around the season. We're required to be hockey all the time for eight months out of the year. But then we get the summer off. Most of us train in the off season, but we have time to relax, travel, do whatever."

In response, Piper shared a benefit of their job. "We accrue a lot of comp time during session since we work such long hours. So after session, it's really great to take some time off to you know... relax, travel, or do whatever."

Dani was watching Marc and saw him smile at her friend as he continued the questioning. "Do you have any big trips planned for after session?" Marc reached for a chip and dipped it generously into the salsa as he asked his question.

Dani assumed Marc was directing the question at Piper, but her friend looked to her to start. Dani assumed that by now Marc knew the specifics about her family, but she figured it would be a good lead-in. "I don't know if Luke told you, but Jake O'Brien is one of my brothers. I try to catch an away series or two in a new city every year. Haven't decided where or when I'm going, but I hope to catch a couple of series this summer."

"Are you RVing?" Piper asked around a grin and a chip. They shared a laugh caused by the inside joke, which left both guys looking a little confused.

Piper knew Dani's family loved to travel in their RV. When they could find coverage for the stores, Dani's parents liked to hit the road for random trips. Depending on their availability, Dani and her brothers would sometimes join them. Some trips were planned far in advance and others were decided by whatever whim took their fancy. The fiascos and breakdowns they'd experienced over the years were legendary.

Dani saw Marc lift his eyebrow as the ladies chuckled. Through a chip-filled mouth he managed, "Did I miss something?"

Piper burst out laughing as she recalled the amazing stories she had heard. She settled back into her chair for the long haul. She was amazed that, considering this was her first double date, she felt remarkably at ease. But then everyone present seemed terribly laid-back. She'd been a ball of nerves all throughout the game, but now she found herself enjoying the company. She looked at Marc to answer his question and was surprised to see how intently he was looking at her. His stare caused her to stumble.

"Th… the… the stories that Dani tells about her family's RV trips are legendary. They have been known to make grown men cry! I've seen it happen. Thanks to word getting out following her first story, Dani has become sought after as a storyteller to help pass time."

Both of the guys forgot about the food and drinks and looked to Dani. Luke asked the obvious question. "Can we hear something now, O Storyteller?"

Dani thought Luke was joking as she looked down at her drink, but she realized he wasn't when she looked up and saw the earnest expression on his face. "I don't tell them nearly as well as my parents. Plus, they're really long. You'll probably be bored to tears."

"Tell them about Iowa!"

Dani jumped a little in her seat at Piper's excited request. Dani thought Piper's plan might be to keep the attention off herself, but glancing at her friend, Dani was happy to see that she seemed calm and relaxed. She was doing just fine.

"Yeah, tell us about Iowa."

This time it was Marc who implored Dani to share a memory.

Looking around at the group, Dani didn't think there was any way she was getting up from this table without sharing a story. "I'm warning you, this may be a letdown after all of this buildup."

No one at the table seemed to mind. Everyone loaded up their appetizer plates and got ready for story time. Taking a sip of water, Dani made sure she swallowed before she set out to make them laugh.

"The summer after I graduated high school, my parents decided that we should do a road trip. And since I'd just graduated, they let me pick the final destination. Being the prim and proper person that I am, I chose Vegas. My two oldest brothers were going to stay and run the stores—we only had two at the time—and then fly out and meet us there for a few days. So my parents and us five younger kids set out on our journey.

"Keep in mind that our RV was thirty-year-old tin can my parents had recently purchased. My dad said he got the deal of the century. He paid $1,500 for it. In Iowa, we found out why!

"We left late in the day and my Dad took the first driving shift to get us out of Minnesota. Once in Iowa, I took over. I'm driving down the interstate and the RV starts chugging. And not just a little chug, but a big heave-ho type of chug, over and over again. I pull off in the middle of nowhere. We find a little garage, but it's the wee hours at this point and it doesn't open for a few hours. Day one, and we're already behind schedule. When the garage opens, my dad and my brothers work with the mechanic to speed things up.

"A couple hours and tons of wrenches later, everything appears to be set. We take off and aren't even to the next exit when it starts to chug again. So we pull off and find another small-town mechanic. Because it's the middle of August and we can't run the air conditioner with a dodgy engine, we're just roasting. My mom and I decide to walk the mile into town to see if there's anything we can get for the boys. We see an ice cream shop in the distance, but just then the boys call us on Mom's cell—which miraculously has a signal—and inform us that it appears to be fixed, so we should head back. All the boys were filthy and they smelled horrible. The RV smelled like a locker room after all the players had eaten a carton full of hard-boiled eggs.

"So we say a prayer that the chugging is done and head into town for ice cream since everyone is so hot. Just as we're pulling up to the ice cream shop, which is closed, we hear this nasty sound of metal twisting. Jake opens the door, heads outside, looks at the back of the RV and says, 'Dad, I don't think you want to come out here.'

"We all pile out of the RV and discover to our dismay that our water tank has fallen out of the bottom of the RV and is now laying in the road a few yards back. Dad is the last to get out and once he does and sees what happened, he just throws his hands in the air and utters with so much misery in his voice, 'What else can go wrong?'

"Just then we hear glass shattering inside the RV. I rush inside to see what it is, and the next thing I'm saying is, 'Dad, Mom, I don't think you want to come in here.' A full-length mirror that had been in the bathroom had, after thirty years, decided to pull away from the wall and shatter. So there's glass all over our nasty brown carpet. Frankly, it made the carpet look better. But anyhow, my parents come back into the RV and I swear to you that my dad shed some tears when he saw the shattered mirror."

As her audience clasped their stomached in fits of laughter, Dani took the opportunity to sip some water.

She smiled at the amusement they found in her family's horrible road trip, so she continued.

"This was all within the first twenty-four hours of our trip. It should have taken us five hours at the most to get through Iowa, but it took a whole day. The RV still wasn't fixed, but that's a story for another day."

"You kept going?" Luke asked incredulously. He was able to choke out his question even though he was still laughing.

Dani nodded. "My mom wanted to turn for home, but my brothers and I had our hearts set on Vegas and the older boys already had their tickets booked to meet us out there. So we kept trucking along! We just had to be careful about using our sinks while trucking down the road since the tank that fell was holding the used water for the bathroom and kitchen sinks. Had it been the toilet tank that had fallen, we would have had to turn around. To this day we try to avoid Iowa."

"I don't blame you!" This time it was Marc who added the commentary.

"Since then my parents have upgraded to a new RV. So to answer your question, Marc, I hope to join my parents for at least one RV trip this summer. We usually end up in some city where Jake is playing. I'd like to visit my brother, Andy, but he's training right now before he heads overseas."

"What does Andy do in the Army?" inquired Luke.

"He's an Army Ranger. I don't know much about his next mission," Dani said truthfully. "I assume he'll be jumping out of planes, blowing stuff up, and doing a bunch of things he can't tell us about."

Luke nodded in understanding.

"Next time you talk to him, please let him know that the Blizzards—especially me—appreciate his service."

Dani was touched by Luke's request, and the sincerity she heard in his voice. It always brought tears to her eyes when people approached Andy while he was in uniform and thanked him for doing what he did. Andy considered it an honor to serve his country and was embarrassed by the attention, which just made Dani all the more proud of him. Although she worried about him and said a prayer for his safety nightly, she knew he was doing what he loved. A sister couldn't want anything more than that for her brother.

She was able to hold back the tears but her voice broke a little when she responded, "Thank you. I'll do that."

Feeling a little bashful, Dani reached for a big mound of nachos and started eating. Having a full mouth was always a good way to keep the tears at bay.

As if sensing Dani's discomfort, Marc took the opportunity to ask Piper what she did outside the House and if she had any plans for the summer.

Piper knew that she was on a pseudo double date, but she'd gotten so distracted by Dani's story that she was caught off guard by Marc's question. She turned to the goalie and saw that he had a warm smile on his face, and was staring very intently at her. Again.

"I teach dance to kids and we have a recital every June. After the final curtain, I hope to sneak away for a bit."

Piper had been watching Marc since he asked the question and couldn't help but notice that he sat up a bit further in his chair and his eyebrows shot up to his hairline at her news. That wasn't the usual reaction people had when she started talking recital details. Most looked like they were trying to find some way to avoid an invitation, but Marc didn't seem scared.

"What type of dance do you teach?"

"I mostly do tap and ballet or jazz. For the older students, we do some lyrical and other specialty dances. I just started teaching a ballroom class that has been a big hit."

At the word *ballroom* Marc offered a wide, and charming, smile. Piper thought it was a very unusual reaction. The few guys she had mentioned it to looked slightly terrified at the prospect.

Piper turned her head sharply as she heard the band start up their second set. Their first set had included a good mix of faster and slower pieces. It sounded like they were starting out the second round with a slower number. Piper turned just in time to see Marc glance at the dance floor and then back to her. She couldn't believe what happened next, although it played out in slow motion for her. Marc pushed his chair back, stood up, moved around the table, and extended his large hand to her. As she looked at the offered appendage, he asked her the question any girl dreams to hear: "Care to dance?"

Piper just stared. She would've stayed that way, had she not felt a very painful jab at her left ankle from her wonderful friend Dani. Lifting her gaze from his hand to his face, Piper fought back her instinct to give Marc a quick "Thanks, but no thanks." Instead she looked to the dance floor once more and knew she had nothing to fear out there. And she needed to do this for herself. She removed the napkin from her lap, smiled at Marc as she put her hand in his, and said, "Why not!"

Marc pulled Piper from her chair and they walked away from the table, leaving Dani and Luke with surprised expressions on their faces. But they were also alone now, which neither of them minded.

Chapter 12

As he led Piper to the dance floor, Marc could not believe his luck. The odds of enjoying this evening and finding the elusive dance partner he'd been seeking had been slim. But he was succeeding on both counts, which did a lot to lift the sour taste he had from the night's loss.

As goalie, he took the final score very seriously. And a loss after a shoot-out was the worst. Unlike a three-period game, a shoot-out showcased the match-up between the shooter and the goalie. In tonight's match-up he'd come up short, but meeting Dani and Piper was helping to ease the ache left from the game.

He understood why his friend Luke was so head over heels for Dani—the girl truly was a stunner. To top it off, she had a killer sense of humor. That RV story had him in tears. And her friend Piper was just as memorable. He'd muttered a "wow" under his breath when he and Luke first saw the two across the cantina. She wasn't a playboy pinup by any means. He'd admit that had been his preference in the past. Piper was more trim and less Barbie (although she did have flowing long brown hair and striking blue eyes), but he found himself attracted to her instantly for no specific reason. And he thought that she had the most infectious laugh. Every time she laughed, he found himself doing the same.

Reaching the dance floor, Marc turned around to face Piper. The floor was dimly lit and even though couples around them appeared to be getting quite intimate, Piper wasn't having any of that. He fought back a smile as she placed her left hand on his shoulder and started raising her right hand, which he automatically grabbed with his left. He was used to women practically climbing him to get closer, but Piper was more reserved. They were close but not quite touching. Marc found Piper refreshing, but he was hoping they would move a bit closer as they started dancing. From what he could tell, she had a beautiful body and he wanted to test his hypothesis that their bodies would fit great together.

As Marc started leading, Piper couldn't help but give her head a little shake in astonishment. When she left for work this morning she was anticipating that after a guaranteed crazy day of work she'd catch a game with her friend, walk to her apartment, and then watch the *Dancing with the Stars* episode she'd recorded earlier in the week. Now instead of being curled up on her couch watching dancing, she was engaging in the very sport with Marc LaFrey. Well, she couldn't really call it dancing; it was more like rocking back and forth, but she was in the arms of Marc LaFrey, which was unfathomable.

Most of her dancing these days involved teaching her choreographed pieces to students in a studio, but she loved opportunities to dance with a partner. And who could complain when their partner was as solid and dreamy as Marc LaFrey, even if his dance skills weren't of John Travolta's caliber.

An even slower song came from the stage and Marc moved a little closer to Piper without missing a beat.

"Do you enjoy working in politics?"

Piper hoped that Marc couldn't feel the shiver that went through her body at his words. As a dancer she was always aware of her body and usually composed, but with Marc leaning into her and asking his question close to her ear, Piper couldn't stop her body's reaction. It had been a long time since she'd danced in such an intimate way and never before with such a virile partner. Taking a breath to calm her reaction, Piper answered his question with a shaky voice.

"Most of the time! Every day is different."

Piper could feel Marc's next question on her skin before her mind was able to process it. "What brought you to the Capitol?"

She smiled into his shoulder as she thought of her entry into the legislative world. "I've always been interested in current affairs and civics. When I took this job a couple of years ago, I thought that I would maybe run for office someday, but I have since discovered that being a legislator is probably not the path for me."

Marc pulled back a small distance to look her in the eyes. "What made you change your mind?"

"A lot of things." Piper stopped speaking for a moment to consider the best way to explain her epiphany. Marc must have seen her internal conflict, because he didn't pressure her to continue.

"It's really, for lack of a better word, awesome to be a part of something that you hope serves the state like good legislation. But your family really sacrifices when you're in office and I don't know if that's something I could ever stomach." Piper gave her shoulders a little shrug. "Plus, politicians' lives are very public."

Piper had dropped her gaze to Marc's neck when admitting her family concerns, but she had to return to looking him in the eyes as she realized the irony of that last statement. "But I guess I don't need to tell you about living in the public eye."

Marc smiled causing his cuteness to increase tenfold. She felt his left hand tighten around her right as his other hand pressed on her back to pull her in a bit closer—their bodies were now practically flush.

"You're right! The lack of privacy is a downside of playing in the pros, but sometimes, like tonight"—Piper saw him glance around the cantina—"we get lucky and people don't recognize us so we can just enjoy ourselves. It doesn't hurt that some of our favorite places, like Tango here, let us come in the back and have special treatment to avoid the fans. But at the end of the day, I love my job enough to live with the interruptions."

"That's good," Piper admitted while nodding her head. "I think I've come to realize that I don't love politics enough."

Marc was gazing at Piper with a look that she thought seemed a lot like admiration. "Then I think you made a good call." They continued dancing in silence as their bodies swayed in perfect harmony. "Do you think you'll be teaching dance for a while?"

Piper was slightly surprised by Marc's question and sudden change in topics. "I hope so. As long as my body will let me, I'd like to keep it up."

From what he was feeling right now, Marc didn't think there was anything wrong with her body. In fact, it felt amazing; she was toned but not hard-bodied. And she was lithe and graceful; she hadn't stepped on his toes once. He silently wondered if she had to wear those skimpy dance outfits for practice. He'd like to see that. Maybe if she said yes to his next question, he'd have the opportunity.

"Do you ever teach private lessons?"

That statement surpassed the last in terms of

surprise. Looking up at his face, Piper was wondering if he was getting at what she thought he was getting at.

"I do," she offered cautiously. "Mostly to students who plan to do solos or duets in competitions. But I've also taught some private ballroom classes for couples' first wedding dances." She lifted an eyebrow as her curiosity piqued. "Why do you ask?"

Marc was hoping she'd say that. "Would you consider taking me on as a private student?" he asked in a matter-of-fact tone.

Jerking away from the shock, Piper felt herself fall out of step as her right foot landed on Marc's left. She still hadn't answered by the time her partner extracted his crushed foot and looked around the dance floor.

"Before you answer, I have to ask that you keep this between us. I've told Luke about my need to learn a dance, but he's the only one. I really don't want this to become public. So even if you don't take me on as a pupil, I'd like to have your word that this discussion doesn't go beyond us."

While processing the requests, Piper looked into Marc's eyes and saw the earnestness there. As an avid fan of *Dancing with the Stars*, she'd seen countless sports athletes take on the ballroom challenge, but she'd certainly never met a hockey player who doubled as a ballroom dancer. "Can I get a bit more information before deciding? What do you need to learn? And when do you need to perform?" And the most important question: "And why?"

Marc had a feeling that Piper was discreet enough to keep this to herself, so he answered.

"My sister is getting married right after the finals. I'm a groomsmen in her wedding and she is a big-time dancer, like you. She's creating an elaborate wedding-party dance and apparently I need to be a part of it. And I mean *need*. She was nice enough to set her wedding date for after the Stanley Cup in case we go all the way, but she absolutely would not waver on me participating in the dance." He rolled his eyes upward. "Heaven forbid that should happen!"

Piper smiled at the sarcasm she heard. "Really?" she asked in her own sarcastic voice. "Athlete or not, I haven't known many sisters who let their brothers off the hook for anything involving their big day."

Marc fought back a grin as he heard the laughter in Piper's comment. "I begged her to leave me out of it since I can't get home to practice. I even called in the big guns, but I think my mom and dad are afraid of her when she's in wedding-planning mode. Plus, my mom thinks it's a great idea! She's taped the practices with my poor dad standing in as me. If I gave you the tapes, could you help me learn my part?"

Piper didn't want to laugh at his story, but it was kind of funny… and endearing. A mighty goalie being brought to his knees by his sister.

They were both silent as she thought about the time commitment it would require. It wouldn't be terrible since she didn't have to choreograph anything, and she could use the extra money. After thinking it over for a few seconds, and still fighting the urge to flee because her body had such a strong reaction to him, Piper decided to help him. She was a professional and this would be a good challenge.

"Sure, when do you need to learn it by?"

Marc smiled at her casual acceptance, though he could tell she'd weighed it mentally. "Her wedding is right after the Stanley Cup, so I have more than a month. But with our travel schedule, and from what I've heard from Luke, the legislature being crazy, it may be hard to pin down some dates. I'll pay you whatever you charge. I'm sure you're worth it."

Piper snapped her head up at that comment, trying to fight back a laugh.

Marc saw the humor in her eyes and realized the error of his last statement but admired her humor even more. He loved a woman with personality. "I didn't mean it in a bad way. I'm sure you charge the going rate—"

Piper's smile stretched to show her teeth and she couldn't help but let out an audible laugh.

Marc was shaking his head but smiling at his teacher. "You have the best laugh!" His statement caused her laugh to fade. She dropped her gaze but her smile remained, which he was happy to see. "I'll pay whatever your private students pay. Sound fair?"

"Sure. I have a business card in my purse that I'll

give you when we get back to the table. It's my House card, but it has my cell number on it."

Piper became a little distracted as she saw her friend come onto the dance floor with Luke. After a few slow numbers, the band picked up their tempo a bit. She pulled away from Marc and immediately felt a loss. It would have been weird trying to mambo with Marc while being flush up against him, but she wasn't opposed to staying in his arms a bit longer. That thought was so foreign to her that she didn't know how to process it.

Marc was bereft when Piper pulled away. As he'd expected, she fit his body perfectly. He was guessing they'd fit perfectly in other positions as well. He'd had one-night stands in the past, but it had been awhile since his last. He didn't find the idea so appealing anymore. He'd only known Piper a few minutes, but Marc was certain that she wasn't the type of girl who would hit the sheets after a drink and a quick proposition — even with a hockey star with a seven-figure contract. And although his body may not like that, his mind did. He appreciated that she wasn't taken with what he was. If anything were to come of this attraction, he wanted it to be because she liked him for who he was.

He followed Piper's gaze and saw that they had company. In an unspoken agreement, the two pairs started moving closer to one another until they had a little circle formed. To anyone watching, it looked like two couples were out on the town and having a good time. Looking at the other three members of his party and seeing the smiles on their faces, Marc couldn't find any objection to that assumption.

Surprised to be left alone when Piper and Marc moved to the dance floor, neither Luke nor Dani minded the personal time it gave them to talk.

"Do you have any plans for the weekend?" Luke thought that throwing out a soft question would be a good way to start. Plus, he really did want to know what she was doing over the weekend. Maybe they could spend some time together. His mind started racing with possibilities until he heard Dani release a sigh. He knew enough of women to know it was a sigh of exasperation, not pleasure.

"I think I'll be at work most of the weekend. We're drafting the first version of the omnibus bill, so I'll be at the Capitol working with the boss and our Senate counterparts."

Definitely not one of the possibilities that had been running through his head, but Luke understood her obligations. The team had to head out for an away game on Sunday anyhow. Maybe they could do something next weekend. He'd heard Jim and Sean talk about the bill process and he was tired of not knowing what they were talking about, so he used this time to edify himself. "So what are the next steps for you from here? And what is an omnibus bill?"

"Basically what happens from here is the boss—that's what I call our rep, the chair of the House bonding committee—puts together his bonding proposal based on what he thinks are the best projects from those submitted. We'll be working with the Senate, but the bills don't have to be identical at first. It just depends on the chairs' preferences. Once the bills are released in the upcoming weeks, the House version will come before our committee for debate. Members can attempt to amend it if something isn't to their liking, but it's difficult. If the bill passes our committee, it may go through another committee before heading to the House floor for a vote."

Pausing to make sure that Luke was still with her, Dani saw that he was following her explanation with interest so she continued. "After it passes the House, it also needs to be taken up by the Senate, or vice versa. Once the bills pass each body the first time, the bills will be conferred. That means members are appointed from each body to develop identical language. The identical bills need to be passed again by a simple yes-or-no vote. If the conferred bill passes both bodies, it heads off to the governor to be signed or vetoed. And that, in a nutshell, is Minnesota's bonding process."

Luke nodded. "That makes sense." He liked seeing Dani smile at his comment. It made his stomach feel the same way it did before he stepped out on the ice before every game, which was unsettling. But he loved seeing her smile. "When Jim asked me—well, threatened is more like it—to be a part of this proposal, I tried to wiggle my way out of it any way I could. Obviously, that didn't work. One of my biggest objections to participating in the proposal—besides my general aversion to politics—was that I had no idea how the process works."

Luke felt comfortable around Dani, so much so that he knew he could admit a flaw and she wouldn't judge him. He'd always been a proud person. "I don't like doing something if I can't do it well. I've been that way since I was a kid."

Dani smiled, remembering him at the Rink practicing his slap shot. There was admiration in her voice when she spoke. "I know."

Luke shot Dani a questioning glance that she returned with an explanation.

Dani rested her forearms on the table and leaned forward. "I saw you at the Rink on a day off. Jake says those are far and few between in the pros. It says a lot about your character and dedication that you were there when you didn't have to be, just because you thought you needed to run drills. And then to begrudgingly succeed at lobbying even though it wasn't something you wanted to do—well, that just confirms my last statement. The Blizzards are lucky to have you, Luke."

It took everything she had to not turn away, but Dani didn't want Luke to doubt the sincerity of her last statement even if it did make her feel bashful. And her reward was priceless. She was able to see the gorgeous face of Luke Coffey go from questioning to pride to peace. Dani could tell that Luke felt comfortable around her and that feeling was completely mutual—another milestone for her. She often felt wary around guys since she wasn't sure if they were interested in her or her family connections.

Suddenly, she wasn't self-conscious. She could feel her guard start to soften. Breathing became a bit easier and her nerves were subsiding. If things went further, she'd have plenty of reasons to be bashful around Luke in the future, but she'd cross that bridge if and when she got there.

Somewhere in the middle of her assessment of him, Luke knew Dani was someone very special. She wasn't judging him and seeing him as an all-star athlete, or millionaire; she saw him just as a guy. And he knew she was sincere. Those gorgeous amber eyes of hers didn't stray from his gaze once during that speech. He could tell it took a lot for her to maintain eye contact, but Luke appreciated it more than she would ever know. Without a doubt, he knew that she was without artifice. Now he just hoped she'd give him a chance, even with all the inevitable challenges ahead.

Many saw the professional hockey world as a glamorous one, but Luke knew it had drawbacks: a crazy travel schedule, lack of privacy, and lots of public appearances. From what he knew of Dani, she tried to avoid the limelight, but hopefully they could make something work. He really wanted something to work. They could figure out the logistics later.

Looking over to the dance floor, Luke saw his friend talking to Piper. The song was just ending, but Luke wanted to get in on some of that closeness. Tipping his head toward the dance floor, Luke smiled at Dani. "Care to dance?"

She couldn't help it. She started laughing, causing Luke's smile to widen.

She shot Luke an uneasy glance. "You know how you mentioned that you don't like doing anything unless you can do it well?" She saw him nod. "Well, I'm the same way. Which is why I don't dance. I never mastered it, so I try to avoid it."

Luke stood and held his hand out. "I may not be the best dancer, but I can hold my own." He could tell Dani was still worried. She hadn't grabbed his hand, but was looking at it consideringly. "I promise. I won't step on your toes or bruise any appendages."

If he was confident enough to joke about it, Dani figured that he must be pretty good. Her smile widened as she lifted her hand. "I can't promise you the same, so proceed at your own risk."

Pulling her up and out of her seat, Luke put his arm around her and leaned in close to her ear. "I'll take my chances. But if you tell any of my teammates about my twinkle toes, I'll tell all of them you're a Chicago fan!"

Chapter 13

Piper sat in the most comfortable leather seat she'd ever been in and wondered, again, how she'd wound up here. She looked out the window of Marc's luxury coupe and smiled as she recalled the rest of their night at Tango Rio.

After working up an appetite dancing, the two pairs had returned to their table and ordered another round of drinks and more food. Then the laughs had really started as they'd shared embarrassing stories.

After some hilarious anecdotes of practical jokes that had been played on them by their teammates, Marc and Luke asked the women to share their most embarrassing stories of each other. Piper knew right away what story she wanted to share, and that she wanted to go first. If she thought about it for too long, she'd start laughing and then she'd never get through it. The guys looked eager for her to begin, and she was never one to keep a captive audience waiting.

"Quick history lesson: I first met Dani last year when she was a page. As you can guess, we became friends instantly and today she is one of my dearest friends. A part of me hates to tell this story, but it's too good not to share. Keep in mind that during the time this story was taking place, Dani was quite sick and we were working around the clock during the last nights of session. Everyone was sleep deprived."

Piper heard Dani moan next to her as she realized what story was being shared, but her good-humored friend also had laughter in her voice. "I can't believe you're doing this to me!"

"Can't wait to hear it!" Luke chimed in as Piper continued.

"Legislators and staffers practically live at the Capitol those last days of session. In order to get all the bills passed, we go into session and take breaks for recess here and there, but we meet around the clock. Well, on one of those last nights it was about two in the morning when recess was called and everyone was just dead tired. Some members who live nearby go home and take naps, others have couches in their offices, but staffers just go wherever we can find room.

"At some point, Dani discovered this great cove in the gallery of the House chambers. It isn't well known or very big, but it's big enough to curl up and even has a drape for privacy. So the House recesses at two a.m.

and everyone goes to try to catch a little shut-eye. I'm able to take a nap on my boss's couch, but it's a small couch so I can't offer Dani a place. I assume she's found somewhere to crash and frankly I'm too tired to worry about her sleeping arrangement.

"Some of us are able to get a couple of hours of sleep, but then word gets out that session is starting back up at four thirty, and I can't find Dani. I look everywhere. I know she's still around since her car is in the parking lot, but the girl is nowhere to be found.

"One of my representative's bills is up on the floor right away so I can't round up people for a search party. As my boss is explaining her bill, the House is pretty quiet. I think most members were still half asleep. All of a sudden, everyone starts looking around because we can hear this ghastly wheezing sound that seems to be coming from the gallery. It sounds like an animal is dying. The Speaker of the House asks my boss to pause for a moment and sends one of the sergeants up to the gallery to see what's making this horrible noise. A minute later we hear the sergeant burst out laughing and the noise stops.

"Every member in the House looks up and sees poor Dani doing the walk of shame across the entire gallery. It took everything I had not to laugh. She looked so rumpled. Her hair was piled on top of her head, she must have been sleeping on an arm because half her face was bright red, and she was sniffling to beat the band from a terrible head cold. Some members couldn't hold their laughter. Dani was so embarrassed. She came down the back stairs, but then had to go on the floor without a chance to pull herself together. She got right to work, though the Speaker did come down from her stand and give Dani a hug. She was blushing for the next hour."

The guys were laughing, but Piper was sending her friend a smile and a sympathetic glance. Dani didn't look too embarrassed. She was laughing just as loudly as the guys.

"So, what's Piper's most embarrassing work story?"

Marc eagerly posed the question to Dani, who just grinned. Piper knew what was coming and started shaking her head at the memory. It was definitely not her finest moment, or her most graceful.

Dani tried starting her story but only got one word out before she started laughing. The guys were grinning in anticipation. Taking a sip of her margarita, Dani took a deep breath and tried again, hoping the tequila would keep the laughs at bay.

"We all know that Piper teaches dance, but what you don't know is just how passionate she is about the sport." Dani motioned with her hand to Luke and Marc. "I'd bet she takes dance as seriously as you take hockey. And although she's a great committee administrator, she's an even better dancer. I've seen her in action and can vouch for her talent."

As she spoke, Dani saw her friend drop her head in embarrassment at the accolade, but she also saw Marc looking at Piper with what appeared to be serious admiration. Dani was so thankful Luke had offered to bring Marc out tonight. He was just what the doctor ordered for her friend. Realizing her pause was becoming unnecessarily long, Dani continued. "But I digress. This story takes place shortly after Piper's story.

"After those horrible last nights of session, our representatives wanted to thank the staff by throwing a little party. Since it was after session in June, Piper was in the peak of her dance season and had her dance recital that very night. Piper teaches, but she also dances herself in the old-timers' class, as she calls it. The rest of us head out to the party after work while Piper goes to her recital, with the intent of joining us afterward.

"After dinner everyone gets into the celebratory mood and the drinks are flowing. A little after ten o'clock, Piper walks in the door and everyone stops what they're doing. She has on this short, slinky red-sequined number. I mean, she walked into the party room of this bar and every guy in the place immediately turned toward Piper."

"Don't lie!" Piper didn't want Dani to get too carried away with the story. "If anyone was looking, it was because I sparkled like a disco ball. In my defense, I was planning to put on my work clothes after the recital, but someone dropped their makeup bag onto my recital bag in the dressing room and the powder broke and got all over my clothes. I texted Dani that I wasn't going to make it, but she and everyone else she told texted back that skipping the party wasn't an option."

Piper saw the guys smirking as her friend continued her story.

"I know you didn't plan on wearing that dress, but the guys saw you in a totally different light after that!"

Piper waved off her friend's comment and hoped the ending was coming soon.

"Looking like she just stepped off of a Las Vegas stage, everyone starts egging on Piper to do some dance moves. Finally, after enough ribbing from our colleagues and various representatives, Piper agrees to do a little turn combination with the stipulation that everyone drops their interest once she finishes. She looks around and finds an open area to do some turns but then one of the members asks her how long she's been dancing. It took some time to answer him and when she went to start turning, a waitress was coming around the corner with a fully loaded tray of drinks."

It took another sip of her margarita before Dani could continue.

"I'm sure you can guess what happened. Piper starts her turn and about halfway through, she collides with the waitress. Her leg catches the waitress's knee and her arm is going straight for the tray." Dani brought her arms up in an exploding motion as she tried to inhale a breath. "Drinks go everywhere. And I mean everywhere. Piper was drenched. Members were soaked with beer. I ended up with someone's cosmopolitan splashed all over my face."

Piper smiled as she saw Luke and Marc both throw back their heads and howl. They obviously found her embarrassment amusing.

"Poor Piper immediately started apologizing to the waitress, who'd taken the majority of the impact. And everyone else was eerily quiet until people started laughing. The place was a liquid mess. We grabbed towels and started wiping, and wiping. It took forever because people had to stop to catch their breath from laughing too hard. Since then, no one has asked Piper to showcase her moves. And I'm sure she's fine with that."

Piper propped her elbow up on the table and rested her forehead on her hand; she closed her eyes and remembered the mess from that night. It had reaffirmed her decision not to dance in public. She never minded that her height kept her to the back of her dance lines; she actually preferred to remain out of the spotlight. The dramatic spill incident solidified her belief that she should keep her dancing to the dance studio. The same studio she'd just agreed to share with Marc LaFrey.

After another round and some laughs, the group decided to call it a night. Marc surprised her by asking where she lived and then offering to drive her home. Apparently he lived by her, and Piper guessed he wanted to discuss the dance partnership. Never had she let a guy drive her home on a first date, but she felt safe with him. Which is how she found herself sitting in the passenger seat of his Mercedes, in the curbside drop-off of Marc's apartment building, while he ran upstairs to grab the dance video.

Piper glanced at the lobby of his apartment building. She had looked at some units in this building when she was searching for her place, but the prices were a little too steep for her state salary, even for a studio. She saw Marc come out of the elevator lobby, say something to the doorman, and then rush to his car. She was thankful that he got in fast enough to save some of the glorious heat pouring from the vents. There was nothing worse than having to sit in a cold car.

"Okay."

Enough heat had escaped from the car that Piper could see Marc's breath as he spoke.

"Where do you live again?" Marc asked as he checked for oncoming traffic and pulled away from the curb.

"I'm not too far. I'm happy to walk if you want to let me out here." Piper's offer was earnest. Although some areas had their quirks, St. Paul was a pretty safe city.

Marc's head whipped toward her. "Not a chance." Piper interpreted Marc's look to say that there was no room for negotiation, so she recited her address and building name in Lowertown. He seemed to know the place, because he didn't ask for any further clarification or directions.

"You live in a great area." Marc maneuvered his way expertly through the streets of St. Paul. "I like to come down here sometimes to grab a drink."

Piper wasn't sure if he threw out that comment to gauge if she did the same, but she filed the information away just in case. "It's developed a lot the couple of years I've been here. It's great for me. I can walk to work and I'm close to everything downtown."

Marc pulled up to the curb in front of her apartment building and put the car in park. He turned toward Piper and held up the DVD. "Here's what my sister sent for me to learn. You'll know who my dad is right away. He's the old geezer of the group."

After she assured him that she would learn the dance that weekend, he asked about their first lesson.

"Are you free Wednesday night?"

Piper took a second to think what her calendar looked like for the week. "Actually, that would work out great. I teach a couple of classes Wednesday so I'll already be there. There will be classes at the dance studio until about eight. Could you meet at eight thirty? Or is that too late?"

Given his game schedule, Marc didn't think that eight thirty was late at all. "Not a problem. Where's your dance studio?"

Piper told him the address and watched as Marc entered the information into his GPS. She thanked him for the ride and opened her door. Before she swung her legs out, Marc spoke. "I really appreciate you helping me with this, Piper."

Closing her door slightly so that it was only partially ajar, Piper turned back to Marc. She heard the sincerity in his voice and couldn't stop her answering nervousness. Marc was looking at her in a way that she couldn't describe, but it caused her body to heat up. If he was causing this reaction already, she had no idea how she was going to get through a whole lesson.

"My pleasure. Happy to help." And Piper meant it. She loved weddings and knew how much these events meant to the families and friends involved. She was glad she could help Marc accommodate his sister and her bridal wish. Smiling at Marc one last time, she thanked him again for the ride and exited the car.

She wouldn't let herself turn around as she walked toward the building, but she could feel someone watching her. It surprised her just how much she hoped it was Marc.

Chapter 14

"Looks like the easiest thing will be to open up the inseam and add a panel for length."

Piper demonstrated her recommendations on the stretchy, shiny, blue hot pants and grabbed the top that made up the other half of the outfit.

"For the top, I'd let the straps out a bit since you have some extra fabric at the seam." Holding the top up to Samantha, one of her dancers, Piper explained her thoughts to Sam's mom, Susan. "By letting out the strap about an inch or so and reattaching it, the top should be long enough to fully cover her torso."

Piper knew dancers loved costume day—she always had at their age too. Not only did her students try on their new costumes and model them, but they also performed shows for each other and their parents before they had to take them off. For parents, costume day was a different story. Although some parents were lucky enough to have dancers who fit perfectly—or close enough—into their costumes, alterations were usually required. Such was the case for Samantha, Piper's tallest dancer.

Some parents found themselves moonlighting as amateur tailors around recital time. Piper shuddered as she remembered some of her mom's creative alterations.

Once all the dancers and parents had left, Piper grabbed a broom and quickly swept up the sequins and feathers that had fallen off the costumes. When the floor was clean, she let herself relax in the teacher's chair for a minute. Rushing from a session and committee day right to teaching was a good recipe for exhaustion, but Piper loved teaching too much to give it up. And for her, dancing was the best way to unwind from everything else that was plaguing her in life. She was able to minimize the stress she had from work by leaving everything she had on the dance floor.

Looking at the clock, Piper saw that she had twenty minutes before Marc was due at the studio. Kicking off her tap shoes to throw on her jazz shoes, she figured she had just enough time to work on a turn combination for her older group and a roll she had to learn for her old-timers' dance.

Five minutes later, Piper had worked out the turn combination she wanted to teach her competition group and was pulling out a mat to work on the roll she couldn't quite master for the dance she'd be performing publicly. In all her years of dancing, she'd never done a car-crash roll—probably because the physics defied her. It was one thing to do a backwards somersault, but then to do the splits while rolling was frustratingly difficult.

Somersaults and splits were two activities Piper could individually do without hesitation, but combining them had proven problematic. If she was going to figure out where she was going wrong, Piper knew she either had to just risk injury and go all out to see if momentum would make the difference, or slowly break the sequence down. In an effort to remain injury free, she opted for the latter.

Ensuring that the mats were properly in place to provide support, Piper started by facing the sidewall and looked at herself in the mirrors that lined the front wall of the studio.

She gave herself some motivational coaching. "Take your time, Piper. Do it right!"

With her right foot in a dig behind her, Piper bent her legs until she was in a sitting-chair position sans the chair. Needing her weight to propel her into a backward somersault, Piper threw herself downward and backward and started to roll. When she felt her weight settling on her shoulder that was pushing against the floor, Piper tried to split her legs as they began to move over her body.

It was barely audible due to her compressed rib cage, but Piper let out a very unladylike, "Fudge!"

Piper could see in the mirror that her legs weren't really splitting. Annoyingly, they straightened above her body, and to make things worse, they were pointing up to the ceiling instead of continuing to roll over to come into contact with the floor. The move was painful at full speed, but slowing it down to make sense of what was going on was surely going to leave bruises.

Not wanting to get stuck with her legs over head again, Piper rolled down into a sitting position. Willing to try anything, Piper bent forward at the waist and threw herself back hard and kept her right leg straight and began lifting it immediately. Although it was slower rotating, Piper noticed that lifting her leg as early as possible helped to keep her rotation going.

Needing that extra momentum to ensure she could get her somersault around completely, Piper stood back up. She thought that she would add a few steps before dropping to the floor. The extra momentum helped, and Piper completed her best car crash to date. She was lying facedown on the floor having just completed the roll, which caused some shoulder burn, when she heard a deep voice behind her.

"I don't remember seeing that move on the wedding video."

Piper groaned into the nasty-smelling mat she was currently plastered to. Of course Marc had to show up early. Rolling onto her back, Piper used her core muscles to pull herself up to a sitting position and rose from the floor as gracefully as she could.

Looking at the clock, Piper saw that Marc was, in fact, eight minutes early.

As Marc propped himself up against the doorframe of the studio with a bemused expression on his face, Piper tried to save as much dignity as possible. She reached down to pick up the mat that was supposed to limit the number of bruises. "This is exactly why I hate dancing in front of people," she lamented into the plastic encasing. That couldn't have been a flattering position to be discovered in at all.

The gruffness hadn't left her voice when she addressed her student and started dragging the mat toward him. "I wasn't expecting you so early."

Marc came forward and grabbed the mat. "I got here quicker than I thought. I saw the light on from outside so I figured you were in here," he explained. Piper noticed he'd already divested himself of his jacket and she assumed he'd been in the lobby for a minute or two, meaning that he'd seen more of her embarrassing attempts at the roll.

"That was quite the move you just did," her student said with admiration in his voice. "There's no way in hell I would be able to do that leg thing over my head."

Without the cantina music drowning it out, Piper was truly hearing Marc's French-Canadian accent and found it very smooth and sensual. Her annoyance was quickly dissipating.

"It's a move I need to perform, but I'm struggling with it. As I'm sure you saw. No doubt I'll have a bruise tomorrow," she began, rubbing her shoulder, "but once I get it down, it should look pretty *sick*." She emphasized the last word just for him.

"Does that move have a name?" Marc asked as his grin grew.

Piper tried to shoot him a mocking look. "It's appropriately named a car crash. You feel the aftereffects for the next few days. And don't worry, you don't have to learn that."

Marc let out an exaggerated sigh. "Good, I had a moment of panic watching you after I got over being impressed."

Although Piper was still slightly mortified by being caught with her butt over her head, his statement oddly flattered her. It helped ease away some of her self-consciousness.

She thought Marc had caught on to her unease because he continued to lighten the conversation. "I'd pay big money to see my sister do that in her poofy wedding dress."

Piper pictured a marshmallow rolling and chuckled. "Don't worry, there are no foreseeable car crashes in your future. Your dance will be less rolling marshmallow and more tango."

Marc groaned. "Leave it to my sister to pick a tango as a group dance." Following his teacher over to the music station, Marc asked the question that had been plaguing him since he first watched the dance. "Isn't the tango a passionate dance?"

Piper shared her opinion of the dance from the few times she had actually done it. "In a true tango you're often skin to skin with your partner. Since this is a group dance, though, it doesn't look as sensual. Unless you're the bride and groom."

Piper saw Marc's eyebrows rise at the word *sensual*. She also hadn't failed to notice that his eyes had dipped a few times to check out her leotard-clad figure when he thought she wasn't looking. He must not have noticed all the mirrors adorning the walls. As soon as she could, she planned to put on her sweatshirt, but she didn't want to be too obvious. She didn't want him to know that he was unsettling her. So with as much suaveness as she could muster, she brought her arms in front of her body to cover as much of her leotard, hot pants, and tights as she could. And then she tried distracting him.

"Do you know who your partner is?"

To his credit, he kept his eyes on hers while he spoke. "*Oui*, my cousin Sophie, who is very beautiful and a great dancer. Hopefully everyone will be watching her and not me."

"I'm sure that won't be the case," Piper muttered.

Apparently Marc also had very good hearing. "Sorry?"

"I just said that I'm sure you'll be great. I looked at the footage and the dance really isn't difficult, but you'll be traveling around the dance floor. That can be tricky—especially since you aren't there to practice with the others."

"Très bien!"

Hearing his language change made Piper smile. "Letting your French slip a little there?" She stepped away to put a new CD in the changer, but her main motive was retrieving her sweatshirt. Once the fleece was firmly in place, she made her way back to the middle of the studio where her unsettling new student had migrated. By the way his lips picked up a bit in the corners and his eyes dropped to her new garment, Piper was assuming that he found her attempt at modesty humorous.

Most women would probably die to have this opportunity to be so close to Marc LaFrey in a super-skimpy outfit, but Piper didn't want her body to send any signals her brain hadn't approved in advance. So she was throwing on layers. And although it may be cold outside, the inside of the studio was anything but.

"I fall back on my native tongue when I'm frustrated. You should hear me when I'm at the net," Marc said with a laugh.

Since she was one of what seemed like only a handful of Minnesotans who didn't play hockey, Piper didn't foresee any face-offs against Marc. "I'll take your word for it."

Rotating to face him, Piper explained the format of the lesson. "My goal today is to teach you the basic tango combination. You'll be doing it frequently in the dance. Then we'll partner up so you can get used to leading your partner. Since you and the group are moving, you're going to have to be spot-on with your leading."

Marc nodded his head. Gone was laughing Marc and in his place was serious Marc, determined to learn what he had to know. He was intently focused on the task at hand—his eyes were locked on her feet.

"Oh no," Piper scolded, successfully raising his eyes from her feet to her face. "Two things. First, I want you to have fun because I'd hate myself if you didn't. Dancing is fun. And second, don't worry about your feet. Ballroom is based on keeping eye contact with your partner and trusting your frame. Your feet will naturally follow."

"Frame?"

"Yes, frame," she said slightly incredulously. "Haven't you ever seen *Dirty Dancing*?"

Marc almost scoffed at the question. "The one with Patrick Swayze dancing? Afraid not."

Piper did scoff at his response. "You're missing out." The look Marc gave her said that he didn't think so.

Grabbing his arms, Piper held them up in the same fashion that Swayze had done for Jennifer Grey a couple of decades prior.

"Your frame is how you hold yourself while dancing. It's important to maintain because this is also how you'll lead your partner. But we'll get back to that later."

Taking his left hand in hers, Piper held it up to his left side and then put his right hand on her back toward her left side and above the small of her back. She could tell he felt a little unsure of himself, but his hold didn't waver. The man radiated masculinity.

"First, we're going to learn the steps but while we do that, I want you to keep your arms just like how they are now so you'll get used to holding your frame."

Marc started laughing, but toned it down as he recognized her seriousness. He looked at himself in the mirror and slouched. Just a little. This time he didn't contain his laughter.

"What's so funny?"

"Seriously?" He looked at her incredulously. "Look familiar?"

Piper had stepped out of his hold so that she could observe him keeping his frame. She didn't get it at first until he crouched down more than was needed for the tango. With his left arm up and his right arm in a wrapped motion around his front, Piper was shocked to realize that he looked like how he did every time he took his place on the ice for the Blizzards.

"Oh my gosh," she chuckled, "You look like—you!"

Marc stood back up to his regular standing height. "I don't think that holding the frame is going to be a problem. If I can hold my own for three-plus periods, I'm sure I can hold it for a two-minute dance."

Piper admitted that the man had a point. "Well," she said sternly to bring her student back to task, "just humor me and keep your arms up. Besides, your left arm should be a little higher for dancing than it is for hockey.

"Facing the mirrors, I'm going to do the basic tango five-step next to you and then in front of you, if you need me to. Typically in ballroom dances, the lead steps forward with his left foot and the partner steps back with her right."

Piper was watching her student to see how well he understood. To her satisfaction, Marc stepped forward with his left foot.

"Wonderful! Now, you will follow that with a step from your right."

Marc did just that.

"Perfect. You have the first two steps: left, right." Piper knew it sounded trivial, but some of her students had a hard time mastering that. "Now the next two are going to be the same, left then right, but you are going to do them double-time and follow it up with one last normal step from your left foot to close out the combination."

Marc started showing a slight bit of unease, but Piper stayed in control of the lesson. She demonstrated the five steps for her student and then motioned for Marc to join her. They started the combination upstage, but after repeating the sequence five times, they were at the mirrors and Marc seemed to have a good understanding of the basic combo.

Moving them back to the center of the studio, Piper felt strongly that Marc would be able to pick up the turn quickly.

"We obviously can't keep going straight with this combination. And the steps themselves don't go in a straight line. As we face the mirror, the first two steps will be forward." Both she and Marc stepped forward with their left feet and then right. "Now on the double-time part, the left foot will be the same but instead of stepping forward with your right, you're going to step to the right. And then bring your left foot to meet it there before starting over again."

Completing the five-step combo, Marc was feeling confident. Looking pleased with himself, Marc dropped his arms and looked toward his instructor. "*Très bien*! Not bad at all," he stated with confidence.

Piper had to fight back a smile. They were far from done. Time to put him back into his place.

"Just a minute there, Swayze!" she said sharply. "You picked up the basic combo quickly. Partnering is next."

Grabbing his shoulders, Piper turned him to face her and felt a ripple of excitement go through her. She never felt uneasy teaching ballroom to other couples. It required getting close to men, but she always stayed professional during the process. Her heartbeat had never picked up like how it was now. She couldn't recall another time when she'd been so aware of her student's breath on her hair. She thought it was a good thing she'd thrown on the sweatshirt since her body was a hot mess.

Sometimes her height was the bane of her existence, but in this case, she appreciated that her genetics kept her from having to strain her neck to make eye contact with her student. Thanks to the heels on her dance shoes, she was only a couple inches shorter than Marc. She was in a perfect position to see that her student had beautiful steel-gray eyes that complimented his black hair perfectly.

"Arms up." Piper tried to jump back into her professional mode. Grabbing Marc's right hand, she pulled it to her back. His hold was strong. Then she placed her hand on his broad shoulder and lifted her right hand to meet his.

Piper tried one last time to convince herself that Marc was just any other ballroom student, but as soon as she moved her gaze from their joined hands to his face, Piper recognized that statement for the lie it was. Most ballroom lessons she gave were to couples who were engaged or older; she never had to worry about losing her composure around those guys. Not the case with Marc. She understood from recently checking his player profile that he was currently single and unless she was sorely mistaken, he'd been admiring her form during the lesson.

She supposed it was vain to think that, but Piper was flattered. She knew she wasn't model-pretty. Truth be told, she always worried she was a bit too muscular, but her dancing had kept her pretty toned. She only had a boyfriend here and there over the years, and none at the moment. Her shyness had been an obstacle she hadn't fully overcome even in her twenties. But this wasn't a date, it was a lesson, and she owed her client his money's worth.

Since they were already poised to dance, Piper thought it was an appropriate time to share what made the tango hold different from other dances.

"Most dances start off how we're standing now. Face to face and parallel. But the tango, as I mentioned, is a more intimate dance. Which means partners get close." Her student obviously had no qualms about that as he tried to move closer. "But we'll start off with this hold for now."

Pushing him to the back of the studio, Piper had given them enough space to run the combination a few times without having to stop.

Looking up at her student, Piper thought that Marc looked ready to go. "We're going to do the basic combination. I'm going to count it out as one, two, three, and four. Five steps, four beats. The third beat is double-timed."

Marc didn't need to be told twice. "Got it. Let's move!"

Piper appreciated his enthusiasm. "All right, here we go. Ready… one, two, three, four."

Marc completed the combination four times with no problems. Piper was impressed and felt confident they could move on.

"Remember how I was talking about using your frame to direct your partner?"

Marc nodded.

"This is a good place to use that. The basic tango step can be used in many directions." She motioned from the back of the room to the front. "We've mastered one direction, but without rotating, you'd run into a wall in no time. With a simple turn during the combo, we can use the same step to move sideways." She started demonstrating as she spoke. "We keep our arms in the same position but turn our bodies toward our joined hands."

Their bodies now parallel to each other, they started heading toward the sidewall.

"We both step forward like we have been, you start on your left foot, and I start on my right. Left, right, but pause here. Now using your right hand, cup my side and back—basically my shoulder blade—and apply a little pressure in the direction you want us to go to lead me. This tells your partner that you want her to turn or just head in another direction. Between the second and third step, when you push me using your frame, I'm going to whirl around to face you." Piper demonstrated the turn and was now facing Marc as before. "From the direction we started, we've now turned ninety degrees. If you're ever running out of room, use your lead to go sideways and then turn your partner and you'll give yourself some more room."

"So I can just push my partner wherever I want her to go?"

Piper eyed Marc suspiciously given his statement. Not certain if he was hoping to push her around or others. "We'll say leading and not pushing. But you have a lot of control as the lead—hence the name. You can just lead your partner, especially me, by directing her with your hold as to where you'd like her to go. Let's try the forward-then-side combo again."

As she directed him, Piper was thinking that Marc was the best student she'd ever had. He had no problem doing the regular combo combined with a side version. Running it a few more times with great success, she decided it was a good time to call it a night.

"I'm impressed, Marc," she announced as she dropped her hands. "You pick up steps quickly. Very quickly."

Marc shrugged at her accolades. "I have good muscle memory. Years of hockey drills."

Piper thought there was probably more to it than that, but she wasn't going to argue with him. She walked over to the teacher's corner and turned off the music she had playing softly in the background. She grabbed her dance bag and headed out of the studio to the lobby. Marc was already there, putting on his jacket. "When should we meet again?" he asked.

Piper mentally pictured her schedule for the next couple of weeks. "Will next Monday work for you? Or do you have a game?"

Marc didn't hesitate in his response. "No, Monday works. Same time?"

"We could meet earlier if you like. The back studio will be open. I can let you in the back door. No one should see you."

"Sounds good. Maybe we could catch dinner or a drink after?"

Piper dropped the water bottle that she had just grabbed from the refrigerator.

She saw Marc's lips form a grin while he raised an eyebrow. "Or do you not do dinner with your students?"

Trying to steal time, Piper took a sip of water. "I've never had a student ask me to dinner." Her immediate reaction was to say no, so she went with it. "That's really nice of you to ask—" And then her mouth just stopped working as his grin faltered.

She knew she sounded like an imbecile stopping mid-sentence, but she was perplexed. She could feel her instinct arguing with her desire. She was twenty-six years old and she needed to start dating. Dani had been encouraging her for months, but she had been too afraid. This wasn't even dating. If anything, Piper thought, she could use this dinner as practice for when the real deal did come along.

"Sure, we can do dinner after." She nodded at Marc. "Thanks for asking."

Piper didn't blame Marc for the confused expression she saw on his face, but thankfully he didn't ask about her roundabout response.

"There are some good restaurants around here. Should we say a seven o'clock lesson?" Piper turned off the studio lights and headed for the outer door. She could hear Marc following her.

"Sure, Monday at seven."

Marc stood beside her as she locked the studio, made sure she got to her car safely, and even opened the door for her. His chivalry didn't go unnoticed. It would have been hard not to notice—a guy had never opened her car door for her before.

She thanked him again, got into her car, and watched him slide as gracefully as a man his size could into his sporty coupe. Figuring that Marc was waiting for her to pull out before leaving, she didn't let her car warm up as long as she normally would. Before reversing, she performed her usual check of her rearview mirror and caught a glimpse of herself. Not so usual: she was smiling like a fool.

Chapter 15

Dani discreetly glanced at the clock on her computer. She tried to hold back an eye roll when she saw that it was already three thirty, but she wasn't sure if she was successful at hiding her irritation. Not that the source of her irritation would have stepped down from her soapbox, so her worry was for naught. Dani had been trapped in her office by the lobbyist in question for the past thirty minutes and it didn't look like an end was anywhere in sight.

She met with lobbyists daily and had quickly learned that some were pushier than others, but the woman currently robbing her of productive work time was the most talkative, aggressive lobbyist she'd ever had the misfortune of being trapped by.

All of Dani's polite attempts to end the conversation in a timely fashion were rudely ignored by the other woman. Every time she tried to bring an end to the tirade, the woman just kept on talking as if the fate of the world depended on what she had to say.

It wasn't uncommon for Dani to make appointments with lobbyists that would run thirty minutes, but this unscheduled drop-in had forced Dani to miss a previously scheduled meeting, which didn't sit well with her.

The lobbyist had already caused her to miss one meeting, so at this point Dani didn't care if she appeared rude. She pulled up the instant messenger on her computer and started typing a silent SOS to Tyler. Even the typing didn't stop the lobbyist from lobbying.

"*Code red. I repeat CODE RED. Rescue required ASAP!*"

It was the first time she was utilizing the SOS mechanism they'd developed earlier in session for situations such as this. To ensure that people didn't catch on to their game, they'd agreed on a respectable time lapse between the message and rescuing interruption.

Receiving a phone call was easier, but this lobbyist had proven that it wasn't always the most effective method. The phone had rung three times in the last thirty minutes and the rude lobbyist hadn't yielded once, even when Dani had motioned to grab it. Initiating the code-red sequence was Dani's only remaining course of action.

Dani wasn't expecting an immediate response from Tyler, but since she wasn't receiving any messages back, she also had no way of knowing if he was still at his desk.

Just as she was getting ready to instant-message Kim, Dani heard the glorious sound of Tyler's chair pushing away from his desk. Seconds later, Ty was pushing her slightly ajar door open all the way.

"Sorry to interrupt the meeting." He looked imploringly at Dani. "Dani, the representative just called; he needs you to swing by committee ASAP!"

Practically jumping out of her chair, Dani grabbed hold of Tyler's lifesaver as tightly as she could. "Thanks, Ty. I'll head down there right now." She tried to look regretful as she approached her time burglar, who was finally also standing up. Dani shot up a silent hallelujah. "Sorry I have to get going, but the boss needs me. Thank you for swinging by," she lied, "and sharing all of this information with me."

As if the last half hour hadn't been enough, Dani found herself at the receiving end of a massive folder filled with information. Just in case there was anything else she needed. Dani threw the folder on her desk and headed down the hallway toward the back staircase. To be safe, Dani thought that keeping up the facade was the safest thing to do, in case the lobbyist poked her head back in.

Wanting to stretch her legs anyhow, Dani walked down a floor and back up a couple times before heading back to her office. She stopped to thank her rescuer.

"Thank you so much! That was absolutely ridiculous. I tried to end that conversation ten times. People who think they're so much more important than everyone else drive me crazy."

Realizing that she was getting more upset the more she thought about the lost thirty minutes, Dani closed her eyes and took a deep breath. "Sorry, now I'm lamenting to you and wasting your time."

"Dani," Ty reassured her, "I'm more than happy to lend an ear if that's what will keep you sane during these crazy weeks. But just an FYI, that woman is known for impromptu meetings like the one you just had. Watch your back, Jack!"

Dani knew she was fortunate to work with someone who was so experienced and sympathetic to her plights. Thanking her stars that she had Tyler as a coworker, she smiled at him one last time and returned to her office.

Sitting down to continue the email she'd been working on when the lobbyist dropped by, Dani first checked to see if she had a message from the Revisor's Office letting her know that the draft of the bonding bill was ready. As luck would have it, she had a new email saying the draft was done and a hard copy would be arriving soon.

Looking at her watch, Dani realized she was due in another meeting. Waiting around for the draft wasn't a viable option. She needed to talk to Kim about logistics. Leaving her office, Dani walked down the hallway toward Kim's desk. Pulling up a chair, Dani grabbed a seat so that she could lean in and speak softly.

"Kim, I have to head off to a meeting, but we're going to be getting the draft of the bonding bill soon. When it's dropped off, grab it and make two copies—keep the original as a back-up and give a copy to the boss and me." Dani wanted to be sure she had Kim's attention for the next part. "People are very interested in seeing this bill, but we're going to look it over one last time over the weekend before it gets introduced next week. We need it to stay under lock and key. When you're done making the copies, put the original and the two copies back in my office and then close the door and make sure it's locked."

Kim was shaking her head in understanding. "No problem! Do you want me to bring your copy to your meeting?"

Dani was tempted to have her do just that, but then decided against it. "It's tempting, but no. People would notice and start asking questions. I'll get it when I come back. Thanks for asking." Dani stood and paused to reinforce the plan. "I'm going to head downstairs. The main thing is to make sure that my door is locked when you close it."

"Will do, Dani."

"Thanks, Kim. And if I don't see you before I get back, have a great night!"

"You too!"

Dani pushed her chair back and headed off to her

meeting with the other CAs. The once-a-week gatherings were a nice time to catch up with her coworkers. They were one of the only opportunities for CAs to get together, have an open forum discussion, and strategize for the upcoming weeks. The meetings were also an ulcer reducer for Dani. It reassured her to know that other CAs weren't having an easy go of it either. She liked knowing it wasn't just her.

The main topic of discussion for this particular meeting was end-of-session planning. A bill was never truly dead in the legislature, so it was a good rule of thumb to try to anticipate curveballs. If a bill failed to pass committee months ago, it could be proposed again as an amendment during a discussion of a similar bill on the floor, and the debate on the failed bill would ensue all over again.

After reiterating the importance of anticipating amendments, Dani was happy to hear their supervisor begin to discuss conference committees. This was a process she'd never undertaken, but knew it would be happening in the near future with the bonding bill. She knew that identical language between the Senate and House bills was developed in these committees, but she wasn't sure about the actual administration required to achieve that.

Dani was already on her second page of "how to run a conference committee" notes when she felt her phone vibrate. Usually she was a stickler about never using her phone in meetings, but she knew that it could be the boss texting something important, or Kim letting her know she'd received the bill. Checking to see that her supervisor wasn't watching her, Dani reached into her pocket and pulled out her phone. She almost dropped it when she saw the sender. It was a text message, but it wasn't from the boss or Kim. It was from Luke. She had to bite the insides of her cheeks to keep from smiling.

It was ridiculous to be so excited about a text from Luke, especially since they'd been texting and talking on the phone a few times this past week, including a quick call last night. And yet she couldn't stop herself. After covertly looking around the room, Dani swiped her phone to get the full message of the text.

"Hey, how are you? Hope you aren't too tired from swimming through all the papers in your office. I didn't get a chance to ask you last night but was wondering if you'd like to get together this weekend? I know you may have to work. I have a game tonight, but I'm free tomorrow and thought we could meet up after you're done?"

Dani knew her supervisor could have been talking about a life-or-death situation with conference committees and she wouldn't have a clue because all her attention was on this text. She could feel her heart beating fast, and her mind started reeling with everything that was going on this weekend. She hadn't gotten more than twenty hours of sleep this whole week thanks in part to work, but also her texting fests with Luke. But it didn't seem like such a big deal now. Apparently for Luke, she'd endure many more sleepless nights.

As soon as her mind processed that thought, more personal and R-rated versions of what she could be doing with Luke at night came to mind. She was sure she didn't even know half of what could go on, which was something she'd have to address with Luke at some point if this went anywhere. She could feel a blush coming on just thinking of the possibilities.

Bringing herself back to the dilemma at hand, she knew that she absolutely had to review the bill draft with a fine-tooth comb over the weekend. If she started tonight and continued bit by bit, she figured she could be done by Sunday night no problem. It probably wouldn't take her as long as she was expecting, but she wanted to be sure she gave herself enough time to be safe. She'd already left her Saturday night open for a family event, but other than that, unless Luke wanted to join her at the laundromat, she had no free time. That is, unless she wanted to take a huge step with Luke, one she'd never taken with a guy.

Dani had to decide if she wanted to invite Luke to join her at her parents' home Saturday night. Meeting the parents when they weren't even dating was a huge step. But she would say that they were friends, and friends met each other's parents. Didn't they? She had a standing invitation to most of her friends' parents' homes.

Her mind flashed back to the conversation she had with Piper in the tunnel. If she wanted the boys to meet Luke, this would be a great opportunity. And she could assess Luke's ability to live up the O'Brien standard. It was a scary thought, though. She'd never brought a guy home. Sean didn't count; he'd just been around since he was friends with her brothers. And although he'd asked, Sean had never been invited to join one of their siblings-only match-ups. But it seemed natural to invite Luke.

Her motive was admittedly twofold: she wanted to spend time with Luke and they were going to be a man down. With baseball season starting up, Jake wouldn't be able to make it back for the last O'Brien match-up of the year.

Usually one of the parents filled in as goalie if they were short, but that wasn't an ideal situation for anyone. Dani and her brothers didn't feel right about shooting pucks at their parents, and neither parent really appreciated having pucks flying at their faces. Plus, it didn't take much to get a puck past Mom or Dad these days. Thinking of those dulled-down hockey games in the past, Dani assumed her brothers would welcome Luke as their seventh player.

Glancing up, Dani was happy to see that the meeting was wrapping up. She started typing away at her screen: *"Hey, long time, no chat! LOL. Papers have receded enough for me to see my nasty carpet and realize that the papers make a better floor covering. I'd love to do something tomorrow, but unfortunately I'll be working the first part of the day and then at my parents' place in the evening. It's our last O'Brien hockey match-up of the year. Would you like to join us? Full disclosure: you'll definitely be recruited to play and will be surrounded by O'Briens."*

Dani pressed "send" and thought about the difficult position she'd put Luke in. She didn't want him to feel duty-bound to meeting her whole family just because he wanted to spend time with her. Wanting to give him a little reprieve, Dani started to type another message.

"Dani?! Hello?! Earth to Dani."

Dani absently realized that someone was standing in front of her seat. Knowing those red pumps anywhere (because she'd been admiring them for weeks), Dani looked up and saw Piper standing above her. Her friend didn't miss her flushed face.

"I think there's something you need to tell me! What's up?"

Looking down at her phone, Dani continued texting while absentmindedly responding to her friend's question. "Yeah, just one second; I'll fill you in. Think we can do a quick lap around the building?"

"Sure, I have committee soon but I can sneak away for a few minutes," Piper told her as she looked at her watch.

"Okay, just a second."

Dani tried to text as quickly as her stubby thumbs

would allow. "If meeting the whole O'Brien clan, sans one brother, sounds a bit daunting, I totally understand. This is your get-out-of-jail-free card. We could always try for another day."

Dani stood up and walked toward her friend, who was waiting at the door. The room was close to an outside side door of the Capitol so they could sneak out unnoticed. Neither minded the crisp air—no longer winter, but not quite spring—that greeted them.

"Was anything substantial said during the second half of the meeting? I got distracted after hearing that we don't have to take minutes for conference committees."

Piper just shrugged. "Not really. I can fill you in. But, Dani, it's so not like you to tune out in a meeting," her friend observed with concern. "What happened?"

Still holding her phone, Dani scrolled up to Luke's original message and passed it to Piper. She couldn't help but grin when her friend started jumping up and down and, predictably, clapping her thigh with her free hand since the other one was occupied with Dani's phone. Not the easiest thing to do when walking in heels.

"Oh my gosh, Dani. You said yes, right?" Dani didn't need to answer since she saw her friend scrolling down through the coversation. "Well, I don't think you needed to send that second message, but—"

"What?" Dani waited for her friend to finish what she'd started to say.

Passing back her phone, Piper started jumping even higher. Dani knew before she looked at the phone that Luke had responded.

"I've never been in jail, nor do I ever intend to be, so I don't need a get-out-of-jail-free card. I'd love to take on the O'Briens. I'm free all day, so let me know the best place and time to meet you. I'll bring my gear. Looking forward to seeing what you've got on the ice."

Now it was Dani's turn to start jumping. Neither woman cared that the governor had just walked by and saw them acting like twelve-year-old girls.

Dani collected herself. "How cute is it that he added the smiley face?" she said in a ridiculously mushy tone. "I'm excited, Pippi. Scared, but also excited."

Piper gave her friend a quick hug. "Oh, Dani, you deserve to find someone great." They had reached the front of the building and started walking up the forty-five steps to the main doors. Doing stairs inside and outside the Capitol was pretty much the only exercise either of them got during the session months. "What are you going to wear?"

Dani started laughing. "Pippi, we're playing hockey. There's no point in me getting dolled up. I'll probably be in leggings, a jersey, and my gear. Trust me, there isn't anything you can do to look sexy in hockey gear."

They had entered the Capitol and were about to go their separate ways. Dani gave her friend and cheerleader one last quick hug. "If I don't see you, have a great weekend. I'll let you know how Saturday goes!"

Piper squeezed back. "I better not have to wait until Monday. I'll be looking for a status text Saturday night or Sunday morning. You can give me all the details later."

"You got it!" Dani promised.

Dani headed down the hall to her office and fought the urge to skip. She was startled when she saw the bill draft and copies Kim had left her. She'd completely forgotten they'd be waiting for her. She couldn't believe that, or the fact that she was going to continue ignoring the bill until she could text Luke her excitement.

"Looking forward to tomorrow too! Let's meet at the Capitol. I can drive us to my parents' and then we can head back when everything is done, if that works for you. I'll plan to meet you in front of the Capitol at five o'clock tomorrow. My parents live about twenty minutes from here. Dinner's part of the deal too. See you then!"

And with that, Dani put her phone in her desk drawer, picked up the ninety-five-page bill, a pencil, and a highlighter, and forced herself to get serious. It was easier said than done.

Chapter 16

It had taken everything she had to leave her apartment while it was still dark out, but it had been a good thing to come into the office. Staying in her pajamas and working from home sounded so appealing, but Dani was too easily distracted at home. History proved it was far too tempting to throw in a *Golden Girls* DVD and hit "play."

And so, for the thirteenth straight day, she was at the Capitol, working her way through a deluge of papers. The boss was there to keep her company, but this sort of work schedule was taking its toll on everyone. People were tired and wanted to be spending their Saturdays with their families and friends. She was keeping her goodie drawer stocked with plenty of chocolate in the hopes it would keep everyone as upbeat as it was possible to be under the circumstances. Dani could see the light at the end of the tunnel; she just wished the light wasn't so far away.

She looked at the clock for about the fiftieth time and saw that it was only three o'clock. Trying to fight back her excitement about her evening plans, Dani checked her phone to make sure she hadn't missed any messages from Luke. Thankfully it appeared that everything was a go, since her last message from him had been the one yesterday saying he'd be in front of the Capitol at five o'clock. She hoped the next two hours would fly by, and when she saw how much of the bill she had left to analyze, she didn't think it was going to be a problem.

The offices had been abuzz all day with staff stopping in to discuss the bill as they all prepared for the upcoming week. The bill was to be introduced and heard in its first committee.

She was a little scared to tell the boss that she had to leave at five, but her worry was wasted. He said that her departure would be a great excuse for him to head home at four thirty. Dani hoped everyone would leave around that time. She didn't want to explain why she was getting in a car with the star player of the Blizzards. Piper told her that this relationship, or pending relationship, wouldn't be an issue. She wasn't the first staffer to date someone from within the government-relations world. But it still made her uneasy.

Keeping a low profile was Dani's goal in life. Considering a few members of her family had more visible careers and lifestyles, that wasn't the easiest thing to do. She'd have to figure out that quandary later, some time when her boss wasn't calling her from down the hall.

"Dani, I need you in here. And please bring some—no, make that a lot—of chocolate with you."

Walking in, she placed her assorted goodies on the boss's desk and sat down on her favorite leather chair. Their Senate counterparts would be joining them soon. They needed to talk timelines.

She leaped up from her chair when she realized she'd uncharacteristically forgotten her notepad. Before returning to the boss's office, she reached into her drawer for a back-up handful of candy and made it to the office just in time to see their counterparts walk in. Welcoming them to the party, Dani made sure to shut the door in case they had any eavesdroppers.

An hour later, they had a good plan on paper. They discussed everything from timing to expected amendments to potential vote counts and media requests. Everyone knew that as soon as the bill was posted for introduction, the press would be all over it. The chief authors and staff had agreed to keep the bill confidential until then and go through their respective media staffers, who Dani and her Senate counterpart would be briefing mid-week.

As the Senate members stood to leave, Dani looked to the clock and saw that it read twenty minutes after four. She breathed easier as she realized they were right on track for getting out on time. Heading back to her desk, Dani reviewed her notes and clarified some points that her shorthand had left vague. She heard the boss before she saw him.

"Dani, I'm heading out for the weekend. You get out of here too. I don't want you to live here."

Upon hearing that news, Dani felt a weight lift as she thought she was in the clear. But then he rounded the corner and stood in her doorframe, causing her shoulders to tense again.

"You're too young and pretty," her boss began arguing, "to be cooped up in this stuffy old office. You need to be out on the town meeting nice guys."

Dani smiled at his compliments. Some women may take offense, but Dani knew that he was being genuine in his own politically incorrect way.

"I will, sir," she reassured him. "I'm staying for another twenty minutes and then heading to my parents' place."

Her boss scoffed and shook his head in dismay. "Dani, your parents' place isn't exactly the best place to meet guys."

Her heart started beating fast in nervousness as she contemplated telling her boss about Luke, but decided against it. There wasn't much to tell right now and she didn't want to jump the gun. They still had a lot to overcome, including his dislike of politics and her aversion to athletes. She felt obligated to tell him something, so she threw her military brother under the figurative bus.

"We have one of our O'Brien matches tonight. That's why I'm heading over there. It's the last one before Andy heads overseas on his next tour." Dani was happy to see that information placated her boss somewhat. She thought it was a good excuse, and since it was mostly true, she didn't feel too bad about misleading him. "Don't worry, sir. I'll have a life after session. Just have to get through the next few weeks, right?"

"You're doing a fantastic job, Dani," her boss said earnestly. "Have fun with your family tonight, and please thank your brother for his service. I'll be keeping him and his battle buddies in my prayers."

"Thank you, sir. I'll be sure to do that," she promised. As her boss headed out the door, Dani wished him a great rest of the weekend and then sat for a moment in the silence. She had about fifteen minutes before meeting Luke, so she started closing things down and using the facilities to freshen up.

Soon she was walking down the forty-five steps of the Capitol entrance to meet Luke, who was lounging against his new luxury SUV. Any other time she'd be skipping down the stairs for fun, but she restrained herself from doing that in front of Luke. She didn't need to put all her quirks out there for him to see immediately, nor did she care to wipe out.

Dani slowed her approach, not quite sure how to greet the man who was looking way too attractive in his jeans and vest for her to be at ease. She debated what greeting to use. Were they at the verbal stage?

A handshake? A hug? Kiss on the cheek? She didn't know. Mercifully, he must have been feeling the same sort of uncertainty, because after a brief moment he leaned in for a quick hug.

Pulling away, Dani was almost breathless by the instant physical attraction as she began talking. "Thanks for being willing to come tonight. I'm sure it wasn't what you had in mind, but I couldn't miss it."

Luke shrugged and had laughter in his voice when he spoke. "Thanks for inviting me. I couldn't pass up a chance to spend time with you. And you look beautiful by the way."

Dani was incredibly grateful that Luke had pulled away because her pulse quickened and she could feel her flesh heating as his words warmed her with their sweetness.

"Do you want to drive? Or should I?" Luke offered next.

"I'm perfectly happy driving," Dani responded. "That is, if you don't mind."

Luke didn't appear to have any qualms with that and it pleased her to know it.

Her brother Andy once told her that a guy who was fine with letting a woman drive was confident with who he was.

"My parents are tucked in by a lake," she explained, "so it's probably easier if I drive us anyhow. I'll put my parking pass in your window so you don't get towed, and we can be off." Dani reached to grab the pass hanging from her rearview mirror and placed it on Luke's dash. "And we need to grab your bag."

Luke was already circling to the back of his SUV. She watched him slide out a bulging Blizzards bag.

"Let's put that in my backseat," she said as she eyed the bag's size. "My bag took up most of the trunk."

Although her compact was reliable, it certainly wasn't as grand or stylish as his ride, but Luke didn't seem to mind. It got her from point A to point B, and that's what mattered. After settling in behind the wheel as Luke threw his bag in the backseat, Dani started the car and turned down the local country station that she'd been jamming to while heading into work that morning. As she watched him climb into the passenger seat, Dani could feel her body heating again with excitement. She was looking forward to this alone time with Luke because she knew that once she got to her parents' place, he was going to be open game for grilling.

"Your family doesn't mind you bringing me along tonight?" Luke asked.

Pulling onto the freeway, Dani merged successfully before answering his question. "No, absolutely not." She stole a quick glace before she continued. "I won't lie; they were surprised when I said you were coming, but they're more than happy that you'll be joining us."

Dani comprehended that the next statement was going to say a lot but she had to let him know. "It's rare for a non-O'Brien to participate in these games, but lucky for you, Jake couldn't make it home and Andy—

the military one—is home on a short leave before heading out on his next tour overseas and he wanted to have a sibling match-up. Of course we had to oblige."

Luke asked the question he'd been pondering all day, especially after her last statement. "I hope you don't mind me asking, but have you ever brought a guy home to play in one of these games?"

Of all the questions he could've asked, Dani was hoping he wouldn't ask that one. She wasn't sure how much he would read into her answer but she couldn't lie. "No," she said honestly, "I haven't."

She could have added again that they needed the extra person, but that wasn't necessarily true. Her parents could have filled in, and they both knew it.

Luke would be lying if he claimed his chest didn't swell a little with the sense of pride he got from Dani's admission. He was honored to be welcomed into such a close-knit environment. And he was relieved to hear that she didn't regularly ask guys to participate in this family activity. He didn't know to what degree yet, but this new piece of information told Luke that he mattered to Dani.

"By the by, since you're in the sports world, can you be careful about who you mention this night to?" Dani could see the quizzical look Luke was sending her way, so she continued. "I only ask because of Jake. He won't be joining us tonight, but he joins when he can. He and his teammates aren't supposed to play any contact sports outside of baseball. As you'll see soon enough, this game is definitely full contact. I wouldn't want him to get in trouble for playing backyard hockey."

"Keeping this under raps is the least I can do," Luke agreed. "And so you know, I'm looking forward to meeting your family—and seeing your moves."

Although she didn't look at him, Luke watched her smile as she drove. Seeing her smile caused him to smile. But just as quickly as her smile appeared, it vanished. "Oh, about that. Forewarning: the boys don't hold back because I'm a girl. If you go easy on me, we don't care if you're an all-star; we'll bench your ass the first chance we get. And if that happens, one of my parents will be subbing for you and that will piss everyone off."

Luke started laughing. What he felt for her was nothing like anything he felt for any of his hockey buddies, but Luke could tell she was being damned serious. He'd never played full out against a member of the opposite sex. Hopefully with her helmet on, he'd be able to convince himself that she was just any other player. He took a peripheral glance at the beauty sitting next to him and knew instinctively that, helmet or no helmet, she wasn't just any other player.

"Go big or go home, right?" he said with all seriousness.

Dani looked his way and raised an eyebrow. "Literally!"

There was a noticeable tinge of respect in his voice as he continued. "You got it. Just like any other hockey player. Maybe we'll be teammates!" Luke prayed that would happen.

"We could be. We'll have to pull checkers when we get there."

He started laughing again. "Checkers? You didn't tell me I should have brushed up on my checker-playing skills!"

Luke's indignation made Dani grin. It probably did sound weird to an outsider. "Nah, you'll be fine. Checkers are the method we developed years ago. We flipped coins once and all got heads, so we opened up our checker set and took out seven pieces. We colored a star on one red piece so that it could be the goalie indicator, but otherwise it's three black and three red. To this day, we use those same checkers to pick teams. It's crazy, but it's tradition."

Luke couldn't wait. This was going to be a very interesting experience. "Checkers it is! Are you excited to let off some steam from this week? How's it been?"

Dani exhaled deeply. "In a word, crazy! I haven't had a day off in weeks, but that's the name of the game. Speaking of game, nice work last night."

Her accolades made Luke feel confident. Not in a cocky way, but in terms of pride. Dani knew the game and he could tell by her voice that she was being sincere. It meant a lot that she was applauding him for his skill at the activity he loved most. "Thanks, it felt good to get another win."

"People are excited for the playoffs to start. Any sense of how they're going to go?"

"It's looking like we may be up against Chicago for the first round. That'll be a tough one. We're pretty even statistically, so it will depend on who brings their A game."

Dani let out a snort from the driver's seat. "I hate them with a passion!"

By the tone of her voice, Luke didn't doubt it for a minute. "Any particular reason?"

"I went to college in Chicago and had some bad fan experiences. A Blizzards' loss in Chicago was always awful."

"Where did you go to school?"

"Loyola University."

Luke was impressed. "I've heard that's a great school, but they don't have a hockey program, right?"

"Sadly, they don't. But I followed other Chicago teams while I was there."

"Did you think about staying in Chicago?"

"I did, but I'm a Minnesota girl at heart."

Luke would be sure to keep that in mind. He loved the state too. "So where do your parents live?"

"Just north of St. Paul in the same house I grew up in. It's a great old house that we've updated a lot over the years."

"Did you do the work yourselves?"

"When we could, we did. My dad always said that having kids meant that you got cheap labor."

Luke laughed, again, reminding him that he hadn't been doing enough of that lately. He liked being so relaxed, and he liked that the camaraderie he and Dani had going felt so organic and not at all forced.

"The worst was the summer we had to reroof." Dani shuddered thinking about the memory. "I have never been in so much pain as I was in the days after that."

Luke knew exactly what she was talking about. After one particular week of grueling training before the Olympics, he found himself in a similar situation. "Don't you love when you work muscles that you never even knew existed?"

"In this case," Dani remembered painfully, "not so much. But every time I look at that roof I get a feeling of pride. A lot of O'Brien sweat, and some blood, went into that project. Speaking of the roof, you'll be able to see it in about thirty seconds."

Dani had been expertly navigating her way along a winding lake road. He figured no one would go to this much trouble unless they were nearing their destination. Just as she'd announced, Dani put on her blinker seconds later as they approached a well-hidden driveway. The boulevard hedges hid the house thoroughly. It was a good thing he hadn't driven; he would have missed it.

"Nice privacy walls," he admired.

Dani started turning into the driveway. "Lilac bushes are great! In a few weeks, all you'll see is purple. When they're in bloom, you'd never know there's a house back here."

As Dani pulled up to a stop, Luke got out of the car and took a look around. Dani was modest in her description. The house was old, but it was a beautiful Craftsman that looked very well maintained. There was a covered porch that started on the side of the house by where they parked and wrapped all the way around to the back. He could see the mini-rink as well as the lake. He just knew that this would have been an amazing place to grow up.

Luke heard Dani pop her trunk, so he quickly walked back to the car and grabbed her bag from the trunk and his from the backseat.

Dani tried to reach for her bag but he wouldn't let her take it. "Oh, you don't have to carry that. I can grab it."

"I got it," Luke said. "Just lead the way."

Realizing that arguing was futile, Dani started leading the way around the house. "We may as well go around to the back and drop off our bags. Then we can head into the kitchen. I have no doubt my brothers are stocking up on carbs before the game."

Luke dropped their bags off next to three others on the back porch. Dani reached for the door handle to the back door, but paused and turned around.

"I'm apologizing in advance if my parents or brothers do or say anything that makes you feel uncomfortable or embarrassed. They're great people, but

Power Play

a little protective—and sometimes just endearingly awkward."

In response, Luke reached forward and put his hand over Dani's on the door handle. "Don't worry, I'm a big boy. I can take anything they throw at me." He stepped closer to her and focused his unwavering gaze on her. "I want to be here, Dani. And I'm honored to be invited." And with that, he pressed down on Dani's hand to release the lock mechanism and started pushing in the door, but not before he placed a quick kiss on her cheek. Her momentary shock allowed him to sneak past her into the house.

Once they were both inside, Dani exhaled the breath she hadn't realized she'd been holding. Her face tingled where he'd placed his lips. Good heavens, she thought. If he was having this effect on her now, she didn't want to think about what kind of inebriated state she'd be in moving forward.

Luke quickly realized that Dani must be right about her brothers already being inside. He was hearing at least a half dozen voices all coming from nearby. Following Dani's lead, Luke took off his shoes and walked toward a set of French doors to the right. They seemed to be following an amazing smell.

The noise dropped slightly as Luke walked through the open double doors that led to the kitchen. Quickly processing the scene, Luke saw Dani walking toward a woman whose resemblance to Dani meant she could only be her mother. She was standing over a massive cooking pot on the stove. When Dani approached, her mom turned around and gave her a big hug. Dani probably would've done the same with her dad, but he was busy digging in the fridge. He must have found what he was searching for because he straightened, closed the door, and then turned toward Luke.

"Mom, Dad, boys, this is Luke Coffey." Motioning around her, Dani made introductions. "Luke, this is the O'Brien clan." Her parents had huge grins on their faces, but the same couldn't be said for her brothers.

One by one, each of the five O'Brien brothers in attendance stood from their perches on the scattered chairs and stools.

Well, he'd either just met the welcoming committee or the firing squad. Taking a deep breath, Luke walked toward Dani's parents. They looked like the safer bet.

Chapter 17

Dani wasn't sure what she should have expected, bringing a guy home for dinner and a match-up, but it wasn't the sight before her. Her brothers were scowling like a pack of hungry wolves. She could detect fluttering to her right and turned to see her mom approach Luke.

"Luke, I'm Kate," her mom announced as she ignored her sons. "Welcome to our home. It's so nice to meet you."

Dani's mom was shaking Luke's hand and motioning to her husband, who was moving away from the fridge.

"This is my other half, Jack," Kate said with affection in her voice.

Jack put his left arm around his wife's waist and reached out to shake Luke's hand with his right. Luke could tell right away where Dani got her warm personality. Her parents exuded friendliness and a deep affection for each other. The verdict was still out on her brothers, but he didn't think he'd have a difficult time with the parents.

"And that sorry lot over there are my brothers." Dani pulled Luke's attention away from her parents and directed it toward the firing squad.

Still standing by her parents, Dani started verbally introducing everyone to keep the guys from approaching Luke. She started from the left and worked her way right.

"You know Sam."

Both men did the acceptable nod of recognition. Growing up, Dani learned that women tended to hug, or at least extend a verbal greeting, whereas men could just get away with a head nod as a greeting. She chuckled as she watched the nod executed with each brother.

"Next to him is Nate, the older twin; then Chris; Patrick—the other twin—and Andrew."

Luke found himself facing five remarkably similar O'Brien scowls. "Nice to meet you, fellas. Dani's told me a story here or there about you all. Thanks for letting me skate in today." Luke scanned the faces and saw that the scowls remained intact. "Should be fun," he added in hopes of breaking the ice.

Dani, watching the interaction between her brothers and Luke, wasn't surprised when Chris spoke first. As the oldest, he was usually the first to speak for the group. He was also the most diplomatic—must be the priest in him.

"Happy you could join us, Luke," Chris announced as his scowl broke into a small smile. "When Dani mentioned you were coming, we were all a little surprised. But you'll be a welcome addition." Chris started walking toward his parents. As he spoke, he nudged his way between the two and slung an arm over each of them. "Otherwise, we were going to get stuck having to play with one of these fools."

"If you're trying to offend me, Chris, I have far thicker skin than you think." Their mom gave her eldest a quick embrace. "Plus, I'm a realist; I know I'm not twenty anymore. I'm a much better cook than hockey player these days."

Chris decided to test his mother's word and scooped out a spoonful of the stew that was simmering in the cooking pot. "That you are, Mom," he said with admiration. "That you are!"

"So, guys, when does the puck drop?" Dani asked, figuring that the sooner she got everyone out onto the ice, the less time they'd have to grill Luke.

Nate started walking toward the kitchen exit. "Right now," he announced as he detoured to shake Luke's hand. "We were just waiting for you kids to get here. Out on the rink in fifteen?"

Dani looked to Luke to get his approval, which she did before speaking. "All right, ice in fifteen."

Grabbing Luke's arm, Dani led him out back through the French doors. "If you need to use the restroom, it's tucked under the stairs. Otherwise, just throw your gear on wherever you like. I have to run up to my room to grab the checkers and change, but I'll see you out there."

Luke enjoyed the view as she ran up the stairs. He pulled his lingering eyes away from her form when he heard people moving behind him. He didn't want to get caught checking out Dani by another O'Brien. That would be awkward.

He decided to make use of Dani's suggestion and headed toward the restroom. Along the way, he checked out what he could see of the O'Brien home. It was nicely decorated, but practical. Luke never understood why people bought houses so big that whole rooms were never used. His idea of the perfect house was something small enough that you could always find someone by yelling out their name, but big enough that you weren't living on top of each other.

As he walked the few steps to the bathroom, he looked at the pictures lining the wall opposite the staircase. He paused when he got to a framed picture of what must have been Dani's first communion. Luke thought she looked adorable in her white dress, shoes, and gloves. Her brothers were lined up next to her in their little suits.

A couple of pictures below, he saw another one of her at what he assumed was her college graduation. She was wearing a maroon robe with a gold sash and ribbon. Instead of being lined up next to her, her brothers were actually holding her up as she lay horizontally across their forearms with her head propped up by one hand, and the other hand showing off her diploma. Every one was all smiles.

Looking at some of the other pictures, Luke could see the love in their family. The feeling of loneliness he sometimes got when thinking about his childhood snuck in as he browsed the photos. He had wished for an environment like this growing up, but his parents had always jokingly told him that they didn't need to have any more kids since they already had the perfect one. They were loving parents, but as an only child, he'd dreamed of growing up with brothers to skate with and sisters to torment.

Realizing that he only had about twelve minutes left, Luke quickly used the restroom and headed outside to don his gear.

The brothers were all on the ice when Luke skated on after dressing. "Where's Dani?"

One of the twins started circling him. "She's always last. Something you should learn now, Luke." Luke thought it was Patrick, not his twin Nate, who shared this bit of information with him.

"Oh shut up, Patti-boy." Yep, Luke thought. He looked over to see Dani crossing the lawn with her skate guards.

"I had to dig out the checkers." Looking at Luke, Dani must have felt the need to defend her honor. "I'm usually very punctual. Except for tonight." He watched in rapture as her face evolved into a guilty smile, "And our first meeting."

"All right, you kids, let's warm up and get this beat-down underway," ordered Andrew. Dani rolled her eyes. Her big brother sometimes forgot that he wasn't on a military base. But no one disagreed with his command and within seconds everyone was skating around the half-sized rink.

Andy called out for teams, so Dani skated to the side and reached down to pick up the old shoe bag that housed the checkers.

"Luke, since you're the guest," Dani offered, "I think it's fitting that you get first pick."

When none of the brothers objected, Luke reached in the bag, tossed around the checkers a bit, and pulled out a red one. Sam was standing next to him and pulled another red checker, this one with a star on it—goalie. He groaned loud enough for everyone to hear. Obviously he didn't want to be guarding the net tonight. Sam headed to the bench to put on his pads, grumbling the whole way.

Nate and Patrick picked black checkers. Andy's checker was red. One black and one red checker remained in the bag, and Chris and Dani still had to draw. Chris reached in and pulled out a black piece. That meant Dani was red. She'd be on Luke's team. Luke let out the breath he was holding. He was happy about not having to body-check her. But as soon as that thought came to mind, another image of Dani and a different kind of body-check surfaced and his body instantly got hot. Grateful they were outside, he pushed the image aside before he started sweating. The two teams broke apart to discuss strategy while Sam headed to the net to warm up.

Andy led Dani and Luke to a bench and cut right to the chase. "Now, you two may be hot for each other—"

"*Andrew*—" Dani scowled.

"What? You could start a fire with the heat you two are throwing at each other. But you'll regret it if you let that get in the way of your play. I play to win, got it?"

Out of all of the brothers, Luke gathered that Andy was the most intense. He also had the loosest tongue. The captain waited to hear their agreement and then turned for the ice.

Dani looked over and saw her parents walking to the makeshift stands with their thermoses. Leaning in to Luke, she apologized for Andy's frankness. "Sorry about that. He needs a muzzle. And there's a perfect example of why I warned you earlier." She let out a low sigh that was part frustration and part embarrassment.

Luke reached out with an ungloved hand to grab her arm. He started rubbing it up and down. "Don't be sorry. He was just being honest," Luke said truthfully.

Looking at Luke with the glint reflecting in his eyes, Dani felt breathless again. She wanted to say more to him in that moment, more about how she felt, but she couldn't risk her brothers overhearing. This was no business of theirs. They needed to get through this game and then they could talk. Suddenly she was eager to get playing.

"Good luck!" she replied as she tried to suck in air. "And remember, go big or go home."

"Always." With a quick wink and a squeeze to her arm, Luke threw on his gloves and skated out onto the ice. Andrew took the right side, Dani played left, which left him at center—his bread and butter. Game on.

Jack and Kate joked that they could make good money selling tickets to these O'Brien matches. Scouts would pay a premium for a match-up between some of their kids, but they wouldn't give up this private time with their brood for anything.

Being small-business owners had its advantages and disadvantages. The family had benefited from financial security, but the constant work schedule for the entire family was a definite disadvantage.

There were times when Jack and Kate worked every single day for months at a time. They tried to have one parent, ideally both, home for dinner every night, but running their own store, which had later expanded to multiple locations, sometimes kept them both away from the dinner table and family time.

Thankfully, their kids enjoyed the family business just as much as they did and understood the sacrifices that were sometimes required. If the kids wanted to, they were allowed to pick up part-time jobs at the stores while they were in high school and college. They'd worked hard and were rewarded for it.

Looking out at the six kids who were present, they couldn't have been more proud of any of them. And their guest appeared to be fitting in just fine.

Kate had been more than surprised when Dani called to ask if either she or Jack would have a problem with her bringing Luke Coffey home. It wasn't like their daughter to bring a guy home, especially one she hadn't even mentioned. But Dani had always been very private with her relationships. No doubt it was a strategy to keep her meddling brothers at bay.

They knew very little about the men she'd dated since high school, but they had complete faith in Dani's choice of guys. They knew enough from her stories to know that she'd had a few not-so-nice boyfriends. But Dani had learned from those mistakes. Plus, they both believed that out of all of their kids, Dani was the best judge of character. If she thought Luke was special, they knew he must be.

No one would argue that he could hold his own on the rink. There were just a few minutes left of play and Dani's team was up by one goal. Like a pro, Dani skated up the left side, executed a spin move that drove her brothers crazy, and slid the puck to Luke. He shot the puck into the net by bypassing the top of Sam's pads and bottom of his glove. Jack and Kate smiled as they watched Luke and Dani embrace—hockey pads and all—in front of the goal. Andrew threw up his hands in celebration and started jeering at his brothers, especially Sam who'd let that "puny" shot slide past him.

With two minutes remaining, Kate stood up and went back inside to get dinner ready. As she stood up to leave, she felt her husband grab her leg. Turning around she saw a pouty look on his face and knew what he wanted. Leaning down, she gave her best friend and partner a kiss that hinted more was in store for later. After thirty years of marriage, she never took for granted the gift that God had given them in each other. Especially since they'd been adversaries when they first met. She smiled thinking of the sparks that flew between them in college.

Her husband was the one person she could count on for everything in life. For a shoulder to cry on, for a laugh, for a confidant—anything that she needed, Jack was there for her. Just like she was always there for him. She prayed every night that each of her children would one day find the same in a partner.

Their eldest, Chris, had already found his life partnership in the church. Now they just had six more to match up. As she walked toward the house, she glanced back at the rink to see the game coming to an end. The boys had obviously warmed up to Luke; she could hear her sons bestowing the title of MVP to him. Instead of reveling in the congratulations, though, Luke seemed to have eyes only for her daughter, as he embraced his teammate. She smiled to herself—maybe they'd soon be down to five out of the seven.

"That is hockey!" exclaimed Luke to no one in particular as he stepped off the ice.

Luke couldn't remember when he'd had so much fun on the rink. Every game he stepped on the ice as a Blizzard was a highlight of his life, but the business side of things often took away from his love of the game. He never had the opportunity these days to play the game because he loved it. But tonight it was the ice, him, and six other really good hockey players.

Luke was impressed as hell with Dani's play, but he didn't know why he was surprised. She had been surprising him since the day they met.

He had treated her just as he would any of his teammates, and she'd definitely proven her worth as a player. Dani had left the actual scoring to him and Andy, but she'd assisted on each goal. She was amazing at finding the openings, and time after time sent the puck exactly where she wanted it. After her passes, he and Andy had no problem doing the rest.

Everyone had taken off their equipment and was heading toward the back door when Luke felt a fist land on his shoulder.

"You did pretty good tonight, Coffey. We may even invite you back at some point."

It was Sam, his potential future teammate, who shared this bit of information with him.

"Happy to oblige. If you do become a Blizzard, we'll have a good rapport already in place."

Sam pushed Luke into the deck spindle. "Keep

dreaming, Coffey. I'm young. There are tons of pretty fish in the sea. That goes for women and teams."

Luke smiled as he looked at the young and naïve college star. He'd thought the same thing when he was younger, but experience had proven that some teams operated differently and, although there were many women at every hotel they stayed in and every restaurant they visited, not all of them were keepers. He'd been bitten by suckerfish one too many times, but Dani was giving him hope that he'd finally found the jewel of the sea.

"Don't let him fool you." Dani's soft voice floated up from behind him as he waited at the top of the deck stairs. "His dream is to play for his hometown team. It's something all of us kids dreamed about when we were younger. We'd all wear jerseys of our favorite Blizzards players and dream that one day our names would be on the backs and we'd be taking the ice at the Rink instead of our own backyard. Even me!" she admitted as she started laughing at the memory.

Dani's eyes drifted away from his as she continued. "For some of us that dream changed, but for Sam it's only grown and solidified over the years. But," she paused tersely, "I probably shouldn't be telling you that."

As she finished talking, Luke could see the worry settle on her beautiful face. He guessed that she was second-guessing sharing so much. "I have nothing to do with acquisitions, but if I did, I'd be recruiting all of you O'Briens—including you. Don't worry, your secret is safe with me."

Her smile was his reward.

"Thanks!" Dani felt the worry ease from her body. "You held up pretty well against our motley crew."

They were standing right outside the door, but neither was motioning to head in yet. "I had a great line out there with me. No joke—your passes were amazing."

Dani gave her shoulders a shrug. "Eh, I'll leave the hockey and power plays to my brothers, and you! I'll stick to my policy plays."

Leaning back to peek into the bay window, Dani saw that the family was crowding around the well-worn table. Taking a deep breath, she wanted to give him one last opportunity to sneak out. "Okay, dinner is probably going to include some interrogation. Are you sure you want to go in? I can come up with an excuse that you had to leave."

Again, he was touched that she was repeatedly worried about him, but he was prepared for any tough question the O'Briens could serve up. As an answer, Luke grabbed Dani's hand, opened the door, and headed in to meet the firing squad. He knew with a certainty that shook him that he'd willingly face the squad for the woman firmly holding his hand.

Chapter 18

After a dinner that was surprisingly free of grilling, Dani offered to show Luke around their property to give him a reprieve from her crazy family. Their home wasn't ostentatious, but it had some gorgeous lake frontage. Borrowing some of her dad's mud boots for Luke, the two suited up and headed outside to stretch their legs. She breathed a little easier when they stepped onto the deck. Her family hadn't said anything terribly embarrassing, but she didn't want to tempt fate. Plus, she wanted some alone time with Luke to continue what had started earlier.

"Well, that was relatively painless," Luke said with humor in his voice as he zipped up his coat. Dani was trying to do the same.

"I'm quite surprised." She zipped her coat all the way up past her chin and looked at Luke. "I thought it was going to be much more intense than that. My brothers can be overprotective." Her statement caused her to start laughing. "Actually that's an understatement, but I guess they already know a bit about you."

Whatever the reason, Luke was happy dinner went the way it did, though he didn't get off scot-free. Luke had to field some personal questions—what his parents did, his long-term goals. They'd even touched on religion. Apparently he'd passed that test, which was a relief. With a priest in the family, he was guessing that was a paramount issue for them. After all, they began dinner by clasping hands and saying grace before indulging in one of the best meals he'd had in a long, long time. He remembered quite a bit from his Sunday school days, but he knew he wouldn't be able to hold his own in a theological debate with a priest. Thankfully, the family seemed more interested in Andrew's upcoming deployment than Luke's profession. He admired and respected the O'Brien's transparent view that family is important—perhaps the *most* important thing.

Luke gathered that Andy was home for another few days before heading back to Georgia and being deployed overseas with his Ranger unit. Just listening to the guy, Luke could tell he loved what he did. He'd asked him if it was difficult choosing between the pros or joining the military. Without blinking, Andy had responded that he had absolutely no regrets about his decision. "I love playing," he'd continued at dinner, "but I knew my career wasn't going to be as a player. I didn't find enough pride in what I was doing. I'd known for years that I wanted to serve, and every time I put on my uniform, I'm humbled."

Luke thought his perspective was humbling. The ranger's confidence and dedication was unquestionable. In the short hours he'd known Andy, he could tell he was a natural leader of men.

Dinner took on a lighter tone when Luke had asked if they were planning any RV trips for the summer. As he began walking down the back porch steps with Dani, Luke couldn't hold back his laugh when he recalled the conversation that had ensued.

Dani was intrigued by his random outburst. "What's so funny?"

"I was just thinking about the RV stories your parents shared at dinner. You guys really had some adventures."

Dani responded to his comment with a smile of her own. "That's an understatement. And there are so many. I'd forgotten that awning incident until tonight."

That only made Luke laugh harder. After he'd broached the topic at dinner, Dani's mother had mentioned they'd be going to a wedding of some family friends in June that was taking place out in Idaho. Of course, they'd drive the RV.

Out of nowhere, Nate had instructed his parents to be sure the awning was secure before heading through South Dakota, which had brought a round of laughs and lots of reminiscing from the O'Brien clan. Luke learned that on a fateful trip through South Dakota, in the middle of a thunderstorm, the awning of their RV had come loose. Half an hour later, after fighting the winds of a nasty storm, they finally were able to retract the awning and be on their way again. But not before five kids were soaked with no clean clothes left to change into.

The whole family was wiping away tears as they reminisced. Luke thought the funniest detail was that the awning fiasco had taken place at the end of the infamous Vegas trip Dani had shared at Tango Rio.

Luke didn't have any similar memories from family vacations. Another result of an only-child childhood. Witnessing the O'Briens, Luke would bet there was never a dull moment in their household. That wasn't Luke's experience. To keep himself from going crazy with boredom, he'd spent hours on end in his basement and driveway, shooting pucks at a net. He couldn't regret his childhood circumstances because all those hours alone with stick, a puck, and a net had led to him being a driven and successful hockey player. But he knew he wanted something different when it came time for him to start his own family.

And wasn't that a telling thought, Luke mused. Family and kids weren't topics that popped into his mind often. Since making the pros, he'd been all hockey, all the time. Something, or rather someone, had recently inspired him to reassess his priorities. In fact, at the moment, she was strolling next to him and pointing to the family rink.

"You've seen the rink side of the yard," Dani explained, "let's walk by the lake and then toward the garden area. It doesn't look like much now, but during the summer it's my mom's pride and joy." The distance sounded great to Luke, but it wasn't. From their place by the rink, they could see the whole yard.

Luke stepped cautiously on the icy, snow-packed ground as he spoke aloud. "This place must have been party central every weekend when you were teenagers."

Dani, also focused on maintaining her balance in the snow, had laughter in her voice as she responded. "You could say that. We always had friends around, but which O'Brien they were visiting depended on the work schedules of the stores, our other side jobs, and our sports and school activities."

They reached the other end of the O'Brien's property when Luke commented on its impressiveness.

"Developers have approached my parents about it and offered amazing amounts of money to buy some of the land, but my parents couldn't do it. Times were tough over the years, especially when they were first starting out and trying to expand the stores, but they wanted a yard we could play in and a place that could be their own personal hideaway. Knowing the sacrifices they made, I'm so thankful they didn't take any of the offers. The privacy and serenity this place offers our family is priceless. Some people probably find it weird that a woman my age likes to visit her parents so often, but I just love it here."

Luke didn't blame her. The place was remarkable, and expansive.

"Do you want to sit down in the gazebo?" Dani asked her guest. At Luke's nod, she walked over to one of the benches, sat down, and waited for Luke to join her. "In the summer," Dani admitted with affection, "I can sit out on the dock and watch the water for hours. When we were younger and before we had the rink in the yard, we'd play pond hockey on the lake. Now I sometimes come in here and sit until my skin starts protesting from the cold."

"What do you think about?" Luke asked.

"Sometimes everything, sometimes nothing," Dani said softly.

They just sat there, each pondering their own private thoughts as they stared out at the frozen tundra that was the melting lake. Minutes later, Dani was the first to break the silence.

"Are you excited for your final week of the regular season?"

"I am. Excited for the playoffs to begin," Luke replied. "We're getting restless to begin the post-season run. How about you? Ready for session to be done?"

Dani couldn't help it. A soft groan escaped before she composed herself and admitted, "Absolutely! I'm looking forward to taking some time off and getting away from the lobbyists, the media, and everyone else."

"Have we," Luke asked softly, "and by that I mean the Blizzards, made your life that miserable this year?"

"No," Dani replied with a laugh. "Well, you have, but I have no other years to compare it to. You aren't the only culprits, but the Rink expansion has taken up more of my time than anything else—but it's also been a great opportunity. That being said, I'll be so happy when it's done and life can settle down."

"Me too!" Luke sighed.

Dani couldn't miss the sigh and slightly begrudging tone in Luke's words. She hoped it wouldn't ruin the great mood they had going, but she wanted to discover why he was so wary of politics.

"Can I ask why do you dislike politics so much?"

Luke knew he had to choose his words carefully. He didn't want to offend Dani. Politics was a world she loved, and even though he'd admit the bonding proposal process wasn't quite what he'd thought it was going to be, he still carried a grudge against politicians.

"When I was fourteen, there was a huge scandal in my hometown. The mayor, a longtime politician and family friend, was caught in an extortion scheme and it threw the town for a loop. I lost faith in public officials, and when I turn on the TV these days, I'm annoyed by the blame game I see on the news and in campaign commercials. In hockey, when you lose, you lose. In politics, it seems like when you lose you just find another way to go about it. It's a never-ending and vicious cycle."

Luke held his breath as he waited for Dani's reaction. He didn't have to wait long. "Fair enough."

Dani almost chuckled at the comic look of surprise on Luke's face. "Don't get me wrong. I may not agree with you, but I can see where you're coming from. I've learned in this profession that you have to be objective, and I can understand why you feel the way you do." Dani dropped her gaze to her lap. "Has your perception changed at all since you've spent time at the Capitol?"

Luke chose his words carefully again. His admission would be telling. "Honestly, yes. And that has a lot to do with you." He looked to Dani to gauge her reaction. "Knowing that people like you—people who truly believe in the mission—are behind the scenes assisting public figures, it has given me a greater sense of confidence in the whole system. Confidence I lost years ago." Luke had a sense of instant satisfaction as Dani smiled at him. "It isn't how I'd prefer to spend my days, but I'm willing to put up with it a bit longer for the team."

"Because you want the expansion?"

Luke contemplated his situation—for about two seconds—and knew he wanted to share it with Dani. He hoped she wouldn't use it against him in the future.

"I know we're still getting to know each other, but I feel like I can trust you."

Dani was ridiculously touched by his words. She had the same feeling.

"But what I'm going to say can't go past this gazebo. If there's a chance it could, I'd rather not say anything."

Dani reached over and grabbed his hand. Her heart picked up its pace as he turned his so they could lace their fingers together. "I'm fine with whatever you're comfortable with, Luke. I can keep a secret like a spy, but I don't want to put you in an awkward position. So if you'd rather not say anything, I completely understand."

Looking down at their laced fingers, Luke knew what he wanted to do. "I want to tell you, since it explains where I'm coming from. I'll try to keep it short," he added with a grin. "You know that I was roped into lobbying. Well, I didn't tell you that it's factoring into my contract negotiations. My contract is set to expire at the end of next year. Playing for this team for my entire career has been a longtime dream. I'm proud to be a Blizzard."

Dani understood his reasons for wanting to stay, but she couldn't understand why the team would risk losing him. "Why aren't they doing everything possible to keep you? You're one of the best centers in the league. And the fans love you."

"I appreciate your vote of confidence, Dani, but there are other centers out there just as good as me and I'm only one player on a very formidable team."

Dani didn't think that was true, but she kept her mouth shut. Privately, she loved that he wasn't cocky about his talents, but she'd also keep that to herself right now. It was pretty amazing to see a player of his caliber without an inflated ego.

"Statistically, I'm a great candidate for a trade and this is a business. I love where I am, though, and like you, I love Minnesota. I love my team, and I think we have a great future. We have some real stars coming up through the minors and prospects we're tracking."

Like her brother, Dani thought.

"Like your brother," confirmed Luke as if he'd read her mind. He was still holding her right hand in his left, but he lifted his other hand to her face to brush back her wayward bangs.

"I find myself in a crappy situation. I support the Rink expansion, but I never wanted to be the poster boy for this project. I don't want management to think they can pull me into any project that comes along. I'm a hockey player, not a puppet. So last week my agent and I went to talk to the suits. I told them I was rescinding my request for a no-trade clause. My agent also let it slip, on purpose, which teams have approached me to sign with them." Luke turned to look Dani in the eyes and saw her unvoiced confusion. "I want to remain a Blizzard, but I don't want to be used — for anything."

Oh gosh, Dani thought, he's leaving for another team. She dropped her eyes from his for a few seconds. Just when she thought things might really get started with Luke. After she'd finally convinced herself that dating an athlete wasn't fatal, he was going to move. She felt the loss in her chest, but she wanted what was best for him. She clasped his hand tighter in hers.

"You have to do what you have to do, Luke. Minnesota will miss you if you leave, but your reasons for leaving—reluctantly or not—are legit. No one could blame you."

Luke moved his right hand to clasp her chin. He moved it slightly so he could look directly into the amber eyes that held him entranced. Then he asked the question he wanted answered most. "Would you miss me if I left?"

Dani knew she'd set herself up for that question. She didn't blink or flinch at all when she told him that she told him softly what her heart knew completely. "Of course."

Luke's smile was brilliant. "I hope you don't think I planned this, because I didn't. I really liked hearing what you said, but I wasn't intentionally fishing for that. I should finish telling you what happened in that meeting last week.

"I told the suits that I loved being a Blizzard, but I didn't want to play for a team that uses its players— off the ice and against their will—for their advantage. So if that's the attitude management was taking toward their players, I'd be rescinding any former contract offers and would respond to other teams' overtures."

Since Sean Williams had helped organize the lobbying project, Luke had specifically asked for him to be present. The look of horror, and later anger, on Sean's face as Luke spoke was something he wouldn't soon forget. It was priceless. But he didn't need to further taint Dani's view of Sean. She still had to work with the jerk.

"Apparently, I called their bluff. Within an hour we came to a no-trade contract that suited everyone's needs. I signed it earlier this week and asked them not to make it public until after your bill is passed—whether the Rink is in it or not."

Seeing the questioning look on Dani's face, Luke continued.

"I don't want it to seem that my contract extension was tied to the expansion proposal. And I'm afraid that's exactly how the press would spin it. I can see the headlines now: 'No Rink, No Coffey.' Management will still have to do some PR wrangling when the details are released."

Dani was elated to hear that Luke wasn't moving. She'd been squeezing his hand so tightly during his story that she could now feel the indentation of one of her rings on the neighboring fingers.

"Luke, I'm so happy for you," she said. "That took courage, but it worked out so well for you."

Luke pulled their hands closer to his body. "And for us," Luke said quietly but confidently. "I'd really like to see if we could be something more, Dani." He turned his body slightly to face her. "I don't think I'm the only one feeling this chemistry between us."

Dani loved looking into his deep eyes and again wondered how he could be so humble. He had hoped, he hadn't assumed.

"No, you're not the only one feeling the chemistry, and I want to see if there could be something more too," Dani replied. Luke's sexy smile threatened to sidetrack her train of thought, but there was something else she wanted to tell him.

"And as long as the cone of silence is over the gazebo, I'd like to share something with you too. You know that I was in the office earlier working on the bill?" Dani asked. Seeing Luke's nod, she continued.

"Well, tomorrow I have to go over all of the projects listed in the bill, and prepare for the mayhem that will ensue when it's introduced. You shared something important about your work with me, and I just wanted to let you know that as of now, the Rink upgrade is in the bill. So your contract probably would have been secure had you not approached management, but you did it on your own terms. I could get in a lot of trouble if anyone found out I told you, but I trust you too and I wanted you to know."

Dani missed a breath when Luke reached out and caressed her cheek with his hand.

"Thank you for trusting me. I'm happy to hear about the Rink, but that news falls short next to hearing that we might have a future. If the Rink expansion wasn't in the bill, I'd still want to be with you. But I guess it's ironic that without the bill, this wouldn't be happening."

Dani reached up to touch the hand that was still caressing her cheek. She felt such wonder and contentment looking into Luke's eyes. She dropped her gaze to his lips, lips that were suddenly moving closer to her own. She didn't know which one of them was moving—maybe both—all she knew was that they were now just a breath apart. Although it was painful to do so, she pulled back suddenly, remembering one last thing she needed to tell him.

"What's wrong?" Luke looked her over to try to determine what had sent her flying back. "Is your family watching?" He glanced toward the house.

She caught both of his hands in her own, and settled them on her leg. "Luke, there's something I need to tell you because it could be a deal breaker for us."

Luke's worry was visible on his face and she debated the best way to tell him.

"I know that the life of an athlete can be a very tempting one. I grew up with six brothers and their many male friends, so I know some guys view relationships differently than women." She knew she wasn't making any sense, and Luke just looked confused by her tangent. She just blurted it out. "I'm a virgin."

Luke's eyebrows shot right up to his hairline. He hadn't been expecting that.

"It's been an issue in the past with guys. Actually, it's the reason Sean and I broke up."

Dani watched as Luke's eyebrows, impossibly, receded further into his hairline and his mouth dropped open. Apparently he didn't know about her past with Sean.

"I thought you knew," Dani explained. "Sean and I dated in high school. He was two grades older, close to my big brothers, and a star athlete." She looked out at the lake. "He was always over at the house as we were growing up. He was my high school sweetheart," she explained. "And then he went off to college, but not before he really turned on the pressure to take our relationship to a more intimate level, even though I'd shared my wishes with him from the beginning. I told him I wasn't ready, and I thought everything between us was great. I sent him care packages, and he visited when he was home. After Christmas I had this great idea to surprise him at school. I worked out the travel details with my parents' help and flew out. You can probably guess what happened next."

Dani felt Luke clasp her hand tighter as he whispered, "Go on."

"I showed up at his dorm. Not knowing what the tie on the handle of his door meant, I started knocking. Sean answered with nothing but a sheet wrapped around him and a disheveled blonde visible in the bed behind him. I ran down the hallway before he could catch me, caught the next flight home, and stayed in my room for days. Sean called constantly, despite my brothers' threats of bodily harm. I later heard from a mutual friend that he said if I'd put out, he wouldn't have been tempted to seek relief elsewhere. I didn't see him or speak to him for years. So you can imagine my surprise, and disdain, when he walked into my office a few weeks ago on behalf of the Blizzards. He insinuated that he was actively collaborating with you on the Rink expansion. Anyway," she confessed, "Sean isn't the only ex-boyfriend who's tried to pressure me into making our relationship physical."

Dani pulled her gaze from the lake and looked directly at Luke again before she continued. "I've dated a number of guys since, but usually the relationships ended in break-ups once I realized that they were more interested in my family connections than they were in me. I have no idea what your dating history is, nor do you have to tell me, but you need to know that I'll stay a virgin until I've married. It's a choice I made years ago. If that changes things for you, I understand. Just because this is my choice doesn't mean it has to be forced onto you. I'm offering you another get-out-of-jail-free card."

Dani figured she'd said enough, so she waited for Luke to respond. He was silent for a long time. She thought that was fair—after all, she'd just thrown him a major curveball—but while she waited, her stomach was twisting and turning with anxiety.

Luke knew that she must think he was an idiot for just sitting there in shock, but his mind couldn't process what she'd just said—not to mention how he should address it. He wasn't a virgin, but in recent years he'd been very selective on the women he took to his bed. When he'd first started off in the pros, he hadn't been as discerning. After being burned by a few user girlfriends, he'd decided it just wasn't worth it. He enjoyed intimacy immensely. What guy didn't? But he'd realized it wasn't worth the loss of privacy to have casual flings anymore.

He just couldn't believe that a woman like Dani, who was so beautiful, funny, and intelligent, was still a virgin. Then he recalled her family and decided it wasn't so surprising. One of her brothers was a priest, after all. But her story about Sean demonstrated her admirable ability to stick to her beliefs, even if doing so was painful. He had a sudden urge to find Sean and beat him to a pulp. He'd been tempted plenty of times in the past, but never for such a compelling reason as mistreating Dani.

Although her news wasn't ideal—he'd been dreaming of making love to Dani since the moment he saw her in the Capitol—Luke respected Dani all the more for staying true to her convictions and even more so for being honest with him from the beginning.

Without saying anything, Luke used their clasped hands to pull Dani closer to him and then settled her so she was facing him, straddling him with the backs of her thighs resting on the top of his.

Dani could feel through her leggings and his jeans that he was aroused. A moment of panic went through her as she tried to figure out what he was doing. He had to know she could feel him. She knew she could defend herself, and if it came to it, she could scream and within seconds her brothers would be out here to help. But she didn't want to believe Luke would do something so awful, especially not after what she had just told him. Would he be like so many of the men she'd encountered before him and try to coerce her into something she wasn't ready for? And was she strong enough to stay true to herself? As so many thoughts raced through her mind, she could feel one of Luke's hands start to rub her back.

"Dani, I know you can feel me. I've pretty much been this way around you since I saw you by that marble pillar—long before I knew you or your story. My body wants to be with yours. I can't change that, and I don't want to. But I want you to know that I'd never force you to do something you didn't want."

Dani immediately exhaled. She felt her body relax and mold itself to his. She never should have doubted him. He'd already shown her his character. She lifted her arms to put them around his neck as he continued.

"You're right, I'm not a virgin. But I am clean. We have to get tested for the team constantly and I've always been safe with my former partners. Unfortunately, I was more lax in my standards when I was younger, but I've grown up. You shared something very personal with me. I'm humbled. I want you to know that I haven't been with another woman for a while. My last girlfriend used me for the fame and I haven't been with anyone since. I can't stop my body's reaction to you, but I'll never use it against you." He lifted a hand to her face to catch a tear that had spilled from her watering eyes. "I'll wait for you, Dani."

Her breath caught as a multitude of emotions came over her. With a sense of peace that was new to her, Dani leaned in and kissed him for all she was worth. He'd never know the love—yes, *love*, she realized—she felt for him in that moment. She'd told her other boyfriends about her decision to remain celibate until marriage, but each had taken it badly. None of them had accepted the news as freely as Luke. She recognized the humor that she, a woman with a self-imposed policy of never dating athletes, was sending up a prayer of thanks for this gorgeous jock.

Her brothers would call what she and Luke were doing tonsil hockey, but she just called it wonderful. There was no awkward nose bumping or neck craning; their bodies seemed to fit perfectly. He was an excellent kisser—not too light, not too firm—just perfect.

She could feel Luke's arm circling her back and moving underneath her jacket. She stopped kissing his lips temporarily and left a path of kisses on his cheek, under his ear, until she got to the base of his neck where she felt his quickened pulse. Giving a lick to his clavicle, Dani heard his groan. He pulled her back and cradled her face in his hands.

"Does this mean we're dating?" Luke started rubbing his thumbs along her cheekbones. He had never felt skin as smooth as hers.

"Isn't that usually the girl's line?" Dani chuckled.

Wrapping one arm around his back to pull him closer, her other arm wrapped around his neck so that her hand could slip into his thick hair. Desire was all Dani could see in Luke's eyes, and she was certain the same was reflected in hers for him to see.

"Well?" he prodded.

"Yes," Dani confirmed. "That's exactly what this means."

Luke made a noise that Dani couldn't interpret, but she didn't give it further thought when she realized his eyes were fixed on her lips. Then his lips came to hers and neither of them said anything else for a long time.

Chapter 19

Dani hadn't known that a day could change so quickly.

It had started off well enough, better than average, actually. She'd practically skipped into work from the just-plowed parking lot and was greeted in her office by Piper, who wouldn't be deterred from her quest for details about Saturday night. After a basic recap, Piper was practically skipping around herself.

"It was pretty spectacular," Dani admitted. "It just felt right."

Tyler had picked up on her sappy mood and had been sending her quizzical glances all morning. Not even her twenty waiting voicemails could derail her giddiness.

Dani knew she should feel guilty for not coming to work yesterday, but she just couldn't muster the sentiment. She'd decided to stay home and review the bill draft, but mostly she found herself daydreaming about what had transpired the night before. Just thinking about it now made her smile like a fool.

She and Luke had stayed outside in the gazebo for far too long. The cold, damp air of the April evening may have run other people indoors, but she and Luke had found other ways to stay warm. In addition to the smile still plastered on her face, she felt a major blush coming as she remembered. She was extremely thankful she had an office door to close—and, come to think of it, relieved that the gazebo wasn't visible from any windows of her parents' home.

But now, five hours after she had arrived at the Capitol, Dani was no longer daydreaming about Saturday night. Now she was wondering how things had turned so rotten in such a short amount of time.

"For the love of Pete, I want to strangle someone!" she exclaimed in frustration.

Somehow, and Dani was determined to find out how, information about the bonding bill draft had been leaked. Her office phone was lit up like a Christmas tree, with everyone from the press to constituents trying to confirm the leaked information.

She bypassed all of the incoming calls and dialed her counterpart in the Senate. "Tom!" Dani was thankful that he picked up. "What's going on? Who spilled?"

"Dani!" Tom sounded equally eager to speak with her. "I have no idea," Tom growled in frustration. "I've been trying to call you for the past ten minutes. I've pretty much barricaded myself in my office. What a cluster-f—" Tom stopped himself before going the distance. "Any ideas who might have loose lips on your end?"

"No clue. I don't think it would've been anyone from our weekend group."

"I don't either. None of us would have said anything. We all knew this would be the result."

Dani felt a pang of guilt at Tom's words. She had told someone, but she squelched the immediate worry that came to mind. Now knowing the man, she knew without a doubt that Luke wouldn't have told anyone the details she shared with him in the gazebo.

"Well, where do we go from here?" Dani wondered out loud. "All the information isn't out, but enough to cause chaos is—including the Rink. And no one is officially responding to the inquiries."

"The way I see it, Dani, we have two options," Tom offered. "We planned to introduce the bill Wednesday; we can dodge questions for a day or so and neither confirm nor deny what's been released. Or we can upload our documents to the web and let them have at it. What do you think?"

Dani thought about the fallouts of each action. It would be nice to stick to the original plan, but at this point her main goal was maintaining the accuracy of the available information and the trust of her coworkers and constituents. Dani didn't want to lose the public's trust. She'd put too much work into this session to have the bill thrown under the bus. In her eyes, everyone had worked way too hard to have the bill marred by misinformation and assumptions.

She ran her hand through her hair as she spoke confidently into the receiver. "At this point, if the bosses are okay with it, I think we should just post them. We can write up a statement explaining that in order to ensure accuracy we were going to wait, but since some information has come out early, we're posting the draft now. We'll also need to remind them that changes might be made in committee, if they're necessary. Thoughts?"

Tom was quiet for a moment. No doubt he was weighing the pros and cons of each proposal as well. "I agree. That's our best option." Dani could hear him sigh. "I wonder how it got leaked though, Dani. It's going to drive me crazy."

"Me too, Tom! I have no idea who could have been such a jerk. I had my copy in my possession all weekend. The only other person who had access to it in my office was Kim. She made two copies."

Kim. Dani thought for a moment. She'd asked Kim to make copies of the bill last week. A sickening feeling was starting to grow inside her. She needed to find Kim. Not wanting to accuse her of something unless she was certain Kim had slipped up, Dani just wanted to get her side of the story.

Tom's voice snapped her back to their conversation. "Well, you know what they say, the best-laid plans go awry."

"Always! I'll work on the statement if you can get the documents ready to post."

"Done!"

"Perfect, I'm going to go talk to the boss on the House floor. I'll send his response to our plan ASAP."

Dani placed the phone back in its receiver and saw that Piper had instant-messaged her. *"You just can't catch a break, can you? Saw the news. Anything I can do to help?"*

Her fingers flew across her keyboard. *"It's a bloody mess! If you could come over and stand watch outside my door, that would be great. (Kidding.) It's chaos, but we're working through it. I may need a drink later. You game?"*

"Wish I could, but I have to be at the studio tonight. Good luck today. Let me know when you need me to stand guard!"

"Will do. Thanks, Pippi!"

Dani locked her computer and grabbed her phone. Just as she was getting ready to leave her office, she heard an unfamiliar voice from the office lobby. "Excuse me, I have a delivery for Dani O'Brien?"

"Her office is right through there," she heard Tyler respond. A second later she saw a deliveryman in a gray coat enter her office with a flower delivery. Her heart skipped a beat as she watched him place the flowers on her desk and then hold out a pad for her to sign. She thanked him for his troubles and eagerly dove into the tissue that covered the arrangement. Her breath escaped in an audible gasp of delight when she saw two dozen red roses.

She read the card and felt her heart melt: "Thank you for Saturday. Can't stop thinking about you! Dinner tonight?"

He hadn't signed it, and Dani was grateful for that thoughtful omission. She didn't have to worry about anyone snooping. She started tapping away on her smartphone.

"The flowers are lovely. Thank you so much! You're too kind. And they couldn't have come at a better time. Day just turned awful—bill details were leaked. (I know it wasn't you!) Trying to sort out how to handle it. Dinner sounds great. Just tell me where and when and I'll be there. Thank you again. Can't stop thinking about you too!"

Still smiling, Dani slipped her phone into her pocket and headed off in search of Kim and the boss. As soon as she stepped into the communal office area, she spotted seven lobbyists. Tyler looked a little frazzled. He didn't lift his gaze as she passed his desk. Had he done so, he would've seen the sympathetic glance she was sending his way. The lobbyists tried to approach her, but she must have been successful in delivering a glare that telegraphed "approach at your own risk" because they all stopped in their tracks. Passing the lobbyists, she slipped into the hallway and walked toward the House floor. With session in, she knew that the boss and Kim would both be there. He was casting votes and Kim was staffing.

Stepping onto the floor, Dani spotted the boss at his assigned desk. She knelt down next to him and started strategizing. They both knew that once he stepped foot outside the chamber, he'd be fair game for the press and advocates. It would be like leading a lamb to the slaughter.

Dani whispered her plan to Representative Johnson. She told him about her conversation with Tom and waited to hear his thoughts.

"Can you get it all done before you leave today?" he asked as he pushed his green button to signal a yes vote.

"Sure can. I'm working on the statement and Tom will post the documents."

Without removing his gaze from the voting board, the boss said thanks and she left his side.

Dani looked for Kim to be circulating on the floor and saw her making copies at the corner machine. Telling herself to be patient enough to hear the whole story, Dani headed toward the copy machine. Kim saw her approach and turned to face her.

"Hey, Dani, what are you doing here?" Kim asked while she laid another document on the glass to copy.

Dani looked around, trying to locate another page, and noticed one just entering the floor. "Hey, Steph," Dani called as she motioned to the young page. "Can you finish this copy job for Kim while I chat with her about committee stuff?"

The young page eagerly agreed as she tagged out Kim at the copier.

"Kim," Dani spoke softly to her colleague, "we need to talk."

"Sure, Dani," Kim replied curiously. "Everything okay?"

Dani pulled her page into the chamber hallway and motioned to a corner under the back stairwell. "No, everything isn't okay. Somehow details of the bill were leaked out." She saw her page cringe at the announcement. "Do you have any idea how that may have happened? I'm not accusing you, Kim. I'm just trying to figure out how it happened. Did you leave the document on the copier while printing? Anything seem off while you were making copies for me and the boss?"

"Well…" she said cautiously. "I did make one extra copy."

"What?" Dani asked incredulously. "I specifically asked you to make two copies. You shouldn't have made more than that." She didn't mean to, but her voice increased in volume during her interrogation.

"But," Kim replied in a shaky voice, "Tyler asked me to make a copy. He's technically my boss too, so I did as he instructed. I'm sorry, Dani. I didn't know. Did I ruin everything?"

Now it was Dani's turn to cringe. The man she viewed as practically a mentor had undermined her. Her anger was quickly replaced by disappointment.

Why would Tyler have asked Kim to do that? She didn't realize she'd posed the question aloud until Kim responded.

"He said he always gets a copy of the bonding bills. When I told him you'd asked me to just make two copies, he seemed upset. He told me he's always received a copy in the past. That's why I didn't think it was a big deal. I'm sorry, Dani."

And Dani knew that she was. Tears had started to form in her eyes. She reached out and gave her coworker a quick hug. "I'm sorry, Kim. I shouldn't have raised my voice. You're right. You were doing as you were asked. I should have spoken with Tyler before. That's where I'm going now. Just so you know, we'll be posting the bill later today since details have already gotten out. But don't share that with anyone just yet. Sound good?"

Dani watched as Kim nodded and took a deep breath, probably to calm her nerves. Giving Kim one more quick hug of reassurance, Dani headed back to the office.

She entered the office and caught Tyler's eye right away. Her usually confident coworker looked visibly uneasy.

"Tyler, may I speak with you in the boss's office?"

Dani entered the office and waited for him to join her. Tyler didn't meet her eyes as he entered the room and closed the door.

"What happened, Ty?" Dani asked in an even, patient voice.

To his credit, Tyler didn't play coy. "I'm sorry, Dani. I was careless. I've always gotten a copy of the bill in years past. I asked Kim to make me a copy when it arrived from the Revisor's Office. When she said you'd instructed her to make just two copies, I got upset and told her to make me one too. This morning I was careless and left the bill on my desk. I took it out to read when I arrived to prepare myself for the expected inquiries. When I came back from our morning meeting, I saw Shirley standing over my desk, writing some notes. When I approached, she made a flimsy excuse that she wanted to see the boss but would track him down herself. Then she ran out. I rounded my desk and knew right away what she'd been looking at. I was praying she hadn't been in the office long, but from the info that's been leaked, she must have had time to peek at the whole thing. I'm sorry, Dani."

He did look sorry. Since the boss wasn't upset, Dani wasn't as stressed as she'd been earlier—but she still felt betrayed.

"Things change, Ty. I know I may manage the bonding-bill process differently than my predecessor, but since I'm responsible for the bill and its content, you should have spoken to me directly instead of directing Kim to disregard my specific instructions."

Tyler was much older than her, and more experienced, but she didn't hesitate in delivering her lecture. What he'd done was wrong and she needed to be sure the same thing wouldn't happen in the future.

Tyler looked at her and nodded his agreement. "You're right. I should have spoken to you first. It won't happen again."

"Thank you," Dani replied.

"How bad is Shirley's damage?" Tyler inquired.

Dani ran her fingers through her hair and let out a sigh. "It's bad, but thankfully the boss isn't too upset. We're going to post the bills later today with a statement that things may still change. Hopefully that will help us save face with the public."

"Smart thinking. Please," Tyler implored, "let me know how I can help, even if it's trivial stuff. I definitely deserve some penance for my screwup."

Dani laughed. "All right. I have a huge stack of contacts I was going to ask Kim to enter into the database," Dani said as she opened the door to exit the office. "But I think that would be a perfect punishment for you."

Dani heard Tyler's groan, but he didn't otherwise object. She smiled as she entered her office again. The two dozen roses greeted her and she forgot all about the Tyler issue. Pausing for a moment to check her phone, Dani saw that Luke had suggested a dinner location and time. Suddenly her day was looking great again.

Chapter 20

Piper was in a much less compromising position when Marc arrived at the studio for his second lesson. She was standing at the back barre doing some stretches. She had texted him earlier to remind him to come to the back door. The front studio was in use, but they could work in peace in the back studio without anyone even knowing they were there.

After she practiced some turns in front of the mirrors before he arrived, Piper stopped to catch her breath and had a strange sense of déjà vu. She could see herself turning in the exact same spot many times over the years. As she caught a glimpse of her current self in the mirror, she realized that even though the studio hadn't changed, or the mirrors, her body definitely had. She couldn't believe the changes that her body had naturally made.

Dance had always been her first love, but Piper had always been aware that she didn't have a typical dancer's body—until she was finishing high school. She'd been an overweight child, despite her love of dance. The taunts of kids in her school had taken a toll on her self-esteem, but she felt empowered when she danced. Until she'd had to do it in a skimpy outfit.

She'd sometimes had to give herself a pep talk before taking the stage in a costume that hugged her curves—the good and the bad—but once she was out on the stage, her awareness of the audience and their potential scrutiny just kind of drifted away, along with her insecurities. When she was dancing, it was just her doing what she loved to do. It was an awesome feeling.

Things changed during her junior year of high school. For whatever reason, her baby fat finally started to fade and she dropped some inches. She was left with a very lean and toned body. The boys started noticing her during senior year, but by then it was already too late. She was annoyed that guys weren't interested in her until she was trim, so she rejected their advances.

College had been a different story because it was a new start. The boys she met only knew her in her new shell. The same with guys today—like Marc. But the insecurities of her younger years still haunted her. That's why she wore loose-fitting clothes and A-line skirts. She didn't want guys showing interest in her strictly for physical reasons; she wanted them to know the real her.

Pulling her eyes away from the mirror, Piper focused on stretching again.

She was standing in first position with her right hand on the barre when she heard a knock on the window. Piper jumped at the sound. It still wasn't the greatest position to be caught in, but at least she didn't have her rear in the air. Seeing a dark-clothed figure outside should have worried Piper since she couldn't make out any facial features, but she could tell it was Marc from his distinctive stature. She rushed to the door, hoping to catch him before he got soaked from the pouring, and cold, spring rain. His saturated coat told her she wasn't quick enough.

She motioned him in and moved to lock the door. "You're turning out to be the most punctual student I've ever had."

Shaking himself off, Marc started unbuttoning his coat. "Not usually, but I had an ulterior motive." Piper shot him a questioning glance. "I was hoping to catch you doing one of those insane, but very sexy, splits moves again."

Although it went against her grain, Piper was surprised to register her desire to play along with his banter. She had a mental stockpile of tons of dance innuendoes that she had amassed over the years but never shared.

"You know what they say," she added, "dance is a vertical expression of a horizontal desire."

His mouth literally dropped. Piper loved it. She'd caught him off guard and this sensual banter gave her a boost of confidence and kick of excitement that she hadn't felt for a while. But they were here for a reason.

Her teacher mode kicked in, as did her no-nonsense voice. "All right, switch your shoes so you aren't squeaking across the floor, and let's get to work. You have a tango to learn."

Marc would admit that it wasn't easy to focus after the visual she'd just given him. He remembered how she'd felt pressed against him, even through her sweatshirt. And now he was picturing how great she'd look in a horizontal position—above or below him, he didn't care.

Not wanting to embarrass himself in front of the woman plaguing his thoughts and getting him excited, Marc took his time removing his coat and turned his back to her as he started to change his shoes.

In the few minutes it took to change into his dress shoes, Marc's body became relaxed enough to join her on the dance floor. During his intentional delay, he snuck glances to admire his teacher from across the room. She was wearing a sweatshirt and leggings again. He knew she tried to hide her body from him by donning extra layers, but her attempts at camouflage were wasted. He was certain that an amazing body was hidden underneath.

Piper had the unshakable feeling that Marc's eyes were on her, so she dived into the task of finding their music and changing her shoes. After reining in her excitement, she walked to the center of the studio as composed as her nervous self could be and waved for Marc to join her. She found it odd that he'd been sitting so long, but didn't give it much thought as she mapped out her agenda for the lesson.

"Let's see what you remember. Please show me your starting position."

Piper almost laughed when Marc crouched down into his goalie position. She rolled her eyes in mock exasperation. "Your other starting position," she instructed in her sternest voice. Marc stood straight and lifted his arms.

He eyed her intently as he said, "Never forget that I'm a hockey player before a dancer."

She shook her head as she returned his intent stare. "Not in this studio you aren't."

Piper stood before him and tested the hold of his frame by pushing down on his forearms. "Please do the basic combination twice going forward, and then one sideways sequence." To her surprise, he performed the requested sequences perfectly. Piper could picture him expertly leading a partner. It wasn't the first time Piper thought he was an outstanding dancer—almost too good for a beginner. She thought back to their time at Tango Rio. Something wasn't adding up here, but she needed a bit more time to test the theory that was forming in her mind.

"Now we'll partner up and dance the two basic combinations around the room just to test your leading." She started the music and completed his frame.

And away they went. Not once did Marc step on her toes or lead her into a wall. "You know, I've never had a student who picked up these steps as quickly as you have." They were still dancing and spotting their moves when Piper threw out the comment as nonchalantly as she could.

Without missing a step, Marc was able to carry the conversation. "I told you, good muscle memory."

"I don't think muscle memory is ever that good!" she muttered.

Prior to Marc arriving, Piper had pulled a TV/DVD player into the studio. She often recorded her students so they could see how their lines and formations looked from an audience perspective. She wanted to watch his sister's dance with Marc to talk through the movement sequences.

They took a few minutes to analyze the choreography together. After discussing the best ways to recreate the wedding dance, they got to work.

Marc had proven an apt student at picking up dance steps; Piper hoped it would be the same when it came to remembering placements in the wedding dance. It would be a challenge to choreograph without the other members of the wedding party present, but spacing was crucial for the dance.

"We're just going to mark the spots right now. Don't worry about the steps, I just want you to know where you're going for now."

A few minutes later, after Piper felt that Marc had a good understanding of where they would be traveling through the space, she coached him around the studio using the two combinations and threw in a pose here or there when warranted by the wedding video.

She was sweating in her sweatshirt but was determined to keep it on. She kept turning up the air conditioning, but it wasn't helping. Piper knew that she could either take off her sweatshirt, or continue sweating and have Marc believing she had a glandular problem.

Unable to stand the feeling of sweat dripping down her back, Piper told Marc her instructions for the first combination sequence and ran over to the music stand to take off her sweatshirt—leaving her torso covered in a modest red leotard and wrap skirt over leggings. As soon as she pulled off the sweatshirt, she sighed in bliss. The cool air felt heavenly on her skin, and with so much time left in their lesson, she would have suffered from heat exhaustion at the rate she was going.

Following Piper's instructions, Marc kept his eyes on his teacher while his feet continued their movement around the dance floor. He was pleased to see that he was right—she had an amazing body. He knew he should be studying his reflection in the mirrors but he couldn't pull his gaze away as she began pulling her sweatshirt overhead. Bit by bit, her toned thighs, rear, and torso were finally revealed. He didn't know why any woman would want to hide a figure as amazing as hers. Once the sweatshirt had cleared her head, he was back to studying himself in the mirror. He didn't want Piper to know he'd been checking her out.

As he stood there doing the five-step combo over and over, it occurred to him that he liked the fact that she didn't use her body to entice attention. Just thinking about other guys ogling her made him grit his teeth in annoyance. The surge of possessiveness surprised him enough to make him stumble his steps. He tried to regain his footing but then he saw Piper heading his way. Watching the smile spread across her face as he completed his combination made him loose his concentration again, and his footing.

"Finally, you got off step. I was beginning to think you were a machine," she exclaimed as she rushed forward. Grabbing his hand, she placed it on the small of her back. She couldn't miss the fact that only a thin piece of Lycra separated his hand from caressing her back. "Just shake that off," she added in a somewhat shaky voice. "We'll go from the top and keep going. Sound good?"

Looking down at Piper, Marc came to the unsettling conclusion that he would agree to just about anything she said.

An hour and a half later, Marc was set for the wedding—he felt confident. He had the steps and line changes down, but Piper kept reiterating that he would need to adjust his positions here and there when he was finally able to practice with the whole group. His sister had told him the whole group would be running the number following the rehearsal dinner the night before the wedding.

"It's great that you're running it when you get home. You've been amazing here, but once you have people moving all around you, it may throw you off. This way, you'll get a chance to get your bearings before the big performance."

Marc was listening as he put his muddy shoes back on to face the rain. "My sister is adamant that everyone do the dance together. I have a feeling she'll want to thank you personally for the time you took to prepare me."

Piper started laughing to cover her nervousness. "It isn't hard to teach someone of your caliber."

Marc swung his coat around to insert his arms when he mumbled his response. "Still, I'd like to tell them about you."

Although he had dropped his voice for that last comment, Piper still heard it. She had no time to reflect on it because the next thing she knew Marc was standing up and asking where they should go for dinner. She had agreed to dinner at their last lesson, but she'd convinced herself nothing would come of it. After all, he probably asked out tons of women. Hearing that dinner was in fact on the agenda, her heartbeat quickened as panic set in.

She looked at Marc, intending to give a bogus excuse for not going. She opened her mouth, but just couldn't get the words out. Instead she found herself saying, "Sure, I just need a minute to change. Where are we going?"

Marc said he'd leave that decision to her and offered to drive, but Piper insisted they go separately. She suggested an Italian place nearby, and ten minutes later they were sitting at a table and ordering drinks. Marc asked for her opinion on dinner choices; Piper had many. It was hard to decide from among so many good choices, so they ordered two dinners to share.

Piper let Marc lead most of the discussion at the beginning, but she found herself chiming in more and more until their sentences just flowed into one another. They covered everything from favorite movies and sports—they discovered they were both huge Green Bay Packer fans—to family, and even favorite vacation spots. Piper was surprised to hear that Marc's favorite place to get away was a cabin he kept in Canada. She would have guessed he'd go for more posh and glitzy locations, and told him as much.

Marc grinned in response. "You haven't seen this cabin!" he declared. "I like what the city has to offer, but my cabin is where I long to go when I have a break."

Marc's enthusiasm was easy to discern. Piper could tell he really loved this cabin. "Is it a family cabin?" she asked.

He nodded. "It's just south of Ottawa—we used to vacation there as a family when we were kids. It's a couple hours outside of Montreal and Toronto and not too far north of the U.S. border."

"Must be lovely. I've been to upstate New York. It's beautiful!"

"Yeah, it's amazing. It was the first thing I bought when I was picked up by a pro team. My family uses it when I'm not there."

Piper couldn't hide her surprise. "Really? A cabin was the first thing you bought?"

"A lot of guys buy cars, but I bought land. Over the years, I designed the cabin, had it built, and now I love to spend as much time there as I can."

"You designed it?"

Marc smiled at her surprise. "Yeah, most people don't know that bit of information."

She gathered that was his polite way of asking that she not spread it around too much.

"I love architecture and enjoy drafting. I designed everything about the place and loved every minute of it."

She was impressed. "You must be very proud of it."

Marc appreciated that she picked up on that. "It's indescribable. No matter how many cities and countries I visit, my favorite place is that cabin." He sat back in his chair a bit more. "How about you? Favorite vacation destination?"

Piper shrugged as she tried to nonchalantly reply, "My family's cabin up north."

Marc's head flew back as his laugh erupted. He obviously found the statement amusing. "Really? Why?"

"It's been in my family for generations. My best memories of growing up happened there. Catching my first fish, running around with my sisters and cousins, and causing mayhem." She shrugged again. "It's paradise."

Marc waited for Piper to look at him before he meaningfully said, "That's exactly how I feel about my place."

Piper was mesmerized by his stare and didn't know what to say. She was rusty at this dating business. Thankfully, the food arrived just then. They agreed that it smelled and looked amazing. Piper spooned some of her baked ravioli on to a separate plate for Marc and then dug in.

"Were you working on those car crashes again before I came tonight?"

Piper was so surprised he remembered the name of her painful new dance move that she accidentally inhaled a bit of cheese and starting coughing.

Marc looked nervous. "Are you okay?"

She nodded her head as she sipped some water. She tested her voice, "I'm okay." She took another sip of water before answering his question. "I wasn't working on those rolls tonight. I was working on some turns before you showed up."

"Why? I saw you doing some à la secondes the last time I was here. You looked great."

Marc jumped in his seat when Piper dropped her utensils on her plate. He'd figured she wouldn't miss the import of his last comment. Taking one last spoonful of pasta, he looked at his beautiful, and currently incredulous, dance teacher. He had to fight back a smile as he saw her leaning back against her chair with her arms folded across her chest.

"What?" he asked with boyish innocence.

Piper studied Marc for a long moment. This was more than a coincidence. She'd been right. "I knew you were too good a dancer to be a beginner. You picked up on the steps way too quickly."

Marc's expression displayed a mix of guilt and humor. "It's your great teaching."

"Ha," she barked aloud, "hardly! And that wouldn't explain how you know what an à la seconde is. Oh, I believe your skills come from some great teaching—but it wasn't mine."

Marc put down his utensils and waited for her to make the next move. He knew she was smart; he was just waiting for her to voice her thoughts.

"You used to take dance lessons, didn't you?"

Marc wasn't expecting her to practically shout her accusation. He started frantically motioning for Piper to keep her voice down as he shushed her. "Don't ever say that out loud again." Marc looked around the restaurant to be sure no one had heard her. Thankfully there was only one elderly couple in the restaurant besides them. Just to be safe, he leaned across the table toward Piper. "If the guys on the team—or any other players—heard about this, I'd never hear the end of it. Agreed?"

Piper immediately nodded, but then she went in for the kill. "Your mom made you take dance lessons, didn't she?"

Marc's eyes opened a bit further due to surprise. She had hit the mark.

She leaned closer. "I'm right, aren't I?"

He shook his head. His lips lifted into a self-mocking smile. "Not quite. My mom did enroll me in dance lessons, but that wasn't the end of it. She was also my teacher," he whispered conspiringly.

Piper couldn't help it; it was her turn to erupt into a fit of laughter. And then she laughed some more. "That is the greatest thing I've ever heard. Your teammates would rip you apart with that information." She knew that it wasn't polite to tease him, but Marc's smug smile suggested he needed to taken down a peg or two.

"Piper—," Marc said, his voice dropping to a warning tone.

"I promise I won't ever say anything. No one else knows about your secret dance expertise, right?"

"No. But I thought I could share that bit of incriminating information with you."

"You shouldn't be embarrassed," Piper chided. "I think it's great. Dance helps with coordination and agility so much. If I'm fortunate enough to have sons, I plan to enroll them in dance."

"What if your husband objects?"

She said the first thing that came to mind. "I'll just have to use my dance skills to convince him otherwise."

Piper wasn't sure if she or Marc were more surprised by her statement. But then she saw Marc's eyes warm. She was amazed that she had actually said it out loud. It wasn't like her to be so free with innuendo, but apparently she was on a roll.

Still, Piper thought it might be safest to change the conversation. "How long did you study?"

Marc didn't miss the change in topic, but he decided to humor her.

"My mom made my sister and I both sign up when we were quite young. I stopped taking lessons when I was about thirteen. Hockey schedules got pretty demanding then, and I didn't want to take any more flack from my guy friends. But my mom used to dance with me and showed me how to do the basic dances so I'd be ready for mixers and formal events."

Piper picked up her fork and started twisting the linguine Marc had shared with her around her plate. "So, if you already knew how to dance, why did you ask me to teach you?"

Marc took a sip of water. Piper didn't hear any hint of regret or apprehension as he spoke.

"Two reasons: first, I'm rusty and needed a partner

to practice with. So thank you for agreeing to do that. I could learn the steps on my own from the video, but it helps to have a partner to practice them. And second: I wanted to get to know you better."

Piper was stunned. "But you didn't know anything about me," she said incredulously. "We'd only just met when you asked me to teach you."

Marc leaned across the table and placed his hand over Piper's. "I knew the minute I saw you that I wanted to get to know you better. Actually, I think I knew before. Luke had been telling me all about Dani and how great he thought she was. I figured any friend of hers had to be just as fantastic. And then listening to your stories at the table, I was hooked. When I heard your infectious laugh, I knew I was a goner. And then when we started dancing to the band, it was as if our bodies already knew each other and I knew you were a strong enough partner to learn the piece and practice with me. But then when I saw you in your element at the studio at our first practice, I was so impressed with your poise and technique. It was selfish and deceptive to not be honest with you up front, but since I did get to know you better, I don't regret it. Do you?"

Piper dropped her eyes and saw that her fork was poking mindlessly at her now mutilated pasta. She'd been just as intrigued by Marc from the minute she first met him. Actually, even before that—he was her favorite Blizzards player. What was she to do? Her mind was already coming up with a million ways to leave the dinner as a single gal—just like she had so many other times in her life. She raised her eyes to Marc's and her mind went quiet. Looking into his steely gray eyes, for the first time in her life Piper let her heart do the talking. But it wasn't quite confident enough to say what it wanted, so she posed another question to him instead.

"After all that you've seen, are you still interested in getting to know me?"

Leaning even closer to Piper, who at this point was doing some leaning of her own, Marc lifted his hand from hers and moved it to the back of her head. Pulling them both closer, he quietly said, "More than ever. Are you?"

He put the ball back in her court. They were only a breath away and Piper didn't want to wait any longer. She had waited too many times in life. Played it safe too often. Let her fear make decisions for her.

Piper knew they were in a restaurant, and she found PDA tacky, but right now she didn't care. Without a word, she closed the distance between them and just lived in the moment.

And what a moment it was, she thought, to start living.

Chapter 21

Words couldn't describe how much Dani was looking forward to the weekend, but she had to get through this one last day to achieve her objective. The bonding bill was set to come before the full committee today. She knew the bill had a ways to go before it could be signed into law, but just passing it out of their committee would be such a load off.

She was walking to the Capitol from the parking lot when she saw Piper pull in. They hadn't seen each for a few days, so Dani was eager to catch up with her friend. As she approached Piper, Dani could tell something was different. It was seven o'clock in the morning and Piper had an ear-to-ear grin plastered on her face as she stepped out of her car. Dani didn't know anyone who was that happy to be at work so early in the morning.

"Whoa, Pipes!" she called out to her friend. "What's up? You look like a kid in a candy store."

Piper was afraid of that. She had to get her grin under control. Her friend knew her well, but at this rate, she wasn't going to be able to fool anyone today and she definitely was not ready to make anything public. She grabbed her purse from her backseat and started walking toward the Capitol. "I'm kind of dating someone."

Dani grabbed her friend and wouldn't let her take another step until she spilled the beans. "You've been holding out on me, Piper. Is it who I think it is?"

Piper looked down at her feet to hide the grin that was widening. "It's Marc. Marc LaFrey."

Dani's response was instant and fierce. *"Shut the front door!"*

A peppering of staffers were starting to arrive at work to get an early start and Piper didn't want to just stand there in the middle of a parking lot—that would draw more attention than anything. "Quick walk?" she offered.

"I have a ton of things to get done before committee, but"—Dani nodded eagerly—"absolutely. Let's go."

They were just a few steps into their walk when Piper began. "Cone of silence?" She didn't have to wait for Dani's agreement to know that her friend would keep this between them. "Marc said that Luke knows, and he said I could share it with you, but let's still keep it on the down-low. When Marc and I were dancing at Tango Rio a few weeks ago, he asked me if I taught dance because he was looking for someone to teach him a tango for his sister's wedding." Piper saw her friend's eyes light up with laughter and she immediately felt the urge to explain. "He's a groomsman, but he can't be home for the practices. So his sister made a recording and sent it to him. He needed to learn the dance before the wedding in June. I told him that I teach ballroom and agreed to take him on as a student."

"And why didn't you tell me any of this?" Dani demanded.

Piper knew Dani wasn't upset—she had raised her voice, but she was trying hard to keep from laughing.

"I'm sorry, Marc made me promise. Anyhow, we've had a couple of lessons and he asked if I wanted to grab something to eat after the last one. I said yes—"

"Really? You did?" Dani started jumping as she walked. "Pippi, that's great. I'm so happy for you. Way to take a chance!"

Dani's recognition of her bold step meant a lot to Piper. It had required courage, but now that she'd taken the risk, she had no regrets.

"Thanks, Dani! We went out and I confronted him on the fact that he is an amazing dancer. I mean really, Dani, despite what we saw at Tango Rio, he is good! His form is great, his hold is strong, and he moves his body so well."

Now Dani did start laughing. Piper knew what her friend was thinking.

"I mean on the dance floor. I have no idea about anything else. What type of girl do you think I am?"

Piper tried to keep a stern edge to her voice but she was laughing as well. It took her a minute before she was able to continue.

"He learned the dance in two lessons—I've never had a ballroom piece picked up by a student so quickly."

"So…" Dani prodded her friend for more details.

"At dinner he admitted that he was forced as a kid to endure some dance lessons—get ready for the best part—by his mother, who was also his teacher."

Dani laughed even harder, and then she stopped herself mid-chuckle as a revelation hit.

"So if he knows how to dance, why did he ask you to teach him?"

Piper threw up her hands in agreement. "I asked the same question. He said he had two reasons. One, he was hoping to find a partner who already knew how to tango so he could practice the steps and positions of the dance. And—he said that from the first time he saw me and heard us telling our stories, he wanted to get to know me better."

"*Shut up!*" Dani almost tackled Piper to the ground by hugging her so tightly. Dani was so happy for her friend. According to Luke, Marc was a stand-up guy. Her friend definitely deserved the best. As she pulled away, she tried to get more details. "So, what did you say after Marc told you?"

"I asked him if he was still interested in getting to know me." Now her voice took on a dreamy tone. She would have cringed had she not been so happy. "In case you're wondering, he said yes."

"And you said?" her friend asked, waiting patiently.

Dani was showcasing the biggest grin Piper had ever seen. She wanted to keep her dear friend in suspense, but she just couldn't do it. Her whole body was humming with excitement.

"I didn't say anything. I just kissed him!"

At that, Dani grabbed her shoulders and practically yelled in her face. "You? Shy Piper. Ms. 'PDA is the worst thing ever'! You kissed him?"

Piper knew it was corny, but she couldn't hold back a contented sigh. "It was so amazing. I'm not going to feel guilty."

Dani moved slightly away from her friend and one of her hands instinctively came up to her chest to parlay the importance of her next statement. "Oh, Piper, I'm so happy for you. You look ecstatic!"

"I am happy. Really happy," her friend confirmed. "I think he's a really good guy, Dani. I mean, what does it say about him that he's going to all this trouble for his sister."

"Everything that I've heard from Luke about Marc has been great. I don't think Luke would be on such good terms with him if he wasn't keeper material."

They were heading back toward the Capitol when Piper stopped in the middle of the sidewalk.

"What's wrong?"

"I just thought of something. His mother, sister, and I all dance. Is that weird? Like some Freudian issue or an Oedipus-complex thing?"

It took Dani a second to process just what it was her friend was asking. "No, I don't think so. I'd actually take it as a high compliment. My brothers have this theory that guys look at girls in one of two ways: as a girl they'd like to have fun with, or as a girl they'd like to have fun with but can also take home to mom. I think sharing this similarity with the women in his family is a good sign that you fall into the latter category and not the former."

Piper liked how that sounded. "I guess," she agreed as she tried to process her friend's insight. "You have brothers, so I'll take your word for it." It dawned on her that their walk was coming to an end and they'd spent the whole time talking about her. "Enough about me. How was your evening? Did you get together with Luke?"

Dani nodded. "Instead of going to a restaurant, he suggested we hang out at one of our places. So he came over and we made dinner and watched a movie. As if he could be any more adorable, he's an amazing cook. He made homemade meatloaf that was a-may-zing!"

Piper just kind of shook her head. "Who would have thought, Dani, that a month ago we'd be having this conversation?"

"Not me. It's"—Dani let out a sound of excitement—"exciting and scary. He's changed my perspective on so many levels. What if—" She stopped herself. The look on her friend's face told Dani that Piper understood her silent question. "Can I let myself dream that big?"

Now it was Piper's turn to give her friend a big hug. "Of course you can, Dani." She paused for a second. "We both can!"

Dani was so happy to hear her friend include herself in that last comment. She was putting herself out there and Dani could only hope and pray that it went well. And if not, she'd be there to help her get through it.

They had made their way around the Capitol and were now pretty much back where they started. "Well, in we go?"

"I guess. The madness awaits! On the plus side, maybe you'll see Luke around here?"

"Yeah, he's supposed to be here, but we're still trying to keep our relationship a secret. So definitely no PDA for us." The disappointment was easy to hear in Dani's voice.

Piper laughed in response. "That would pique the interest of the Capitol press corps! Have a good one, sweetie. Keep me updated."

"You too, Pipes. Love ya!"

The last time Luke was in the committee room for the Bonding Committee, he found himself at the testifiers' table. This time he was able to sit against the sidewall and enjoy the show—management just wanted him at the hearing as something of a novelty.

Dani's boss was walking through the bill and explaining the reasoning behind the accumulation of projects. Resting his head against the wall, Luke let himself gaze lazily at the beautiful blonde at the head table. He couldn't help but notice how gorgeous Dani looked sitting next to her boss. She was wearing a purple blouse that highlighted her amber eyes, making their distinctive color visible even across the room.

He'd never felt this attracted to a woman before. But it wasn't just a physical attraction; she resonated with him on so many different levels. Luke found himself thinking about her constantly. That fact alone should put him on edge, but the opposite was true. He could be himself when he was around her, and that brought a sense of peace to his life that he'd never experienced.

As he watched her discreetly, he willed her to turn her head his way so he could catch her gaze for a second. But she was in professional mode. She had hardly looked anywhere but at the committee table. Members were offering up amendments and he now knew it was her duty to track all of them. Just as he was lecturing himself to quit ogling her, she looked his way and gave him a quick smile. It came and went so quickly that he almost missed it, but thankfully he caught just enough of it to get that sense of ease he found whenever he was with her.

And he needed a shot of calm to get through the next few hours as the committee continued. Finally, the amendments stopped and the members stopped debating. The bill passed the committee by a pretty uncontentious vote, which Luke appreciated. His faith in the process was somewhat restored at seeing the bipartisan effort.

He was glad that he stuck around for the whole committee. That hadn't been his intention, but he found he loathed leaving Dani's presence.

As the audience and Blizzards contingent, including Sean and Jim, exited the committee room, Luke stole one last look at Dani, who was talking to Zach, a sports reporter Luke knew was with the St. Paul paper. He was going to approach her to say congratulations, but Sean grabbed his arm and pulled him toward the hallway to speak to the media. Luke hated being so close to Dani's ex after hearing how their relationship ended, but he'd promised Dani last night that he wouldn't give Sean any indication that he knew about their history.

Flashes started going off as soon as the Blizzards' contingent exited the room.

"Luke, are you happy to see the Rink provision included?" one reported called out.

"What did you think of committee?" said another.

"Weren't you asked to testify? Why not?" came from a third voice.

Luke couldn't make out which reporter had asked what question. Sean dove right in.

"On behalf of the Blizzards," Sean began, "I'd like to say that we're very excited to see the Rink provision included. Luke, would you like to say a few words?"

Luke cleared his throat and started rattling off the talking points that he'd been coached on prior to the committee. "We're very excited to be included in this year's bonding proposal. And we're extremely grateful for the work put forward by the legislators and staff of the Bonding Committees. Their dedication to the entire bill is immeasurable." Luke added that last part but got back on track. "We look forward to sharing the game experience with more fans in the future and want to thank everyone for their assistance and dedication to moving this project forward."

"You seem to understand the process well, Luke," one of the reporters observed. "Do you foresee a career in politics in the future?"

Luke shook his head and flashed a grin. "I've enjoyed this experience,"—more than any of them would know, thanks to Dani, Luke thought—"and have learned a lot along the way, but I'll stick to hockey. Thanks for the vote of confidence though."

Luke watched Zach, the reporter he last saw talking to Dani, push his way to the front of the crowd.

Over the years, Luke had developed a love-hate relationship with the reporter. He wasn't sure which end of the spectrum he'd land on today.

"Luke, I heard that a contingency of your contract extension required your participation in this bonding process. Is that the only reason you've been a spokesperson for this proposal? Are you waiting for an expansion before you finalize your contract? And now that it's been included, does this mean you'll be staying with the Blizzards?"

Today, it was definitely a hate relationship. Luke was furious. He wanted to know how Zach had been tipped off. Everything he'd been trying to avoid was about to come to fruition. He was going to look like a greedy son of a bitch and he had no idea how to get out of it.

He was trying to formulate a response as the other reporters were shouting follow-up questions. Luke looked over at Sean and saw the slimeball look back at him with a blank expression. The man who looked for every opportunity to get in the press suddenly had nothing to say. As if sensing Luke's panic, and Sean's hesitation, Jim stepped in.

"Luke has been an absolute asset to this process and the Blizzards. As an instrumental member of the Blizzards, we were fortunate to have his support—even during the height of the hockey season. Contract negotiations are not a public matter, so for legal reasons, we have no further comment. But again, I cannot stress what an asset Luke has been to us on this proposal. Thank you for your interest on this legislation, we should get back to the Rink now so Luke can get on the ice and get ready for those playoffs."

Reporters started yelling more questions, but Jim was leading Luke toward the door. Luke looked at Jim and, in a tone that invited no argument, announced, "I'll meet you at the car in ten minutes." Then Luke turned and headed down the hall that led to the back stairwell, while Jim played guard.

He didn't look back even once. His mind was too busy processing the fact that he'd been played: Dani had lied to him. She was the only person he'd told about the contract negotiation, and she was talking to Zach right before he'd lobbed his damaging question. Had she done it on purpose? Was it an accident? If so, why hadn't she warned him? He needed answers.

He wasn't sure what he'd do when she admitted it, but he had to know. Luke stalked into the office and was happy to see Tyler wasn't at his desk. He went straight to her office. She was settling into her chair as he entered. She'd obviously just made her way back from committee. He saw her shoulders relax and her face break into a beautiful grin when she saw him. As he watched her watch him, he saw her face turn to concern and his stomach started to hurt.

"Can I talk to you?" he asked, with no intention of stopping if she said no.

Dani could hear the animosity in his voice and became worried. "Sure, close the door." They'd agreed to keep things professional at work, so she hadn't expected to see him up here. But once she did, she wasn't worried about professionalism. She was just happy to see him, until she realized that something wasn't right. "What's wrong?"

Luke didn't keep her waiting. "We were just hounded by reporters downstairs. One of them asked me in front of everyone why I was holding out on my contract until the Rink proposal had been finalized."

Dani sagged against the closed door; she felt sick for him. The reason for his mood change made perfect sense. "Oh no! Luke, I'm so sorry. This is exactly what you were afraid would happen."

Luke cut to the chase; he didn't let her concern and empathy affect him. "Dani, you were the only person outside of the team that I told."

She'd been approaching him to give him a hug, but his comment made her stop cold with her arms half raised. It wasn't a question; it wasn't an inquiry; it was a statement. He thought she was the leak. And that meant he didn't trust her. Pain unlike anything she'd ever known ripped through her as she dropped her arms.

When her bill was leaked, she hadn't suspected him. She'd pushed through her insecurities and trusted him. But Luke had just proven that he didn't have the same level of trust in her as she did in him.

As Luke watched Dani's expression change, he felt his certainty waning quickly. He saw the anger flash in Dani's eyes, but it was the hurt that made him call himself a fool ten times over. He could feel his face soften. It wasn't her. He could see it in her face. Realizing the mistake he'd made, Luke started to explain himself, but she cut him off before he could begin.

Looking him dead in the eye, Dani answered his question very clearly and slowly. "Luke, it wasn't me, and I'm sorry that I had to say that." Her eyes stung with tears, but she'd honed the skill of fighting back tears at an early age. She wouldn't let her brothers see her cry then and, by all that was holy, she wouldn't let Luke see her cry now. "I think you should leave." Her voice was surprisingly unwavering, despite her volatile emotions. "Now."

Luke lifted his arms as if to motion her toward him, but Dani didn't move.

"Dani, I'm sorry." And he was. The regret was there in his voice. "I didn't think. It was my first impulse to assume the worst—that you had used me."

Damn, damn, damn. More tears were filling her eyes. They were about to spill over. "Luke, I know you've been used before, but so have I. You've just proven that you don't trust me, not the same way that I trust you. We aren't meeting each other on an even playing field and I'm not okay with that." She fought hard to keep her voice from breaking. She tried taking a deep breath, but it wasn't working. "You need to leave now." She turned to open the door, but paused for a second. The tears were so close to spilling but she needed to say one last thing. "This isn't going to work, Luke."

Luke approached her from behind. He put his hand on hers over the door handle and leaned his head above hers against the door. "Don't say that, Dani," he pleaded. "I made a mistake. We can get past this. I reverted to my insecurities, but I know now that I never have to where you're concerned. I'm sorry, Dani. More sorry than you'll ever know."

Dani turned around and let Luke see her tears. This had cut her to the core like nothing else. "I have a history too, Luke. You know I do. But I didn't let those terrible experiences cloud my judgment toward you — at least not once I got to know you. Now," she said with as much poise as she could muster, "you really have to leave." She turned the knob and opened her office door.

"Dani" — Luke knew his voice was cracking but he didn't care — "please don't do this. I'm so sorry."

Dani could hear the regret in Luke's voice and see that has his eyes had become misty as well, but her pride wouldn't let her back down. She held the door and waited for him to leave.

Luke stood there for a moment, debating what to do. How had it come to this so quickly? Last night his mind had been racing with thoughts of the two of them together for years to come; now he was trying to find a way to keep Dani in his life for the next five minutes.

Dani was relieved when he finally stepped through the door. He looked back once when he got to the outer office door, but then he turned and walked away.

Dani closed her door, and sent an instant message asking Tyler, who still wasn't back, not to bother her. Then she put her head down on her desk and let the tears fall freely.

Again she had opened her heart and it had been ripped out. But this time made any past experience seem like a bruise compared to this gaping wound.

Chapter 22

Over the years, Luke's coaches had told him that he must have an incredible pain threshold to play in the condition he did sometimes. But the pain he felt when remembering Dani's crestfallen face as he looked at her one last time almost paralyzed him.

The team was heading into the playoffs. He should be elated. He'd imagined spending more time with Dani when and if she could join him on the road. But instead of spending the past week with her, he'd spent it drowning his stupidity and sorrow in beer. Marc had tried to pull him out of his funk, but to no avail.

It didn't help his pity party that Marc was happier than a kid in a candy store about his new relationship with Piper. It made him a terrible friend, but Luke was doing everything he could to avoid girl talk with Marc. Hearing his Canadian friend's excitement when he talked about Piper just reminded Luke of his own stupidity.

Dani had been the real thing, and he'd let his insecurities ruin the greatest thing he'd ever been a part of—hockey included.

Sitting at his locker, getting dressed for a scrimmage skate, Luke should have been concentrating on his job. But that final image of Dani just wouldn't leave his mind.

His mood soured even more when he realized he wasn't likely to get a reprieve from reminiscing about Dani for the next couple of hours. The guy sitting across from him in the locker room lacing up his skates was sure to keep her fresh in his mind.

With the first playoff game happening tomorrow, the Blizzards had invited their top prospects to join today's practice. It wouldn't be a full-out scrimmage since they didn't want to risk injury to their playoff line-up, but the front office was hoping some of the excitement and anticipation about the post-season would rub off favorably on their prospects. As the team's top prospect, Sam O'Brien had received a hand-delivered invitation to take part.

Luke noticed that Sam had managed to take in the whole locker room, but avoid meeting his gaze every time he scanned the room.

The few times he'd inadvertently made eye contact, Luke had been at the receiving end of what could only be called a death stare. He was definitely not the easygoing, joke-making goalie he remembered from their match at the O'Brien compound.

Luke had become a big fan of the O'Brien clan. His shoulders slumped even more as he reminded himself that his actions probably severed his fledgling ties to Dani's exceptional family. Her parents and brothers clearly loved Dani, and Luke wasn't stupid enough to believe that they wouldn't hold some ill feelings toward him for upsetting their girl.

He was hoping to speak to Sam and explain the situation. Maybe he'd be able to offer Luke some advice about how to get Dani back. But he missed out on his chance when the guys were called out onto the ice and Sam headed out before Luke had his skates laced up. He tried calling out to him to wait up, but the prospect just kept trudging toward the ice.

When Luke skated onto the ice, Coach Nelson had just finished welcoming the prospects to the Rink and began introducing the seven veterans who'd been recruited to participate in the scrimmage—Luke and Marc included. The guys were broken up into two teams; Sam and Luke would be playing against each other.

The scrimmage got underway. Luke couldn't help but be proud at seeing Sam play up to his potential. He wasn't, however, feeling the same affinity for Sam a minute later when O'Brien checked him into the boards.

Not expecting to kiss the boards today, Luke took the hit hard and was slow to recover.

In his stunned state, Luke heard a whistle blow.

"O'Brien," Coach barked, "nice hit. Do it again and I'll escort you out of the building myself!"

Luke was now lucid enough to hear Sam's apology—to Coach, not to him—and his explanation that all the excitement was getting to him. Luke knew the real reason for the check—Luke had hurt one of his family and Sam was out for blood. And, Luke thought begrudgingly, he couldn't blame the guy.

Stepping off the ice an hour later, Luke was determined to speak to Sam. As he waited for the recruit to enter the locker room, Luke scanned the talent the Blizzards had invited in today. All in all, Luke was impressed with the players the team was courting. If a few members of this scrimmage squad signed with the Blizzards, their team would be formidable.

Luke was starting to unlace his skates when he saw Sam stride into the locker room. Much to his chagrin, Coach called Sam into his office and diverted him off a path that would have led him right by Luke.

Needing to stall, Luke took his sweet time getting ready. He wanted to catch Sam after his meeting with Coach and the trainers.

Sam came out of the showers in a towel just as Luke was throwing on his sweater. Sam hesitated a moment when he realized they were the last two players in the locker room, but he continued toward his borrowed locker. He didn't have much choice—he needed his clothes.

"Sam, can I talk to you for a second?" Luke asked.

Without turning away from his locker, Sam answered the question with obvious disdain in his voice. "Screw you, Coffey. I don't have anything to say to you."

Not surprised by the animosity, Luke continued anyway. "Yes, you do, and I don't blame you. I know—"

"You hurt my sister, which means you've royally pissed me off. She may be my big sister, but all six of us boys would go to hell and back for her."

Luke didn't doubt it for a minute. Sam pulled on his pants and looked at Luke like he'd do battle with him in a heartbeat if he said the wrong thing.

"Sam, I know I hurt your sister," Luke admitted with remorse. "You'll never know how sorry and angry I am at myself for being an ass. I've tried calling her more times than I care to admit, but she won't pick up." He was wearing his heart on his sleeve—the feeling of vulnerability was frightening, but he didn't care. Dani was more important than his pride. "How is she?"

Luke couldn't sleep at night, not knowing how she was doing. He thought about her constantly. Luke wanted—no, he *needed*—to know he hadn't done something irrevocable.

After a long silence, Sam answered. "She's rough. You really did a number on her," he answered, sounding sad. "It doesn't help that this is about the busiest week of her whole year." Sam was quiet for a while, as if he were fighting with himself about how much to say. His voice was noticeably quieter as he continued.

"I never saw her happier than the weeks she was with you. Then I saw her Sunday at church and brunch after." Sam took a deep breath. "It was painful to look at her. She seemed so defeated. And you know that's not Dani—she's so full of life."

That description broke Luke's heart and caused his eyes to moisten. He didn't know how he could hate himself anymore than he did at that moment. His voice broke as he fought back tears. "Sam, you'll never know how sorry I am. If I could, I'd go to Dani and beg her to take me back, but I can't do that if she won't talk to me. I love her, Sam."

That caused the prospect's head to pop up as Sam eyed Luke suspiciously.

"I do. The weeks with her were the best of my life. I need to get her back, Sam. Please," he begged Sam. "Will you help me?"

Sam heard the plea from the powerful center and weighed his options. He knew his sister loved Luke. Seeing them together reminded him of his parents, which was saying a lot. His parents had set a high standard when it came to relationships, and he and his siblings all hoped to find the same kind of love one day.

Knowing that he should be on his sister's side, Sam thought about letting Luke wallow in his misery. But after seeing his sister on Sunday, and hearing what Luke had just said, he knew that getting his sister and his future teammate back together was the right thing to do. Luke had made a stupid mistake, but he and his brothers had made plenty of stupid mistakes over the years, especially when it came to their sister. Dani, with her big heart, had always forgiven them even when she had reasons not to. When it came to his family, Sam never faltered—his sister and Luke belonged together. He'd help in any way he could.

"Your timing sucks. She's stressed to the max right now. I spoke with her earlier today for a few seconds because that's all she could spare, and she said that the plan is to take the bill up for a vote tomorrow night. You may be able to get her to reconsider, but I wouldn't even try until after tomorrow."

Luke felt his chest inflate and rise as he realized that Sam was willing to help him.

"Dani didn't say anything about your contract." Sam's tone had taken back on a slight edge. "She wouldn't say anything." In a move that seemed to surprise them both, Sam reached forward and put his hand on Luke's shoulder. "For the record, man, she's the most private person you'll ever meet. But I don't think she knows anything about it—she didn't say anything to us."

Again, Luke silently berated himself as he shrugged off Sam's attempt at comfort. Even though he'd hurt her, she'd still protected him by keeping his contract information from her family. How could he have ever doubted her, he wondered yet again. He knew he'd never repeat that mistake as long as he lived. First she had to take him back, and then he'd spend the rest of his life proving that to her.

"Do you know who it was?" Sam asked.

Just as Luke was getting ready to share his suspicion, a familiar voice came from the office side of the locker room. Luke turned to see Sean Williams round the corner.

"Well, who ever thought we'd see the mighty Luke Coffey practically on his knees for some chick. Even if she is one hot piece of ass."

Sam swung around at Sean's first statement and started for him on the second. "Hey, dickhead, that's my sister you're talking about."

Luke held back Sam, and put himself between him and the douchebag that was the bane of his existence. "It was you, wasn't it, Sean?" Luke challenged. "You knew all about the contract. Just like you knew about the silence agreement, but you leaked it anyway, didn't you?" He didn't let his accused answer. "You selfish son of a bitch!"

To Luke's growing fury, Sean slouched against the locker room wall and delivered a smug grin. "You were getting off too good. You were going to be seen as the hero of this expansion process, not those of us who spent hours over reports and analyses, but you—the poster boy of the Blizzards. That contract agreement you inked out is so much more than you deserve. You needed to be knocked off your pedestal a bit. The fact that you blamed Dani was just the icing on the cake.

I knew you were hot for her. I wasn't asleep on that plane, lover boy. But not even I could have planned an outcome as perfect as this."

Luke lunged for Sean, but now it was Sam's turn to hold him back. He was about to spit on the weasel, since he couldn't punch him, when he saw Jim come into the locker room. Luke was positive that Sean's boss wasn't aware of his subordinate's deception. He never would have stood for it. With his back turned to the door, Sean was unaware that his boss had entered the room. Jim remained motionless by the door as he took in the scene.

"So how did you tip off Zach?" Luke intentionally prompted Sean.

Sean had the audacity to laugh. "I work in public affairs, Luke. This is what I do for a living. I spun the details about your contract and let Zach do what he does best."

"What if it would've hurt the Blizzard's chances of getting an expansion?"

"This is Minnesota, Luke. Hockey isn't the state sport for no reason. Like I knew it would, the leak made you seem like a selfish bastard, holding out for more money while the team looked like the martyr, trying to find a way to keep their star player while expanding their facilities to meet the fans' needs. The Blizzards came out on top, and precious Luke Coffey didn't."

Sean was literally snickering at Luke until he heard the fourth voice enter the conversation.

"I don't think you had this cleared by the higher ranks, Sean," Jim announced as he approached his protégé. He made sure to address Luke for his next statement. "In fact, I know you didn't, because this is the first I'm hearing about it."

Sean flinched at Jim's words, realizing he'd been caught. He lunged for Luke, the one who'd put him in this intentionally compromising situation. Sam and Luke were ready. Both men stepped in and decked Sean, one in the head and one in the gut, before he could make contact with either.

Jim walked closer as Sean lay curled in the fetal position on the locker room floor, reeling from the two blows.

Looking at the two men who'd just brought Sean down, literally, Jim took out his smartphone and started typing feverishly as he spoke. "I suspected he was the leak, but I couldn't prove it. I also couldn't figure out what he had to gain from it. Everyone upstairs knows of his animosity toward you, but not even I knew that it had grown into a full-out vendetta. I heard Sean's earlier statements too; I know that it cost you, Luke, but I'm glad we got to the bottom of it."

Sam and Luke both felt a great sense of satisfaction as they watched Jim look down at Sean and tell him to pack his things immediately and wait for security to escort him off the premises—because he was fired.

Luke had every right to be smug at the idea of Sean Williams being out of his life, but again the truth came back to haunt him. How could he ever have thought Dani was capable of such an act? This had Sean's name written all over it. Had he taken even a minute to process everything, he'd have come to that conclusion. But instead he'd acted impulsively—and foolishly. He hadn't listened to his gut, or his heart, and it had cost him everything.

They watched as Sean peeled himself from the floor. Responding to Jim's text, two security guards entered the room to escort the traitor from their lives once and for all.

But Sean wasn't going to go quietly. "You are so overrated, Luke. You're an overpaid, idolized asshole. But that's fitting—Dani always was a righteous, spoiled bitch." It was obvious that Sean believed he was striking a chord with Luke. "She only liked you because you're a player with lots of money. But even the great and powerful Luke Coffey wasn't enough to satisfy her."

Luke could feel Sam shaking with anger next to him. But Luke was calm and collected when he responded to the jerk being manhandled by security.

"Whatever the reason, Sean, she still chose me over you." Luke saw Sean's eyes and nostrils flare open even more. "And you're wrong. She didn't choose me because I'm a player and I have money. She chose me in spite of it. And don't kid yourself, she saw you for the lowlife you are. You never stood a real chance with someone as amazing as Dani O'Brien."

And with that, the security crew escorted a reluctant Sean from the locker room with Jim following.

Once again, Luke and Sam found themselves alone in the locker room. Sam was finally fully clothed and both men headed out to the parking structure.

"Thank you for what you said about my sister. I know her well and although she doesn't hold grudges, she never forgets when she's been wronged. You're going to have to do something big to overcome her hurt that you didn't trust her. You're going to have to grow a pair and put yourself out there. I don't know how you're going to win her back, but you better think of something. And hey," Sam added, "we might need you for another O'Brien match-up in the future. So make it good."

Luke's heart was beating so quickly at the possibility of being with Dani again, but a worry began developing—what gesture would be big enough?

"I'd love nothing more than to help you out there." Both men were now at their cars, conveniently located only a few stalls from each other. Before getting into his SUV, Luke paused and turned to Sam. "Thanks, Sam."

"Good luck. You're going to need it. That goes for tomorrow's game too. Give 'em hell!"

Chapter 23

Dani was willing to give up her favorite pair of shoes to have this night over.

She wanted nothing more than to curl up in bed for the whole weekend and forget these past weeks ever happened. The only thing standing in her way of doing just that was the bonding bill, otherwise known as the bane of her existence. It was set to come before the House sometime before tonight's adjournment. She was praying it came up before midnight.

She was so tired and emotionally drained that she could hardly keep her eyes open. And whenever they were open, they threatened to leak. Weepy seemed to be a permanent state right now. It didn't help that they were in the final days of session, and days were turning into very long nights. It was already six o'clock when the House decided to recess for a few hours before taking up the bonding bill.

Officially, the break was for members to catch a nap or grab dinner before coming back to take up the bonding bill. Unofficially, the break was for everyone to watch the Blizzards as they began their playoff run for the Stanley Cup.

"Dani!"

Dani spun around on her heels to see Piper jogging toward her across the Rotunda hallway.

"What are you doing for dinner?" her friend asked in a breathless whisper.

Dani was planning to order in since she'd gone through her mom's leftovers by Wednesday and downtown was flooded with people attending the game.

"I was going to order from our standby. Care to join me?"

"Sure!" Piper agreed. "I'll have my usual."

"Great. I'll order. They'll probably get here just in time for the puck to drop."

Dani saw the surprise register on her friend's face. "You're okay with watching the game?"

"They're still my team, Pipes." She was silent for a second. "And I want him to do well. He's worked so hard and deserves a good series. And I can't wait to see Marc shut out Chicago."

"Me too! So sandwiches and hockey—sounds like a perfect way to spend a Friday night at work. Oh, don't we just love what we do? Even though it keeps us here instead of the Rink."

With that, Dani gave her friend a smile and continued walking back to her office. Just as Dani had guessed, the sandwiches arrived in time for the puck to drop.

The commentators predicted that this series would be a fight to the end, and the period's zero-zero score seemed to indicate they were accurate. Dani and Piper talked during the first period and intermission. Dani didn't fail to notice that her friend must have asked her five different times how she was doing. Piper had been shocked when Dani told her about the falling-out with Luke. Being the unfailing friend that she was, Piper had hugged her, shared her tears, and offered to slash Luke's tires.

The second period started out just as strong as the first, but then both girls watched as Marc got tangled up with a right winger who'd gone down in front of the net, and the center used that opportunity to score a goal. Piper was dutifully outraged by the cheap shot on her guy. Dani even smiled when she heard the uncharacteristic litany of insults Piper was directing toward Chicago.

"Deep breaths, Pipes. That was a crap shot but there's still plenty of game left. Marc is fine and I'm sure that pissed off a lot of the Blizzards."

Just as she had even before they'd met, Dani watched Luke closely throughout the game. He was playing well, but he wasn't getting as many shooting opportunities as he normally would. Chicago's defense was doing a pro job of covering him.

Watching him on TV made her heart ache. Not for the first time, she wondered if she'd been too quick to react to Luke's accusation. It couldn't have been easy for Luke to be confronted by the journalist's question, but his lack of trust in her had struck deep.

The second period ended with the Blizzards down by one. The Speaker of the House's office sent out an email informing members and staff that the House would be going back into session in forty-five minutes. Just in time for the game to end—unless they went into overtime.

The final period started and Dani was transfixed by the action. Three minutes into the period and the Blizzards had their first power play of the game. A Chicago player had taken a slash at one of the Blizzards' forwards and, thankfully, a referee had been nearby to see. The Blizzards had two minutes of five on four to make something happen.

Chicago was doing a great job of killing the power play, but with thirty seconds left of the two minutes, the Blizzards scored with Luke's line on the ice and tied the game up. Dani muted the TV and both she and Piper started laughing when they heard clapping coming from elsewhere in the Capitol.

The period was winding down and it looked like the game was going to go into an extra period. Only eighty seconds remained when Luke and his line hopped out on the ice. They would finish off the period.

The Blizzards were trying to get the puck out of their own zone when Marc made a stick save and shot it off toward center ice. Luke had been playing back and was hustling to get to it before one of the Chicago defenders. He crossed center ice, took aim, and sent a slap shot soaring toward the net—he aimed right and low. The referee pointed at the net signaling the goal as the net light starting flashing red with three seconds left in the third period. Blizzards win!

Dani and Piper started clapping and looked out the window to make sure the goal was official. They gave each other a high five when they saw the lights going off on top of the Rink.

"Dani, are you crying?"

She couldn't help it. She was an emotional wreck lately. But, unlike the last few nights, these were tears of joy. She was still hurt, and had a lot of resentment toward Luke, but nonetheless she was happy for him. He and his boys had worked so hard for this moment. And he'd taken the toughest shot he could.

Grabbing her phone, Dani seriously thought about sending him a congratulatory text, but she decided against it. She could see on the TV that his teammates were hounding him on the ice and she was pretty certain the press would be doing the same when he got into the locker room.

Her computer beeped, alerting her of a new email. The House session was starting back up in five minutes. She turned off her TV, grabbed her massive accordion file, slipped her high heels back on, and turned to Piper.

"Let's get this over with."

Luke had done it—he'd hit the lower-right corner right when he needed to. He knew he had to get a shot off before the buzzer sounded. Chicago's goalie was covering the left side of the net much more than the right. He knew Luke hated shooting for the lower right side, so he tried to capitalize on that fact. He'd shot low and right and watched as the puck sailed just to the right of the goalie's glove and leg pad and hit the back netting—just where he wanted it to go. He lifted his arms, stick and all, into the air and within seconds he was bombarded by his teammates.

The Rink was in an uproar. Everyone was celebrating their victory, but Luke knew he was missing something, or rather someone. As he felt the numerous pounds on his back from his teammates, he looked around the faces of the Rink and waved to the fans. There were more than sixteen thousand people cheering him on, but he'd trade those sixteen thousand cheers for just one special one. He was missing the support of the one person he couldn't live without. In a somewhat unexpected moment of clarity given the mayhem, he knew what he had to do.

The team quickly skated a round on the ice and then he ran, as fast as his skates would let him, into the locker room. He bypassed the media—much to their chagrin—and took the quickest shower of his life. Heading out of the players' entrance, he quickly realized that getting to his car wasn't the problem; it was getting onto the street outside the Rink that would be difficult.

Using the traffic stalemate to his advantage, Luke took out his phone and looked up the status of the House. He wasn't able to find a current update, so he found the number of someone he was praying would be there.

"Office of Representative Johnson, Tyler speaking."

Luke sighed with relief. "Tyler, this is Luke Coffey."

"Luke? Great game!" Tyler's tone indicated his surprise but also his excitement.

"Tyler, I'm sorry, man, but I can't talk right now. Is the House still in?"

"Yeah, they're taking up the bonding bill right now."

"Right now? Thanks, that's what I needed to know."

Before Ty could respond, Luke hung up. He saw a break in the traffic and he took it.

He finally got to the Capitol an hour after the game ended. He parked illegally and took the front steps two at a time. Once inside, he headed for the third floor. Taking no time to catch his breath, he headed for the House Gallery door. Once inside, he ran to the railing past the people who were actually trying to pay attention to what was happening and bellowed, "*Stop!*"

People on the House floor lifted their heads to locate the cause of the unusual interruption. The room became eerily quiet as people stared up at him in surprise and confusion.

Scanning the floor, he found Dani immediately. She was standing behind her boss's desk along the sidewall and was looking up at him in shock. She dropped her file when she realized who was shouting. It pained him to see how tired and sad she looked, but he didn't have time to mull that over too long because he knew he only had a few moments before the sergeants were on him.

"Members, I'm sorry to interrupt, but I need you to do something. I need you to not vote for the Rink expansion."

The murmurs and talk started happening in both the gallery and on the floor; the Speaker started rapping her gavel. He saw Dani run off the floor and wondered if she was heading up to him. He didn't have to wait long—she came flying down the catwalk to the gallery and shouting loud enough for everyone to hear.

"Have you lost your ever-loving mind? What are you doing?"

She had reached him but stopped a few feet shy of meeting him. She glanced down at the House floor and then raised her eyes to his as she dropped her voice to a quiet plea. "Why are you here? Are you trying to ruin the bill I've spent the last year helping to create? Are you doing this because of what happened with us?"

He did what he'd been longing to do since he last saw her. Before she could protest, his hands grasped her upper arms and he pulled her into a tight embrace. She didn't resist, but she didn't welcome the embrace either. "Don't think that, Dani," Luke instructed as he felt his body shake with emotion. "I've missed you so much." He pulled back and tried to explain his sudden outburst. "We won the game."

Dani didn't try to hide her exasperation. "I know. Congratulations," she said as she tried to push his hands away. "But that doesn't give you the right to derail my bill."

"Dani," Luke implored, "I need you to know something about your bill. That's why I'm here. I realized something. My teammates, my parents, and thousands of fans were cheering me on, surrounding me." Luke let Dani pull back a bit so he could look into her eyes. "But the woman I wanted there more than anyone else wasn't—in body or spirit. I wanted to see you there, Dani. I know that even if we were still together you wouldn't have been able to attend, but I wanted to know you were cheering and celebrating as my better half."

Luke raised his hands to cradle Dani's face. She was taking quick, shallow breaths. "I know I hurt you, Dani, and for that I'll always be sorry, but I need you to know this: I love you! I've loved you from the day you smacked me with that door. You're the best person I know. I let an old insecurity rear its ugly head and I gave you good reason to leave me. I need you to know that my love comes unconditionally. It doesn't come with a contract, or a good media story, or even a rink expansion. That's why I need members to vote down the Rink proposal. I need you to know that these feelings I have are for you, not an arena or a prospect for the team. You."

Luke wasn't the only one shaking, he realized; Dani was quivering in his arms. His angel, who could hold her own with six brawny brothers, started to cry. He quickly wiped the few tears that had slipped from her eyes with the pads of his thumbs. "You are my everything, Dani. I can live without the Blizzards, I can live without the Rink, but I can't live without you. Can you ever forgive me?"

Luke stood there for what was actually seconds but felt like hours. He had no idea what to expect; he only knew that he had to do this. Dani dropped her eyes from his and his heart hit the floor. He did not take that as a good sign. But then she lifted her beautiful amber eyes to him and said proudly and clearly, "I love you too."

She leaned in and kissed him for all she was worth. Luke lifted her off the ground and held her so close, he couldn't tell where his body stopped and hers began.

After what could have been seconds or minutes of kissing, Luke registered the sound of clapping beginning to crescendo. Dani must have realized it too, because she pulled back. They realized they were still in the House balcony and visible to everyone. The members on the House floor and the visitors in the gallery were clapping and cheering their public performance. Dani flushed scarlet and hid her face in Luke's neck.

Still holding Dani, Luke waved at their audience and pulled Dani away from the prying eyes. He heard the Speaker rapping her gavel with more force, and he quickly scanned the gallery. Seeing his target, he led Dani over to the wall and pulled back the heavy drapes to reveal the hidden window seat that he'd heard about in Piper's story about Dani's embarrassing moment. He sat down with Dani in his lap and shut the curtains to create a private cocoon.

They could still hear the members and audience clapping and laughing, as the Speaker reopened discussion of the bonding bill. Dani should have been on the floor, but she didn't want to leave their little nest. They needed a few moments alone.

"Dani, I love you so much."

Dani rested her head on his shoulder and again gave him the words she'd wanted to say in her parents' gazebo. "I love you too, Luke."

His hand came up to cup her head as she felt him inhale. "I'm sorry again for what happened. It haunts me."

She leaned back in his embrace and brought a finger to his lips to silence him. "It's over and done with. Let's not talk about it again. We've both admitted to our trust issues, but I think we've overcome them. Forever. There's no reason to rehash it." Her eyebrow rose suggestively. "I'm sure we can find much more enjoyable activities to occupy our time."

Luke's answer was to kiss her passionately. They weren't sure how much time had passed when they heard some forceful throat-clearing from the other side of the curtain. Smiling at each other and stealing one more kiss, they pulled back the curtain and found that Marc and Piper had discovered their hiding place and were patiently waiting with matching bemused expressions on their faces.

Marc lifted his arm and put it around Piper as he tried to stare down his friend. "You don't do anything half-assed, do you, my friend?"

Piper was grinning from ear to ear. "Sorry to interrupt you two; Dani, they need you on the floor. The bill is going to be voted on any minute now."

Luke had reluctantly just extracted them both from the window cocoon. "No, but what about the Rink?"

Dani silenced him this time with a quick kiss. "Absolutely not, Luke. You'll never know how much your balcony performance meant to me, but it was futile. It has passed the Senate and will most likely pass the House in a few minutes, which means it'll probably go all the way. And when all is said and done, it's good policy for the state. You know my mantra: you can't argue with good policy!"

"Excuse me, sir. But I'm going to have to ask you to leave."

All four turned to see Tom, the head sergeant, waiting to escort Luke from the gallery. As much as Minnesotans loves their hockey, they weren't going to let Luke skate by after his horribly inappropriate—but lovely, thought Dani—performance.

Dani wrapped her arms around Luke. "Oh, Tom, he isn't going to get in trouble, is he?"

"I don't know, Dani, but I have an order from the Speaker to extract him from the gallery."

"It's okay. I'd better go. You and Piper have work to do. Marc and I will go chill at my place. Why don't you two come over when you're done here?"

Both women quickly agreed, gave their boyfriends good-bye kisses, and headed down the back stairs to the House floor.

Exiting the House Gallery, Marc, Luke, and their escort stopped to view the monitor stationed right outside the exit door in a quiet hallway. The cameras were on Dani, who was flaming red and trying to talk to her boss. She was grinning from ear to ear and hugging Representative Johnson. Everything seemed fine between them.

A few seconds later, the Speaker asked the clerk to take the roll on the bill. The cameras panned to the voting board, which was predominately green as it displayed the favorable votes on the bill. Luke wasn't crushed that his speech hadn't swayed members. As long as Dani understood his intent, that was all that mattered. He'd have to answer to the suits at the Blizzards, but knowing that Dani was back in his life made any other worries seem trivial.

Marc nudged him forcefully in his arm. "Well, it looks like the Blizzards got what they wanted. You did it, Luke. You helped us get the expansion funding."

They watched as the vote was closed and the bill was passed. Luke and Marc turned to head down the spiral staircase, where they saw reporters waiting on the next landing. Normally Luke would be annoyed with the relentless media, but he was so content after making peace with Dani that nothing could turn his mood sour.

"The Blizzards may have gotten what they wanted," Luke corrected his friend, "but I got what I needed."

Epilogue

"Think you can get it out today?"

Dani sat in her chair, listening to her boss through the receiver while she twirled the phone cord around her fingers.

"No problem," she confirmed, "I'll send it out before I leave."

"Just wanted to be sure you remember how to write a press release. Seems like you're never around anymore."

Dani knew her boss wasn't upset about that. In fact, he encouraged her absence. This was her first full week in the office since session ended weeks ago in May. Since their reconciliation after Luke's very public declaration the night the bonding bill passed—a clip of which had even made the news—the two of them had hardly spent a day apart.

She played along with her boss's good-natured ribbing. "It's like riding a bike—no problem!"

"I believe you. You could be in the office for one day and get done what it would take some people a week to do. I probably won't talk to you for the rest of the day, so have a good weekend. Doing anything exciting?"

Dani tried to recall what she and Luke had planned. "Nope, nothing much. Just chilling with the beau."

"I'm happy for you, Dani." She could hear he was. "Have a great time."

"Thank you, sir."

Hanging up the phone, Dani got back to editing the press release. It was a follow-up to the bonding bill. She wanted to get it done as soon as possible because she knew Luke was due to arrive shortly and she didn't want to keep him waiting.

Luke hadn't been to the Capitol since he stormed the gallery, so Dani was surprised when he mentioned wanting to take a tour. But she was happy to join him. They spent as much time as they could together, but none of it had been at the Capitol.

Right after the balcony episode, the Blizzards had a second home game, which they won, before heading off to Chicago. Since her bill had passed after clearing conference committee with little debate and was signed by the governor, the boss gave Dani his blessing to take a couple of days off to watch her "beau"—as he now referred to Luke—play in the Windy City.

Shortly after winning the Chicago series, the Blizzards were on to the next stage of the playoffs, competing against Denver. Thanks to telecommuting and red-eye flights, Dani was able to join Luke again. She'd also been able to spend some quality time with his parents who were also catching the series.

The Blizzards had a rough series against Colorado, but they squeaked out the series win after a close seventh game back home. They weren't so lucky in the third round of the Stanley Cup playoffs; they lost in five games to Toronto. Luke was understandably upset about missing out on making the finals, but he regained his good humor quickly and was spending as much time with Dani as he could in the few months he had off.

For the first time in her life, Dani was taking a day or two off from work each week to spend time with Luke.

They had a blast packing a cooler and taking the boat out. Sometimes they fished, sometimes they just sunbathed, and sometimes they got out the water toys—the skis and tubes. A few times they were joined by her brothers, but most often it was just the two of them, which they loved.

Now back at work, Dani couldn't wait for Luke to arrive. She was turning into one of those girls she always used to roll her eyes at, the giddy girlfriend. She couldn't stop leaning over to smell the flowers Luke had spontaneously sent her earlier in the week, and she couldn't help grinning every time she looked at her screen saver. It was a picture of the two of them at Château Frontenac while they were in Quebec City for Marc's sister's wedding.

That was another adventure in recent weeks: an RV trip to Quebec for the LaFrey wedding. Since Luke had become such a close family friend, he'd been invited to the big celebration and had asked Dani to join him. She would've accompanied him anyway, but she was especially excited when she heard Piper was also going.

The four of them had gone on another double date to Tango Rio during the playoffs and were discussing travel and lodging options for the wedding. Since the Stanley Cup Finals no longer prohibited him from attending, Marc had to be there a week early for family events. Piper asked to be Dani and Luke's traveling companion. Dani jokingly threw out the idea of taking the RV, not really expecting anyone to hop on the bandwagon, but Luke thought that was the best idea he'd ever heard.

He practically shouted his agreement. "That would be great! We could drive out there, spend sometime in Quebec, and Marc could join us for the journey back. We could drive through Canada on the way and drive back on the U.S. side for a change of scenery."

Looking at the two ladies, Luke tried to gauge their interest. "What do you think?"

Dani thought Luke was being sarcastic at first, but then she realized he was dead serious. And she was in heaven—she'd always wanted a guy who RVed. "I'm game. Piper, how about you? I know you aren't much of an outdoors girl."

Piper wasn't deterred. "This is an RV; it is far from roughing it. I'm in."

"Zut alors!"

They smiled at Marc's French lament.

"While you're having a fun time exploring my great country, I'm going to be stuck with a bunch of wedding-crazed family members putting together party favors. Trade you?"

No one took Marc up on his offer.

"What do you think," Luke asked Dani with a smile, "the chances are that we can borrow your parents' RV? And how likely is it to break down?"

Dani grinned at the worry in his voice. "Don't worry, my parents got rid of that Vegas RV last year. Now we'll be riding in style. They won't mind if we take it, but we'll probably have to endure an instruction session from my dad."

"Sounds fair," Luke agreed.

Dani was right. Her parents were fine with loaning the RV to their sensible daughter, and her dad did insist on showing them a few things. In fact, the tutorial lasted four hours.

In the end, the trip had gone smoothly, the scenery was lovely, the wedding was gorgeous, and the company better. Dani was disappointed she couldn't muster up enough of her high-school French to speak with most of the locals, though. They loved seeing Marc demonstrate his fancy tango skills in the choreographed group dance his sister had created. He showed off more of his moves later on the dance floor with Piper after requesting a tango piece from the band.

And now Dani had returned to a full week at work, which seemed never-ending. She couldn't wait for Luke to arrive.

She'd just finished sending the press release to her media contacts when she heard a knock on her door. Looking up, she saw her gorgeous boyfriend waiting to enter and she melted at the sight. Dani thought she was tougher than that, but she was forced to admit that he just made her giddy. She waved him in and stood up to greet him with a hug and kiss. Tyler had taken off and Kim was no longer around since session had ended, so it was just the two of them.

Keeping her arms around his neck, Dani leaned back to look into Luke's handsome face. "I was just admiring the flowers you sent for, like, the fiftieth time." Leaning in, she thanked him with a lingering kiss. "Thank you, again," she said breathlessly, "they're beautiful."

"So are you," Luke responded, a little breathless himself as he buried his face in her hair and inhaled the smell of her that he loved so much. "And, again, you're welcome."

Luke couldn't believe he was able to remain so calm. He was incredibly excited for this tour. Well, he was excited for what he had planned for after the tour. He reluctantly pulled away from Dani and asked if she was ready to go. After locking up her office, they headed downstairs to meet their tour guide. Unbeknownst to Dani, Luke had met Sophie a few minutes earlier to go over the plan. He'd been strategizing for weeks.

Dani had seen Sophie around the Capitol many times, but never had the privilege of taking one of her tours. As they began, just the three of them, Sophie told them she'd been giving tours of the Capitol for the past thirty years. Dani thought she was adorable, the spitting image of Sophia from *The Golden Girls*. Things were off to a great start.

Luke tried to pay attention to all the interesting information Sophie was telling them, he really was, but none of it was registering. He was looking at the beautiful paintings depicting Minnesota's pivotal role in the Civil War that lined the walls of the governor's retiring room. He felt a little guilty for not paying sufficient attention, but his mind just wouldn't stop reviewing the rest of his plan.

Sophie took them up to the third floor and approached a door that looked like nothing more than a coat closet. They watched as she swiped a key card to gain access. As she opened it, Dani and Luke saw that the minimalist door led to a massive staircase. After climbing dozens of steps, the trio stepped out onto the roof level that was showcased on the tour so visitors could see the Quadriga.

Luke may not have set foot in the Capitol until a few months ago, but even he recognized the gold-leaf-covered statuary group that adorned the top of the building. Most people knew the sculpture simply as "the golden horses," but as Sophie was explaining, it was officially titled "Progress of the State" and signified the state's prosperity.

Like many aspects of the Capitol, Luke was amazed at the beauty of the sculpture, but he was even more taken by the woman standing next to the guardrail admiring it. With the sun reflecting off of the golden statue and her hair, he found himself breathless just looking at her. He hoped that he'd remember this moment for the rest of his days.

Using the moment to his advantage, Luke silently signaled to Sophie. Without a sound, their tour guide smiled and left them on the Capitol roof as she headed down the many steps alone.

Approaching the unsuspecting Dani, Luke was reluctant to break this peaceful moment but he had an important question to ask.

"You seem to be quite taken with those horses," he joked.

Turning to face Luke, Dani shared a peaceful smile. "I've seen this statue thousands of times since I was a little girl. I've been in this building so many hours these past few months and I'm still amazed at the beauty of this place. Have you ever seen anything so beautiful?"

Luke's eyes didn't stray from Dani's as he pulled her into his arms. "Yes, I have."

Dani tried to retreat from Luke's piercing gaze, but he wouldn't let her. He was referring to her, of that she had no doubt. The intensity of his gaze was breathtaking. How had she gotten so lucky to meet a man as wonderful as Luke? She didn't know what good deeds she'd done in her life to deserve him; she just knew that she was extremely blessed. Belatedly remembering that they had an audience, Dani looked around for their *Golden Girls* look-alike.

"Where did Sophie go?"

Luke used one of the lines he'd practiced. "Didn't you hear her?" he asked with a straight face. "She said she was going to leave us up here to look around and she went back down."

"She just left us up here?" Dani pulled away to look around. "Can she do that?"

"Guess so!"

Trying to distract her, and just because he wanted to, Luke clasped his hands behind her back and pulled her in for a hot kiss. When he pulled back, Dani was breathing hard and had a slightly dazed expression. She reached up to run her hand above his eyebrow and down his cheek.

"I know that you didn't want to do it, Luke, and I know it could have cost you your career with the Blizzards, but I'm so happy that you were roped into the arena proposal. It's selfish of me, but I just can't imagine not having met you. Not loving you."

Luke was struck speechless by Dani's words. He was thrilled to be hearing them, of course—but she was stealing his material! He'd been toying with what to say to her for weeks and she'd just pirated two of his top picks. Afraid that she was going to continue and completely derail him, he swept in for another quick kiss.

"Dani, you're the most selfless person I know. And if for some reason I ever had to pick between you and hockey again, I'd pick you every day of the week and twice on Sunday. I love you, Dani O'Brien."

Reluctantly, he let go of her hands to lean over the railing of the balcony to grab the bag he'd arranged to be placed on the roof before their tour. Reaching for it, Luke was amazed at the sense of peace he was feeling. He wasn't nervous at all. He was excited.

"I have a gift for you." He loved seeing her eyes light up.

"Luke, you didn't have to get me—"

He wouldn't let her finish. She was always giving him a hard time when he bought her things or wanted to pick up their dinner tab. Just another thing he loved about her.

"I wanted to get you this, Dani." He reached into the bag and pulled out a Blizzards jersey.

"Oh, Luke, a jersey! How great." He loved that she

was excited about a jersey. She didn't expect anything lavish. But before he could let her take over, he pulled it out of her reach to finish what he started to say.

"Remember that day at your parents' place when you told me how you and all your brothers dreamed about playing professionally one day, each of you with *O'Brien* emblazoned on the back of your jersey?"

He saw her beautiful head shake up and down and her smile widen.

"Well, if it were up to me, I'd draft you to be on my team in a heartbeat, but the league has rules about women in the league. So I wanted to give you a little something that I thought might be the next-best thing."

Although the NHL draft was right around the corner, Dani had no idea where Sam would end up playing. And Luke was staying with the Blizzards, so she didn't understand his last comment. She reached for the jersey again and raised it up in the sunlight to admire the front. She turned it around, expecting to see Luke's name and number on the back and she froze.

It was Luke's number, but instead of the name reading "Coffey," it read "O'Brien Coffey." She lowered the jersey and saw Luke on his knee facing her.

Without her noticing, he'd pulled out a little box and was holding it up to her. Her heart started beating frantically as he continued talking.

"I thought hockey was my life, Dani. But then I met you and realized how empty that idea was. Hockey was my life before I met you, Dani, but you've shown me what life really is. Being with you is like breathing. You are my life."

He lifted the lid of the box just as Dani raised her hand to her mouth. The diamond was sparkling every which way in the sunlight.

"I went to your parents and brothers last week and told them that I'd met my soul mate the day you hit me with your boss's door. I asked them for their blessing and they gave it wholeheartedly. So now I'm asking you, Danielle O'Brien. Will you please make me the happiest man on earth and do me the honor of becoming my wife?"

Dani could feel the tears pouring down her face. She had dreamed of this day, but she never imagined the heart-stopping reality. She leaned down to kiss her future husband's lips and put her hand under his chin to urge him to stand.

Luke thought the kiss was a good sign, but he was an athlete and he needed an audible. He didn't have to wait long.

"Luke, is there even a doubt about how you feel about me or how I feel about you? I thank God daily for sending you my way! I would be honored to marry you."

Luke swooped Dani up and swung her around as they both laughed and wept. Putting her down, he took the ring out of the box and gently placed it on her finger—a perfect fit. And although the diamond did sparkle, it didn't come close to the love he saw shining in Dani's eyes. She was his future.

When the last tour of the day came to view the Quadriga thirty minutes later, Dani and Luke were still up on the roof kissing, embracing, and being at peace with each other as they looked out over the capital city. Dani was shocked to realize that the last tour was comprised entirely of her family, Luke's parents, and Marc and Piper. Everyone rushed to congratulate them. At some point she put the jersey on and had everyone admiring the new pairing.

An hour later, the family had retreated down to the Rotunda since it was well past touring hours, but Dani and Luke stayed on the roof for a few last minutes alone. Holding each other close, they looked out over the cityscape. In the distance, they could see the crane still working over the Rink area. The expansion construction was already underway.

As Luke had told Marc, the Blizzards and the state may have gotten what they wanted, but holding Dani in his arms, he knew that they got what they both needed—each other.

Acknowledgments

It has been an absolutely amazing journey bringing *Power Play* to fruition, and I'm so thankful and grateful that I was able to share it with so many people.

The final product wouldn't be what it is without the wonderful team at Beaver's Pond Press who helped steer me through the quagmire that is the publishing world. Katy Jo Turner, you've been a great mentor and brainstorming partner, and are incredibly patient with my many questions. Wendy Weckwerth, my editor, and Alicia Ester, my proofreader, the time and diligence you spent editing *Power Play* has produced a wonderful product that I am immensely proud of. And Laura Drew, your imagination and creativity have given *Power Play* the best physical image possible. Thank you, team!

I can't count the number of friends who have listened to me rant, rave, laugh, and cry (okay, maybe not cry) about this project. Without the constructive feedback, words of wisdom, and cheering, this product likely never would have come to be. Thank you, my friends, for supporting me on this journey. Special thanks to Sheila, Nicky, Crystal, Amy, Lydia, and Sandra for ever-so-delicately providing feedback in those early days and ensuring that I wasn't just inarticulately writing a manual on how to pass a bill into law. Nina, Vicky, Nushky, and Mandy, thank you for being my perennial cheerleaders over the years. And to my friends in the pod-quad and the SBMT, you know who you are, thank you for your awesome insight and red-pen editing.

Although this idea had floated through my mind for years, I never may have put pen to paper if I hadn't had the opportunity to work on some very interesting and unique pieces of legislation. For that, I'd like to say thanks to my many friends in the Minnesota Legislature, and a special thank you to Senator Julie Rosen. Thank you for being a wonderful boss, mentor, legislator, public servant, and most importantly, a friend. My Capitol friends will know that I switched things around by putting the House offices in the Capitol and not the SOB, but I did this intentionally to switch things up, given that it is fiction. I thought the change would be nice.

There are also a few authors I would like to acknowledge. Mary Bracho and Kathleen Eagle, I so appreciated our discussions and your feedback at the Loft. Lauren Willig, thank you for sharing information early on about how to get started and for inspiring me to become a writer just from reading *The Secret History of the Pink Carnation*. And thanks to Jayne Jones, who along with Alicia Long, wrote a fabulous page-turner in *Capitol Hell* and provided invaluable insight into the publishing process and helped steer me toward Beaver's Pond Press.

And lastly, I'd like to thank my family. A girl couldn't ask for better brothers, sisters-in-law, and parents. Especially when those same people offer to read, edit, and keep me on track all while cheering for my success. Thank you for not thinking I had gone too far off the deep end after hearing I was writing a novel. How many people have told us over the years that we need to write a book about our RV trips? Well, I tried to include some of them in *Power Play*. Thank you for everything—love you!

And thank you, dear reader, for taking time to join me on this journey. I hope you enjoyed *Power Play*.